RUIN ME, DADDY

TWISTED DESIRES
BOOK 1

JENNIFER O'MALLEY

Cover Design © 2025 GetCovers

Beta Reading: Abrianna Denae Proofreading

Developmental Editing: Bev Rosenbaum

Line Editing: Lawrence Editing

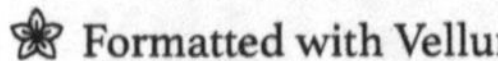

INTRODUCTON

Thank you for taking the time to read *Ruin Me, Daddy*!

As you read it, it may seem a little familiar. This originally started out as a 30k word novella, *Killer Attraction*, for an anthology. But it has now blossomed into a full-length book of over 94k words!

So, if you read it before, there is plenty of new content to lose yourself in!

Honey To-Do List of Tropes, Content, and Trigger Warnings:

- Daddy/boy
- Age gap
- Cop/Serial Killer
- Opposite Sides of the Law
- Forbidden Romance
- Possessive/Obsessive MC
- Murder Discussion
- Language
- Sexual Situations
- Graphic Violence

- On Page Murder
- Touch Him and Die
- Breeding Kink (briefly mentioned, no mpreg)
- Brief Implied Homophobia
- Dubcon
- Stalking
- Breath Play
- Mental Health Rep (Mentions of ASPD, Panic Attacks, Anxiety)

1
NATHAN

Tonight was the night I was going to make him mine.

I took a deep breath as I stood outside the door to the hotel bar and went over the plan in my head again. For the last three weeks, I'd been popping in to see Duncan while he worked, watching him, waiting for the perfect moment.

Everything was planned out, and I'd even booked a suite at the hotel for the evening so I could give him the night he deserved. All I had to do now was walk in there and convince him to give me a chance.

Not that I thought it would be difficult. We'd been flirting for most of the time I'd been coming into the bar to see him, and I'd made it clear I had money. But if I couldn't, then I had other methods of persuasion.

With a final shake of my shoulders, I flung off any doubt I had and walked through the doors with a smile on my face. A smile that slowly slipped as my eyes darted around behind the bar and I didn't see Duncan.

I took in the cheap Halloween decorations, the colored

lights pulsing throughout the bar instead of the usual annoying fluorescent beams, the red runner down the length of the bar, and the supposedly *festive* cobwebs and plastic spiders strategically placed along the glass on the back wall.

But there was something—no, *someone*, missing.

My steps slowed as I got closer to the bar, my head cocking to the side as I replayed our conversation from the other night in my head.

My eyes drifted closed and I could see him clear as day. Duncan McCallister, a pretty boy with blond hair and a killer smile that he flashed as he served me drinks from behind the bar. He'd told me he was working tonight. I knew he did. So why wasn't he where he was supposed to be?

The betrayal was like a knife, carving out my soul.

"Nathan?"

My eyes flashed open and I turned to see who had called my name. There weren't many people here who knew my name. I'd made sure of that. I spied the bartender at the other end, in the middle of taking care of another customer, giving me a nod and holding up a finger indicating for me to wait a moment.

I stood there, watching him work. His hands were large but handled the glassware with a delicacy that spoke of experience and his smile was easy and effortless. But it did nothing for me. Not the way his athletic build filled out his tight-fitting black T-shirt and tight jeans that seemed to be the bar's uniform or his olive complexion and dark eyes and long, wavy hair that he had tied back in a bun.

Then again, he would do, to work off some steam and tension that suddenly filled my body.

But that hadn't been the plan and I hated to deviate from a plan. He had me curious, though, so I crossed my arms over my chest and leaned against the bar and waited for him to finish with his customer. I watched him like a lion stalking a gazelle as he made his way to where I stood.

He watched me with equal curiosity and I wondered what all Duncan had told him about me. Considering he knew my name, it was obvious he'd talked to his coworkers about me and a part of me preened at the thought, while another part cursed at the inconvenience.

"Duncan's not here tonight," the bartender, whose name I wasn't sure I ever knew, told me as he continued to look me up and down. The gleam in his eyes was a giveaway to the fact he thought he was the one on the prowl, but he had no idea the danger he'd just walked into by approaching me.

"Yeah, I can see that." My fist clenched at my side, and no matter how much I tried, I couldn't keep the harsh bitterness from my tone. It wasn't this man's fault, but I didn't care about that. What I cared about was the fact Duncan had lied to me. He'd ruined what I had so carefully planned for the two of us.

The other man gave me a grin as he slid my usual beer order my way.

"Doesn't mean you have to leave. First one's on me." He shot me a wink as another customer flagged him down from a few stools away.

I sneered at the drink as though it had personally offended me, refusing to drink it.

"Did he say why he wasn't coming in tonight?" I asked before he was able to get too far away.

He shot me another grin as he threw the reply over his shoulder and kept walking. "Oh, he's working tonight. He just got bumped up to bartend a wedding in the ballroom tonight because the original bartender got the flu."

What the fuck?

I stormed out of the bar, furious with the way the asshole bartender had been jerking me around. I wanted to kill him just for fucking with me, but I knew I couldn't draw that much attention to myself. I roamed the halls of the hotel, slipping into the employees only section.

There had to be a way into that ballroom where the wedding reception was taking place. He was in there. And he was *mine*, whether he knew it or not, his life was mine for the taking.

From the first moment I had laid eyes on him at the bar, I knew he was meant to be mine. I'd watched him, wanted him, waited for him. The timing had to be perfect.

And it had been.

Until it wasn't.

My thoughts raced and I paced along the hall, wondering why *tonight* of all nights he had to be pulled from where he was supposed to be. I'd planned everything so carefully.

Looking up into the bright lights that hung from the ceiling, as though they would deliver me a solution, I wondered how everything had gotten so fucked up. Wondered why the universe was mocking me, taunting me.

A low growl tore from my chest as I darted down another hallway in the back of the hotel. It was a risk being in public, especially when I was feeling agitated, but I was desperate. I'd watched him for so long, this was supposed to be my chance to get him. The thought of letting him slide through my fingers made my heart clench in my chest. It was an ache that stole my breath.

My phone vibrated in my pocket, drawing me out of my spiral. I yanked it out so hard and fast, I almost flung it across the hall, not even bothering to look at who was trying to get ahold of me as I powered it off before shoving it back into my pants. Whoever it was could wait.

Fuck. I needed to get a hold of myself.

Taking a deep breath, I put my palms flat against the wall

and leaned back. If I didn't calm down, I would lose control and that was how mistakes happened.

And I didn't make mistakes.

Ever.

An itch started to work its way across my body and it took every ounce of control I had to not scratch my skin raw, to bleed myself dry to get rid of the feeling of uneasiness crawling beneath my skin.

The instinct to rush back and grab the bartender was overwhelming. It wouldn't be as satisfying to take him, fuck him, and kill him, but it would still ease the primal urge in me that lusted to exert that power and control over a human being. There was nothing more thrilling than watching the life slip out of a well-fucked man and know *I did that*, on both counts.

But the beast inside me didn't crave that nobody back there. It craved Duncan and it wouldn't be satisfied until he was ours.

The sting of betrayal since finding out he wasn't at the bar had slowly faded, but it still poked at the surface. I couldn't help but wonder if he had known he'd be tending bar at the wedding rather than the bar and hadn't told me, because I didn't believe his coworker when he said it was last minute.

But I couldn't figure out why Duncan would do that, except that he hadn't trusted me.

And if he didn't trust me, then I couldn't get him where I needed him to be, to go with me.

"Sir? You're not supposed to be back here." A young man had appeared in one of the doorways off to my right. His face was pinched with concern and confusion as he peeked over my shoulder. I assumed he was trying to figure out how I had gotten back there and what I was doing there.

Join the club, because I had still been trying to figure that out myself.

"Sorry. I think I got turned around." I let go of the wall and glanced around, giving him my best helpless look.

He opened his mouth, ready to say something, before he looked back over his shoulder for a moment. When he refocused back on me, the apprehension was clear in his face, making me wonder just what he'd noticed before he'd said something to me.

"Where are you trying to get to? I'm sure no one will miss me if I'm gone for a couple minutes to help you." The smile he offered me paled in comparison to the ones Duncan usually gave me, but then again, nothing about this kid shone as bright as Duncan's star.

A slow smile slid across my face as I reached into my pocket, putting my phone back and wrapping my fingers around the stiletto blade I kept hidden there.

"That would be great. Thanks." I made sure no one was around before I took a step toward him. His eyes darted to the side before coming back up to my face, and I could tell the unease was starting to creep in, as though he had just realized he might have made a mistake.

He had. But I wouldn't let him go now.

I smiled as I took another step, my fingers tightening on my hidden blade. "I'm trying to find the ballroom. I'm supposed to pick up my friend from a wedding, but he's not answering."

With a shrug I hoped came across as nonchalant and maybe a little flirty, I closed the final distance between us and got right in his personal space. "What's your name?"

It wasn't that I cared. But I was meticulous and I wasn't used to killing without stalking and a plan. So I knew I'd have to keep an eye on this man's life for a little while after the deed was done.

The man nodded, but it didn't seem to be at anything I'd said and went to take a step back.

I frowned, my arm reaching out to grab his wrist so he couldn't run, but I didn't hold on tight. Not yet.

"You still didn't tell me your name, sweetheart." I swiped my thumb along his wrist and offered up a shy smile, suppressing the urge to wipe my hand on my pants and get his germs, his scent, off me.

Even though I knew something about me had already spooked him, I had to try to get the situation back under control. Because even though he wasn't the one I was after, he was the ticket I needed to get to my Duncan. My boy was waiting for me in that ballroom and I couldn't disappoint him. So, for the moment, I had to pretend to want this man, who meant nothing, at least while he could give me what I needed.

"Thomas." The name came out in a whisper as he looked back down the hall. And I could tell the moment he was going to run, just before he took the step back.

I reached out and grabbed his wrists, pressing him against the wall, pinning his hands to the wall in a grip so tight I swore I could feel a bone or two snap. The way he whimpered under me, with his big brown eyes staring up at me, wide and full of tears, only confirmed I must have broken something.

With a sigh, I leaned in and brought my lips to his ear. "Tsk tsk, Thomas. You've been a very naughty boy."

The young man let out another whimper as he squirmed and tried to pull free of my grasp, but it was no use.

"Please. Just let me go. Whatever you want, you can have it," he tried to reason. "I won't tell anyone you were back here. No one has to know anything."

"You're right, you won't tell anyone that I was back here." I rubbed my stubbled cheek against the smooth baby soft skin of his neck before I pulled him away from the wall, clasping his hands behind his back, and marched him down to the exit and into the alley. By the time I pushed the door open, Thomas worked himself into a frenzy.

I hated criers. Why couldn't people greet the end of their lives with a little dignity?

"Please," he tried to beg again as I pushed him out the door, "I don't even know who you are. You don't have to do this."

My hand went into my pocket and twisted along the thin cylinder there as I slowly pulled it out.

"That's where you're wrong, Thomas. I do have to do this. It wasn't supposed to be you. Honestly, you just ended up in the wrong place at the wrong time. But, your death will serve a purpose." I gave him a smile as I stepped closer, but my words seemed to have caught him off guard, since he hadn't tried to run.

"A purpose?" He looked up at me, all wide-eyed and innocent, completely bypassing the fact we were talking about his death.

I reached out and cupped his cheek, swiping my thumb over his cheekbone. It was a shame. He really was very pretty.

"You're going to help me get to my Duncan."

He stared at me, confused, before I made my move, but by then, it was too late.

My arms wrapped around him, pulling him into a tight embrace as my arm came up and the needle pricked the side of his neck.

Thomas' eyes widened with fear and his mouth went slack as his body went weightless in my arms. I gently laid him down on the ground and watched as he struggled to move. His breathing slowed as he reached out to me. I stood, waiting against the wall with my arms and legs crossed, before his breathing finally stopped.

When I was sure he was dead, I stripped him of his uniform and pulled it on over my clothes. It was a little snug, but I didn't think anyone would be paying close enough attention this late in the evening.

The wedding reception had to be winding down by now. I just needed to blend in enough to slip by unnoticed through the back halls. Then I could sneak into the reception and pretend to be a guest.

At least, until I made my way to the bar. To *him*. And claimed my prize.

Duncan was mine.

He wasn't going to escape me. There was no escaping the beast that lived under my skin.

It was time to make my move and get Duncan out of the ballroom without anyone seeing.

2

AIDEN

Tension and booze flowed through my veins. It wasn't an ideal combination, but then again, I hadn't asked to attend *thee* social event of the season. Instead, I'd been unceremoniously kidnapped by my best friend, who insisted I was the perfect plus-one for the occasion.

What Victoria had failed to mention as she dragged me along to her cousin's wedding, was the fact it was Halloween-themed. And not just color scheme and a few tasteful decorations.

The asshole who came up with the bright idea of holiday-themed weddings, *especially* Halloween-themed weddings, needed to be shot. Pronto.

My fingers picked at the stringy cobwebs draped across the edge of the bar and flicked at a plastic spider. It skittered across the shiny blood red bar top, until it slid off the edge on the other side of the bar. Damn. Maybe I shouldn't have done that, considering that was the only company I had for the evening.

I snorted into my drink, the bartender giving me the side-eye. Honestly, half the night I thought he was hitting on me and the other half I thought he was trying to get rid of me. It had left me half hard and fully frustrated that I couldn't get a read on the guy. He politely smiled at most of my flirting but didn't give me much to work with.

Knowing my luck, he was probably straight and thought I was a creep.

Hell, he probably thought I was just another dumb guy at a wedding who wouldn't leave him alone, but since I was tipping him well, he kept his mouth shut. Couldn't blame the dude for that.

Fuck. That *did* make me a creep.

Despite the fact the wedding had mostly died down to just a couple dozen guests, the loud bass of the music continued to blare, grating on my nerves. My jaw twitched as I clung to the glass in my hand and willed myself not to beg the bartender to leave the whole damn bottle—despite the fact I was usually a two-drink max kind of guy.

I swear, there was nothing worse than being stuck at a social event that you couldn't leave.

Scratch that. Being stuck at a social event *alone* when you don't really know anyone else should definitely be its own circle of hell.

When I agreed to come as my best friend's plus-one to her cousin's wedding, I assumed she'd stick with me most of the time. And to her credit, she had. Right until a tall, dark, gorgeous six-and-a-half-foot god came up and asked her to dance. Not that I could blame her, because if she hadn't been interested, I might have tried my luck to see if the guy also swung my way.

But alas, Victoria seemed as enamored with the man as he was with her.

I flicked my gaze up to the mirror behind the bar and sought out my potentially former bestie. She was easy to spot with her red curls that had come loose and now flowed over her shoulder and her bright orange creamsicle-colored dress.

My lips twitched and my heart fluttered as she clung to the man at her side. Even with the distance between us, I could hear it when she let out a laugh I'd never heard from her before.

It wasn't that I wasn't happy for Vic. She deserved the world and if this guy was willing to give it to her, then she deserved him.

But if he broke her heart, well, then he better hope he doesn't meet me when I have my gun on me. Because I wasn't afraid to use it.

So, I found myself sitting at the bar, sipping top-shelf liquor and mixed drinks that went down way too smooth. If I didn't stop soon, I'd definitely end up embarrassing myself. And that was the last thing I wanted to do, especially in front of Victoria's family. She'd never let me live it down. And considering I had to put up with her at work, giving my partner ammunition she could use to get the entire precinct to tease me over, was the last thing I wanted to do.

As I sat at the bar, sipping my third—no, fourth—martini, I scanned the crowd that had considerably thinned since the evening had started. I knew some of Victoria's family, since we had been partners for almost a decade. But most of them had already turned in for the night. Besides the bride and groom, Victoria, and Shelby, Victoria's sister, there wasn't anyone else who was still mingling through the crowd that I knew.

By the way Victoria and her man were moving on the dance floor, it was obvious I was going to go back to the room by myself. With a sigh, I turned back in my stool to lean against the bar.

I brought my drink to my lips and drained the glass dry.

"I'll have another one of these, whatever you wanna call them."

The bartender raised a brow but didn't make a move toward

me as he continued cleaning out the glass in his hand. "You really think that's a good idea?"

His smirk sent butterflies crashing through my stomach. Maybe I hadn't lost my touch after all and still had a chance with him.

I leaned forward against the bar and gave him my best charming smile. But the way he snorted and shook his head had me frowning and second-guessing myself. I knew I'd had more to drink than usual, but I hadn't thought I was *that* drunk.

Dammit.

"I could think of a few better ideas."

The bartender leaned down on his elbows and his eyes slid over me in a slow caress. "Sorry, handsome. I don't date cops."

It was my turn to raise an eyebrow at him as I lifted my glass for another drink, only to realize I was still empty.

"That so? Why? You a criminal or something?"

He smirked as he refilled my glass and dropped it in front of me, but didn't answer my question. It shouldn't have made him even more interesting, but fuck, it made me want to drag him back to my room even more.

"Oh, that's a dangerous question," came a deep voice from my right.

I turned and saw a man in an impressive-looking, well-tailored charcoal suit. He grinned and let out a chuckle, at my expense, no doubt. His deep chocolate eyes didn't quite match the warmth in his voice, but they were still hypnotizing as I found myself letting out a chuckle in return.

"Is that so?" Out of the corner of my eye, I saw the bartender cast a glance between us with a frown before he turned his back to us and moved off before I could say anything to him. I wasn't sure what it was about the newcomer that had sent him scampering, but there was a tangle of nerves I couldn't define that clenched in my gut.

When I glanced back over at the man who had joined me at

the bar, his eyes also seemed to track the bartender's movements.

He turned back to me and gave a shrug as he swiped my glass and took a sip before giving it back with a grimace. I grinned at his obvious distaste and pulled the glass back toward me, only mildly disappointed we wouldn't be sharing.

"Yeah." He shot me a grin as he tried to catch the bartender's eye, I assumed to order his own drink. "I learned a long time ago that it's never a good idea to ask a question you don't already have the answer to. Especially, if you aren't sure you want the answer."

I leaned back in the chair and studied the man before me, his answer seeming a bit too serious for a silly question at a wedding. And while there was a niggling at the back of my brain that there was *something*, I couldn't quite put my finger on it. But it was enough to have me intrigued.

The detective in me needed to know more, not to mention the man. Unanswered questions were like my kryptonite.

Not to mention, there seemed to be something familiar about him, and I couldn't quite put my finger on it. I assumed I'd probably met him at one of Vic's family gatherings, considering we were at her cousin's wedding. But it only made my curiosity increase the more I watched him and thought about him.

"Who says I didn't already know the answer?" I quirked an eyebrow at him as I raised my glass to my lips, never breaking eye contact.

He let out a chuckle as he cast another glance at the bartender with a frown. There was something about the way they'd glanced at each other, or carefully kept from looking at each other at the same time, I couldn't help but wonder if they knew each other. The thought twisted my gut in an unpleasant way.

I let out a soft hum as I turned away from him and rested my elbows on the bar, focusing on my drink once again.

When the bartender brought over a beer and slid it over to the stranger next to me, without him having to ask for anything in particular, it only reinforced my suspicions. I had no reason for the way jealousy clouded my vision and clawed at my insides, but it tended to be an irrational bitch.

I squashed down the voice yelling *mine!* and tried to ignore the handsome man, instead keeping my gaze on Victoria in the mirror.

"Waiting for your wife?"

My drink sputtered out of my mouth as I tried not to choke any more than I already had at his words.

"What?" I turned and looked at him, my brows drawn in confusion.

He shrugged. His dark eyes roaming over me, assessing. Caressing… possessing. Like he owned me.

Which was ridiculous, considering he didn't even know me.

I didn't even know his name.

So why did I want it to be true?

"The way you're watching that mirror. It's obvious you're watching someone." His voice was a low growl. The jealousy was obvious and it sent a spike of arousal and need through me.

It couldn't be wrong to be happy he was just as jealous as I had been just moments ago, right?

I thought about teasing him. But the way my cock was quickly plumping had me ready to squirm in my seat and I didn't think I'd last much longer. He seemed like a sure thing to take back to my room.

"Honestly, I'm just wondering if I need to wait for my friend to tell me she's ditching me or if I can ditch her first. But it doesn't seem very gentlemanly to leave her alone." Not that I would ever insinuate to Victoria that she was incapable of taking care of herself. She'd been a cop before me, but my instinct would always be to look after and protect my partner, even in a social situation that comprised mostly of her family members.

"So, not a girlfriend, then?" Tall, dark, and handsome quirked up an eyebrow. I let out a full-bellied laugh that left him looking perplexed yet amused.

"Oh, God no. Just a friend. We work together. I'm a hundred percent gay." I felt my cheeks darken, unsure as to what prompted me to blurt out that declaration. Not that it was a secret. But it wasn't usually something I led with before I even exchanged names with a stranger. The tug of his lips at the information left me thinking maybe it hadn't been such a bad thing, though.

The way we'd been dancing around each other, flirting, I was sure he'd picked up what I was putting down already. But I still wasn't used to being so blunt about it.

"Sorry," I muttered, turning back to my drink.

I was such an idiot. I didn't know this guy, despite the flirting, or being at my bestie's family event. Not that I was overly worried. While I wasn't the biggest guy, I had almost a decade as a cop with more than my share of experience where I had to be able to handle myself in a fight.

"For what?" the guy next to me asked, the puzzled expression clear on his face.

"It's not usually something I just blurt out, especially to random men. Sometimes people get the wrong idea." I tried to shrug it off, not feeling as confident as I had a few minutes ago, but the way he stared at me made me feel exposed and vulnerable, but I wasn't sure if it was in a sexy way.

He continued to study me for another moment before he gave a slight nod and took a sip of his drink. "What about when the wrong idea is the right idea?"

My head snapped in his direction, sure I had heard him incorrectly.

"I'm sorry. What?" I felt like an idiot as the other man sat there and smirked at me.

"Nathan Turner," the man said, extending his hand.

Flustered, I slid my hand into his, my eyes widening at the way I would have sworn literal sparks flew when we made contact.

"A-Aiden. Aiden Cooper," I replied, tripping over my own name. I wasn't sure what it was about this man, but he left me feeling tied up in knots. While I usually didn't have much game when it came to flirting, there was something about Nathan Turner that left me feeling equally relaxed and on edge.

Or maybe it was just that I wanted him to put me on edge.

Over. And over. And over.

I shook my head, eradicating the stray thought.

"It's nice to meet you, Aiden." His voice was low and raspy, deep in a way that turned my insides to jello. "What do you say we live a little and get out of here?"

My breathing hitched. There had been no way I'd heard right, that this gorgeous, put-together man wanted *me*. Despite the way we had flirted when he first sat down, I never thought I'd actually stood a chance. Pushing my reservations aside, I knew the last thing I planned to do was let a man like him slip through my fingertips, even if it was only going to be for one night.

"Your room or mine?" I asked, barely able to recognize the sound of my own voice.

3

NATHAN

A fine tremor buzzed just below the surface that took all my strength to squash. Of all the hotels and all the bars.

I couldn't believe I ran into *him*. I never thought I was going to see him again, but there he was right in front of me.

Living. Breathing.

Wanting me.

Every instinct in me was screaming to take him and make him mine. To claim him and never let him go.

To keep him or kill him, that was the question.

I wasn't used to wrestling my instincts when I found someone and I had to squash the urge to fidget in my seat. He shouldn't have been different than any of the others, but all my wires were getting crossed when it came to him. This boy was unraveling me and I reveled in it while it also made me want to tear him apart for making me feel.

Out of the corner of my eye, I caught Duncan, who was barely a blimp on my radar, though my senses and instincts wouldn't let me forget him for long. The part of my brain that took one look at a person and categorized them as prey, a threat, a fuck, or nothing had claimed Duncan as prey. It wouldn't be happy until his blood was on my hands, so I needed to make it happen. And soon.

Especially since he was also pinging as a threat—a threat to my beautiful boy who sat in front of me with wide, blue eyes that stared up at me like he couldn't believe I was real.

Join the club, baby.

My focus zeroed in on Aiden, as I could sense his hesitation when I asked him if he wanted to leave. Maybe I had pushed too hard, too fast. The way he looked at me made me think otherwise. But if I had to, I'd stay and chat with him for a bit first. Something told me he was looking for a good fuck just as much as I was, though.

Still, the wariness rolled off him in waves. His eyes darted back to the mirror and my gut twisted, knowing he was looking at the woman on the dance floor. Despite his rushed admission that he was gay, I knew I'd have to look into her, and him, and find out just what their connection was and make sure she wasn't a threat to my boy.

Nothing was going to get in between us. He was *mine* and he would be until his body was food for the worms deep in the earth. Even then, he would still belong to me.

With a smile tugging on the corner of my lips, I stood and reached my hand out to him, giving him the illusion of having a choice. When he placed his smaller hand in mine, my heart felt like it had started to beat for the first time in my life.

My eyes never left his as I raised our joined hands to my lips and left a soft kiss across his knuckles. The way he blushed and nibbled on his bottom lip left me desperately wishing I were the one who had that lip between my teeth.

I reached up with my free hand and cupped his cheek before I slowly leaned in and claimed his lips in a kiss, ignoring the crowd of the party—and Duncan—around us. No one else existed with him in my arms as the feel of his lips against mine seared itself into my soul. My heart kicked in my chest, almost causing me to stumble back, it was so unexpected.

Then again, everything about Aiden Cooper was unexpected.

"Come on, baby," I urged as my hand caressed his side. He shuddered and when he looked back up at me, his eyes dark with lust, I knew I had him. With a smile, I tugged Aiden's hand and led him out of the ballroom. When we got to the door, he hesitated and glanced behind him. My hand clenched and I needed to glance away from him so he wouldn't see the jealous monster that lurked beneath the surface.

When he took another step, tugging my hand this time, I let out a silent sigh of relief. The soft chuckle coming from Aiden let me know I wasn't as put together as I thought I was and he had seen through a crack in my armor.

It should have scared me, but it oddly eased something within me.

When we made it to the elevators, I pressed the button, then slid my hand to the small of his back. I needed to touch him, to know he was real and was with me. A low groan caught in my throat and it took all the restraint I could muster not to push him against the wall and devour him while we waited for the elevator to arrive.

My body was taut like a wire, ready to snap at any moment. I needed him close to me, but I also needed to keep him away so I didn't get arrested for public indecency. Because the things I wanted to do to my boy, they were definitely indecent.

I watched him out of the corner of my eye as we waited. He kept fidgeting and tugging on the sleeve of his shirt. Every couple of seconds, he'd sneak a look at me from under his long lashes and bite his lip.

My hands were itching to reach out and touch him, more so than I already was. But I had to behave. We were in public after all. Anyone could see us. There was a buzzing spreading through my body in anticipation.

It had been too long.

"Nathan." My name was a whimper on his lips as he cocked his head in my direction. I wasn't sure what he was thinking or feeling, but his eyes were pleading for salvation as he shuffled closer.

A salvation he knew only I could give to him.

"Shhh, little bird. I've got you."

Aiden's eyes widened before narrowing for a brief moment. A myriad of emotions flickered across his face, but I couldn't decipher any of them. But then a naked look of *need* settled over him and he gazed at me as though I had the answer to all his prayers and I let out a relieved breath.

The elevator finally opened and with my hand still on his back, I guided him closer, so he was flush against my side as we entered the car.

"Where's your room?" I breathed the words into the top of his head as his arms instinctively went around my waist.

He stared at me, wide-eyed, tugging that irresistible bottom lip back between his teeth. With a look at the number panel and then back at me, he straightened his shoulders. "I'm on floor twelve."

I nodded and offered him a reassuring smile as I reached over and pressed the button. His arms tightened around me and he didn't let go for the entire elevator ride. When the doors finally opened to his floor, I kept him close as we made our way to his room.

He hadn't said a word since we'd gotten off the elevator. I couldn't help but wonder what he was thinking as his fingers held tight to mine and he led me down the hall to his room. Despite his obvious nervousness that I didn't understand but attributed to the fact that I was a stranger, there was blatant desire painted across his features as we stopped in front of what I assumed was his room.

"Key?" I whispered as I gazed down at his face that was tilted up to look at me, afraid to break whatever spell we had found ourselves under.

Without a word, he slid his hand into the inner pocket of his suit jacket. It didn't escape my notice that his fingers were trembling as he pulled out the key and reached out in front of him to unlock the door.

The moment we were across the threshold, I descended like a madman, taking what I wanted.

What I needed.

"Nate." My name left his mouth in a gasp as my lips caught his in a bruising kiss. I pushed him against the closed hotel room door. My heart thudded as I let out a low growl. It had been a long time since I heard anyone call me that.

Usually, I hated being called anything but Nathan. But hearing it fall from his lips was like a balm to my tattered and corrupt soul.

"My little bird," I said, nipping at his ear as my hand wrapped around his delicate throat. "I'm going to make you fly."

A low groan escaped from Aiden as his head fell back at my words. The movement gave me the access I needed to lick a stripe up the side of his neck.

"Yes." He let out a hiss as my teeth sank into his tender flesh, marking him as *mine*.

I took a step back and tugged him forward so he would follow me as I led him over to the bed. As he stood there, I took a step back, admiring him like a piece of art. He had a blissed-out look on his face and I was sure the room could catch on fire and he wouldn't even notice.

My hand flew up and pushed against his chest when he

tried to take a step toward me. He frowned, his confusion almost palpable.

"Strip." I leaned back and issued the command, my eyes locking with his and refusing to look away.

His Adam's apple bobbed as he swallowed and hastily nodded at my directive. My drifted down, taking in his body as he slowly started to shed himself from the confines of his suit.

"Aren't you going to undress, too?" His voice was unsteady and I wasn't sure if it was from horniness or nerves. He paused, eyes still on mine, but I gave him nothing but a raised eyebrow, silently commanding him to continue.

With a deep breath, Aiden shrugged out of his dress shirt and kicked off his shoes. A slow smile spread across my face and he flinched as my eyes dropped to where his hands stopped for a moment before fumbling with his belt buckle.

"Don't worry. I will. First, I want to watch you." Without looking back, I sat in the chair that was behind me and faced the bed. Aiden's nerves were on full display once he realized he was the only one getting naked and putting on a show.

But I needed to see all that delicious flesh on display just for me. He was mine. And I always got what I wanted in the end. It was a lesson he'd do well to learn early on and remember. It would make things much easier for him.

Aiden bit his lip before he pulled the belt free and dropped it to the floor. My eyes raked over the skin and muscle that he was offering up for me to feast upon. He was much more defined than the frumpy, ill-fitting suit indicated. The urge to reach out and touch him was strong, but I stilled my hand as he stepped out of his pants.

When Aiden went to bend to take his socks off, I surprised us both by sliding to my knees in front of him. After a moment, I brushed aside the confusion that swirled in me and placed my hands on his thighs and pushed back, indicating I wanted him to sit on the bed.

Thankfully, he complied without comment. I slid my hands down his thighs and caressed his legs until I reached the top of his socks. Slowly, I slid his socks off, and he let out a soft gasp. Clanging up, the frown between his eyes made me pause. A feeling I wasn't used to made me want to surge up and press my lips to his. I wanted to climb on top of him, drive into him, and claim him, wiping that frown away.

My boy should never frown.

I'd never been one to want to be the one to make someone else smile. To demand their happiness, to be the reason for their joy.

That wasn't who I was.

"Nate." My name was almost a question, bringing my attention back to my boy, as I fought the primal urge to fuck and claim. I promised to make my little bird fly and I was more determined than ever that he would soar.

Instead of responding, I pressed a soft kiss to the first one, and then the other knee that I was bracketed between. My eyes never left his as I worked my way up until I met the fabric of his boxers. Aiden let out a whimper and his head fell back as I teased the band before I slid my fingers in and pulled them down, releasing his leaking cock.

A soft hiss escaped from my lips as I watched it bob against his stomach.

I didn't know what was wrong with me. Never before had I felt so impatient, so ready to fuck. But I didn't want that with him. Not with Aiden.

My little bird.

He was mine and I wanted to make him feel good.

The opposing needs warred within me. But I didn't get to where I was in life by being sloppy or careless. And I wasn't going to start with Aiden.

"Turn around," I ordered, practically grinding my teeth. "On all fours."

The wary look he gave me set off a low-sounding alarm in my head. But too many things were already in motion for me to turn back now.

4

AIDEN

My pulse pounded in my ears as the voice inside my head screamed at me that I was smarter than that. I was a cop, for crying out loud. I didn't wander off with strange men to my hotel room for one-night stands.

The only thing that kept me on the brink of sanity and feeling like I was going off the deep end, was knowing that I had picked him up at my partner's cousin's wedding. I'd ask Vic about him next time I saw her and get the scoop on him.

But that didn't stop my heart from bottoming out to my ass as his hand slid up my naked back.

I wasn't sure what to expect with Nate. One glance and I knew he'd be the dominant type, which I didn't mind at all. I had a stressful job and an even more stressful life, so if I could relax and let go when it came to sex, I was down.

But there was also something about him that made me wary. I couldn't put my finger on it, but I felt like there was something I couldn't trust. It was an instinct I'd learned a long time ago not to ignore. One that'd saved my skin more than a couple times.

So when he told me to turn around, I wasn't sure if I wanted to turn my back on him. I realized that if I didn't feel safe and comfortable with him, then I probably shouldn't let him fuck me.

But that was where I was getting tripped up. As I swallowed the lump in my throat and turned to settle on my elbows and knees, I realized the problem wasn't that I thought I didn't feel safe with him, because I did, but I did recognize I didn't exactly trust him. And the seesawing feelings were fucking with my head.

But something besides horniness was tickling my lizard brain. Something that told me this man was dangerous. I wasn't sure if it was my instincts as a homicide detective or just a man who was able to identify the dangers in another man.

But did I care?

No.

The only thing I cared about at that moment was getting his dick. Then he'd be gone and I wouldn't have to see him again or worry about what it was about him that made me uneasy.

When Nate's hand softly stroked down my spine, I jumped but also leaned into the touch as though I were a cat getting petted. I practically purred with the way his hand was rubbing up and down my body.

Fuck, that felt good.

It had been a long time since I'd had sex. Definitely too long if just that simple touch made me feel like I was going to blow.

"Please," I panted, my head falling onto my clasped hands on the bed. My ass wiggled with my desire and I was too needy to even feel any shame at my desperation.

He hummed, his hands still slowly gliding over my heated flesh. "What do you need, little bird?"

Fuck. I didn't know what it was about him calling me *little bird*, but it made me shiver. Except, I wasn't sure if it was a good shiver or not. It felt almost like a chill—possessive yet dark.

I also didn't want him to stop.

"You, need you." I gasped as his hand slid down the curve of my ass, grazing over my crease but not getting anywhere near close enough. My cock was hard and leaking between my legs, suspended over the bed and unable to get any friction.

"I'm right here," he teased, swatting my ass and eliciting a sharp cry.

"Fuck me. Please. I need you to fuck me." I knew I sounded desperate, but I couldn't find it in myself to care. There was no pretext as to what we went to the room for. We both knew we were looking for sex, so there was no need to be coy about it. Especially since he already had me naked and presenting my ass for him.

Nate's hand stroked up my side, fingers gliding over the ruined flesh of the scars that were there, and I stilled. My brain started to scream and rebel against the touch.

"Lube? Condoms?" he asked, moving away as though he sensed my discomfort.

I let out a shaky breath and needed to gulp in several lungfuls of air before I was able to answer him. "Nightstand drawer," I gasped out, still feeling overwhelmed.

It was so stupid. I didn't even really remember what happened when I got the scars, but I couldn't handle them being touched or talking about it. But there was a sense of shame that rolled over me at how I reacted. I thought I had a better grip on it than that.

I mentally slapped myself. I needed to get it together. Opportunities like this didn't present themselves that often for me. I let out a slow breath and willed my body to relax.

My head fell to the side and I watched Nate take what he needed from the drawer. He caught me watching him and gave me a wink before he settled behind me. Usually, I didn't like it like this. I needed to see what was going on and feel like I had some control, even if I longed to give it up and have all the choices taken out of my hands.

When I heard the snap of the cap from the lube, my hips rocked back, eager to get the show on the road.

A soft chuckle came from behind me and I let out a groan as his palms spread my cheeks, exposing my tight pink hole. He echoed my groan with one of his own as one of his lubed-up fingers lightly circled around my rim.

I squirmed as I let out a gasp, needing more than the light teasing touch he was giving me. More than anything, I needed him to fill me and take me out of my own head. Even if it was only for one night.

"So fucking perfect," Nate whispered as his finger tapped at my entrance before the tip slid in.

A shiver ran down my body as he breached me. My hips rocked, desperately trying to get him deeper. It didn't take long before he was sliding in and grazing my prostate.

I let out a yelp and bucked on the bed. The way he hit that hidden spot felt like there was an electric current bolting through me.

"More," I begged. "Please, Nate." The bastard ignored me and kept slowly sliding the one finger in and out of my tight ass. I was going to explode if he didn't get moving.

His lips grazed the curve of my ass and he bit down as he slid a second finger deep inside. It'd been so long, just the two thick fingers inside made me feel full. But still, I needed more. I needed it all. Needed his cock.

"Relax, little bird. Gonna make you feel so good."

I let out a whimper at his words and the way his fingers just barely stroked against my prostate as he glided in and out. There was no way he wasn't doing it on purpose.

The way he played with me and I responded in turn, it felt like I was meant to be his. I shook that thought away. Thinking like that was dangerous. This was one night. No sense in embarrassing myself by thinking it could ever be more than it was.

After a few more minutes, Nate added another finger and I let out the sluttiest groan known to man. He felt perfect as he filled me, and that was just his fingers. I could only imagine what it would feel like to be stuffed with his cock.

The bed shifted and out of the corner of my eye, I saw him reaching for the condom he'd put off to the side. Excitement zapped through my body as I heard the foil wrapper tear and the snap of the lube cap.

"You ready for me, little one?" he asked.

I nodded emphatically and he let out a chuckle.

But his words had rendered me speechless. He was really fucking with my head, with talk like that. I wasn't necessarily a small guy at a little under six feet tall, but I was slender and toned. Compared to Nate, though, I was like a little bird. He was broad and had to be close to six and a half feet.

His words made me feel small, though, but not in a bad way. Rather, in a way that made me feel protected and cared for, which was crazy.

A shudder wracked my body as he slid his cock along my crease. It was the first feel I got of it and he was *huge*. I let out a groan as I began to rock my hips. There was nothing more that I needed than for him to tear me apart with his monster cock.

As he guided it to my hole, Nate made soothing noises and rubbed his other hand over my hip in long, firm strokes that helped to calm the nerves that began to creep up as the head of his dick breached the first ring of muscles.

"Breathe," he reminded me and I let out a deep gasping breath. I bore down, trying to help ease him in and let out a gasp. He was so fucking big and for a moment, I wondered if he would truly tear me apart.

After a minute or so of him slowly rocking his hips and moving deeper inch by agonizing inch, I couldn't take it anymore and rocked back, slamming him down the rest of the way. I let out a strangled scream but rocked my hips to work myself through the burn.

Nate grabbed my hips in a bruising grip.

"What was that?" His harsh words were bit out, strangled and worried. The frown that creased his forehead when I glanced back made my stomach sink with regret. The last thing I wanted was for him to be upset with me.

"You're going to fucking hurt yourself. You're not the one in charge here, little bird." He slapped my ass, hard. Twice.

I let out a whimper as I tried to still my hips against the sting. The last thing I wanted was for Nate to be mad at me, especially over something so stupid.

He pulled back a little and slapped my ass again, making us both let out a groan.

"Who's in charge?"

I let out a whimper, but I couldn't find my voice. His palm snaked up my body and wrapped around my throat, pulling me up so I was flush against his chest.

"I didn't hear you, little bird." His breath against my ear and the way his hips were grinding against my ass had me melting against him. There was no way he could have expected an actual answer.

Nate snapped his hips, lodging his cock deep in my ass, and kept himself there, planting himself deep inside me. I cried out against the sharp sting of his teeth clamping down on my ear.

"I can't hear you, sweet boy," he whispered. "The correct answer is that Daddy's in charge, little one."

My breath caught in my throat and I would have fallen flat on my face if his hand weren't still on my throat and I hadn't reached out to grab ahold of his arms after that declaration that made my brain blue screen.

Nate grabbed my fists and eased me back down onto the mattress, pinning my hands above my head, and set a punishing pace as he pounded into me over and over. My fists twisted in the sheets, needing to hold on to something as he plundered away at my hole, making me cry out with each stroke.

But he refused to hit my prostate. He was making me pay for my impatience and it made me want to weep. I was so hard and I couldn't find any relief for my aching cock as he held me in place, leaving me unable to fall and grind against the bed.

"Please, please let me come." I was a begging mess, willing to sell my soul for release.

He didn't say anything and I thought he was going to continue to ignore my pleas. But then the angle changed, just ever so slightly, and he was pegging my prostate over and over.

"Fuck! Oh, oh, fuuuuck, yes." Tears streamed down my face as frustration and relief intermingled. "Please, oh God, Nate, please."

Nate leaned over me, bracing his arms on either side of me, and swiped his tongue over my neck. One of his arms snaked around my neck and he pulled us up so we were both kneeling.

"Beg again for me, little bird."

My head lolled back against his shoulder as my body had gone boneless. "Please. Fuck, Nate—"

"No."

I went rigid and blinked, trying to figure out what it was he wanted. He wanted me to beg, which was what I had been doing.

"Nate—"

"No." He cut me off again when I said his name, and it clicked, causing my cheeks to flame.

Daddy.

I glanced up at him from where my head rested on his shoulder and the look on his face told me he was serious. Fuck. Could I call another man Daddy? That had never been my thing, but I couldn't deny that the thought of calling him Daddy turned me on.

A shiver ran down my spine as I realized I wanted nothing more than to be soooo good for him. To give up the control I needed in my every day life and trust him to take care of me.

To make me fall apart and put me back together even better than I was before he touched me.

"Please, Daddy... let me come." My voice was low, barely more than a whisper, but the way he smiled at me as he bent his head and gave me a soft kiss made me soar.

"Fly for me. Fly so high for me, little bird. Higher than ever before," he whispered as he wrapped his arm around my throat and squeezed.

His words triggered my climax and my load shot out of me so hard and far that I thought I was going to pass out. It took a few seconds for me to realize the spots dancing behind my eyes were because I couldn't breathe. My hands reached up and tapped Nate's arm.

I could hear him behind me as he pistoned into my ass and the low groan he let out as the muscles in his arm tightened, marked his release.

"Fuck, Aiden," he groaned out.

For a moment, I didn't move, wanting to give him a second to get his bearings and come down and let me go.

But he didn't let go. I gasped his name and wrapped my hands around Nate's arm, trying to pull him off when he continued to squeeze. The most embarrassing thing about that moment was the way my cock let out another jet of cum.

Nate immediately let go and I fell down onto the bed, landing in the mess I had made as I wasn't able to brace myself. Stunned, I lay there while he held my hips and slowly pulled himself out. I wasn't sure where he went, but I felt the bed move and it took a moment before I realized he'd gone to the bathroom when I heard the sink turn on.

I moved my head so I was facing the opposite direction, not wanting him to see the angry and embarrassed tears that streamed down my face. Sex had never been like that for me and I wasn't sure I had liked it. Except, I couldn't fool either one of us because we both knew how hard I came—untouched—and that I'd come again when he choked me.

When the warm cloth unexpectedly touched my used and abused ass, I let out a hiss.

"Sorry," he murmured, but I couldn't tell if he really meant it or not. Or what exactly he was apologizing for—there were a few things that immediately came to mind. He didn't stop wiping down my ass and thighs, though, tapping my hip when he wanted me to turn over so he could clean my front.

Which just added to my embarrassment even more. I'd never had a guy stop and clean me up after we had sex. Not even boyfriends ever took the time to take that step for me.

It immediately made me think of him as Daddy and an irrational spike of anger shot through me. Then again, maybe it wasn't so irrational.

"I can do that myself," I snarked and he looked up at me in surprise, his brown eyes wide but unreadable.

"Oh," he said, dropping the washcloth on the bed.

He stood there as we stared at each other, and I was unsure what I should do or say. Part of me felt stupid, but then another part of me reminded me that I had felt something uneasy in him from the beginning. And it wasn't as though the sex was bad. It was great.

I didn't know why I was mad. Except maybe I was mad at myself because I liked when he choked me. Not to mention the whole *Daddy* thing. But I wasn't sure if that was real or just a power move. Maybe I was just mad he hadn't discussed any of it prior to us having sex. I wasn't one to kink shame, but I also thought you should have an open dialogue with a partner before unleashing something like that. Particularly something as dangerous as choking.

Nate tore his eyes away from mine and rubbed the back of his neck.

"Ummm. Sorry. I can...I can go, if you want. I'd understand."

My eyes tracked Nate's movements as he picked up his discarded suit and started to haphazardly pull it on. I let out a sigh.

"Don't be stupid," I muttered as I swung my legs off the side of the bed.

I wasn't sure what came over me, but I had a sudden pang of need for the mystifying man in front of me. Something that told me I didn't want to let him go. But that was silly because it was only a one-night stand. I had to let him go eventually.

Right?

He looked up at me like he wasn't sure if he could trust my words, which I didn't want to analyze the irony at the moment. So I stood up and reached my hand out to him and tugged him along to the bathroom. We could both use a shower and I was running on pure instinct.

I had a feeling he didn't want to leave just as much as I didn't want him to leave. And that was something I could work with.

Once the water got warm, I urged him to get in the shower and then I got in behind him and grabbed the soap and started to wash him.

"I...umm...you don't have to do that." The tentative tone in his voice made me pause and I wondered if he didn't like it or perhaps he just wasn't used to someone taking care of him.

"What if I want to?" I asked, trying to sound as nonchalant as possible.

His breathing picked up, but only slightly, before he turned to face me. I wasn't sure what he was looking for as he searched my eyes for the answer to his unasked question.

"Nate," I said softly.

He hummed. "Why do you call me that?"

I pulled back from him, my eyes furrowed. "I...I'm not sure. Do you not like it?" The more I thought about it, after he asked, I realized he'd introduced himself as Nathan and I just jumped right into calling him Nate, not even bothering to find out what he preferred to be called. "I'm sorry. I don't have to—"

His lips cut me off, stopping me mid-ramble, for which I was grateful.

"I like it coming from you. Or Daddy." He looked away, the words so low I almost didn't hear them. "Which is weird, because normally I don't like nicknames."

I ignored the Daddy thing for the moment and smirked. "Really? I wouldn't have guessed from the way you keep calling me *little bird*."

Nate scoffed. "That's different."

"How so?" I asked, laughing at his ridiculousness. "It's still a nickname."

He crossed his big, bulky arms over his chest and tried to level me with an intimidating glare. But it wasn't working.

"It just is." And with that, he turned back around and moved under the spray to wet his hair, effectively ending the conversation.

I rolled my eyes and grabbed the shampoo left out by housekeeping and reached up to massage it into his scalp. He let out a low groan that had my dick twitching. Once he had the shampoo rinsed out, I concentrated on lathering up the body-wash and spreading it all over his body.

When I was done, he maneuvered me so we switched places and he gave me the same treatment.

"How did you get these?" he asked quietly, running his hand up my left side again.

I went still and tried to move away, but there was nowhere for me to go—not in the small confines of the hotel shower.

"Don't," I said, voice stern as I pushed his hand away. "It was something that happened a long time ago. I don't even really remember it. And I definitely don't talk about it, or think about it."

My head turned away. It was the only way I had to hide in the small space. I refused to feel like a victim when I was with him. I wasn't that lost boy anymore, no matter how fucked up my brain and body still were.

"Don't," I repeated softly.

Nate just stared at me for a moment, as though trying to figure out what to say to my mini outburst. I didn't think he was going to say anything else on the subject, as he turned off the water and grabbed a towel to dry me off. When we were dry, he led me back to the bed, where he stripped the dirty sheets and got out the extra linens from the closet to remake the bed.

"You shouldn't hide yourself. There's nothing to be ashamed of. We all have our scars. Some are just more visible than others. Do you know what scars are?" he asked as he got into bed behind me, pulling me flush against his chest.

I shook my head.

He kissed the spot right behind my ear before whispering, "They're a reminder you survived, little bird."

5

NATHAN

I ghosted my fingertips over his skin, barely caressing his heated flesh. There was an itch under my skin to take him, claim him, mark him. To make him mine and never let him go.

My little bird.

But I had to be careful not to wake him as I pulled my clothes back on from the night before. In the end, the disguise to get into the wedding hadn't been necessary, but I couldn't find it in me to care that I had killed an innocent man for nothing.

There wasn't much at all in this world that I cared about.

Except him.

My little bird.

In the light of the day, I thought maybe I'd have some clarity. But, if anything, I felt more unsure than ever. It wasn't something I was used to feeling. Feelings, in general, weren't something I was used to dealing with too often.

When I'd woken with Aiden's body wrapped around me, my first thought was about how I would do anything for him, anything to protect him, anything to *keep him*. That he was *mine* and I was never going to let him go.

Not again.

And those feelings had only grown and intensified as I'd wandered around his room, looking through his things before I had finally gotten dressed and decided I needed to get out.

I didn't need to get caught. Not that I didn't think I could distract him with my dick. But I had other things I needed to take care of before I could focus on Aiden.

The obsession I had with him was unnerving. It tingled along my nerves, setting me on fire. I was used to feeling this way with my victims. It was how they all made me feel.

When I found them, there was something about them that tugged at me. An inner voice that told me they were *mine* and only they could calm the beast that raged within me. I felt that same obsession with Aiden, to know him, to possess him.

But it was different this time in ways I didn't understand. He shouldn't have been different. There was only one way this could end, and that was with me bathing in his blood.

So, why does the idea of killing him make me sick?

With the need to know more driving me, I kept my eyes on him as I moved around the room and made my way to where he'd discarded his clothes. Reaching into his pocket, I pulled out his wallet and flipped through the contents. It was pretty standard. Some business cards, a debit card, a couple credit cards.

His driver's license slid out of the protective sleeve easily enough and I snapped a picture of the front and back. After I put his wallet back, I searched his other pockets, including his suit jacket, and my heart beat in triple time when I saw his badge. Of course, I'd heard him and Duncan mention it the night before. But I refused to let myself think about it too hard.

There was a slight tremble to my hand that made me frown as I took a picture of the badge as well, just in case.

After I put everything back, I moved over and I stood next to the bed, watching his prone body cling to the pillow I'd shoved in his arms to take my place. I tried to figure out what was wrong with me. I'd never hesitated when I found someone before. I took what I wanted and there was nothing, and no one, to stop me.

My hand reached out and stopped just above him. I wanted to run my hands down his scars, wanted to worship them and revel in their beauty.

He was a work of art. Perfection.

I'd crossed a line with him the night before and I was still surprised he hadn't kicked me out after he came. When I'd had my arm wrapped around him, holding his life in my hands, nothing could have compared to the rush I'd felt. It had been a high like no other.

Why did I let go?

Anyone else would have been dead. I still couldn't figure out why I hesitated and left him alive.

I continued to stare at him as I tried to work the puzzle out. There was something about this man that I couldn't take his life. And it almost pissed me off. I liked things a certain way and I never deviated from how I did things.

Until Aiden Cooper came into my life.

I moved my hand up and softly stroked the messy tendrils of his silky hair. The act had me puzzled. I wasn't an overly touchy person. I didn't usually do affection, at all. Yet I could barely resist the urge to touch him.

Before I was able to move back, Aiden stirred under my hand. When his eyes fluttered, I knew I needed to get out of there before I did something stupid—or rather, something even stupider than I already did.

With a quiet sigh, I let my index finger graze over his smooth cheek one last time before I silently slipped out the door before he realized how close he had come to death, more than once.

When I reached the elevator at the end of the hall, I pressed the button and waited while I tried to come up with a new game plan. Nothing had gone down the way I had intended the night before.

Duncan was still alive. He was a loose thread I couldn't risk leaving alive. It was an itch under my skin that I couldn't scratch. The compulsion and desire I needed to quell while I was in public, until I could find a new way to get to him.

Now that he'd seen me with Aiden, he wouldn't let me near him to seduce him to be able to get to him that way. I didn't like when I needed to go to my victims because it made things appear less random. They were harder to explain away. But I would do what I had to do.

But first things first, I needed to get the fuck out of that hotel. I'd already spent too much time there and could be associated with too many people connected to it.

When the doors opened to the elevator, I dashed inside and pressed the button to close the door before anyone could get the idea to come along and try to get in with me. It was the slowest ride down to the lobby. It was a novelty, being so impatient. Usually, I was calm and cool under pressure, but too many things had gone off script.

I needed to find a way to get things back on track.

The doors finally opened and I let out a breath of relief as I stepped into the lobby and quickened my steps as I neared the doors. My freedom was only a few feet away.

At the desk, there was a group of employees huddled around, talking in excited, hushed whispers. My steps faltered as I tried to hear what they were saying, but my eyes never left the prize in front of me.

"Excuse me! Sir!"

Ah. Fuck.

My steps slowed and my back went rigid, shoulders squaring. I wasn't sure what the desk clerk was frantically calling after me about, but I was sure I didn't give a fuck about it. I cast a mournful glance at the door before I turned to glare at the man a few feet away.

"Yes?" My voice dripped with annoyance and boredom, which was hopefully a clear indicator that I wanted whatever this interaction was to hurry up and be done with.

He glanced around, his hands wringing in front of him. The look in his eyes was as if he'd seen a ghost, but I lived with ghosts every day.

"Um... I'm sorry, sir, but you can't leave the hotel right now."

I scoffed. That was when I noticed a few other guests were milling around the lobby.

"Why the hell not?"

The man, who looked like he was barely a day over eighteen, flinched at the demanding tone, but I was beyond caring. Whatever drama was going on at the hotel, it wasn't my drama and I wasn't about to get roped into it. I had my own shit to deal with.

My brows furrowed as I scowled and tried to figure out what was going on. But the sirens off in the distance that were quickly getting closer were a disturbing clue.

There was no reason to panic, and I didn't. The racing of my heart was natural, even if it wasn't a reaction I was accustomed to.

I wonder if Aiden has been woken up with the call yet.

A soft gasp from in front of me had me quirking a brow at one of the women behind the desk. It was obvious she knew who I was. I hoped I could use that to my advantage.

"Can I help you?" I offered her an easy, almost flirtatious smile that made her blush and giggle.

She bit her lip and offered me a coy smile that turned my stomach. "You're Nathan Turner."

I shrugged. "Guilty. How do you know who I am, sweetheart?"

"I'm a business major at Cardell," she said with a shrug. "I've been trying to get your office to arrange an interview for one of my classes, but they keep pushing me off."

She let out a sigh and bit her lip, looking away, as though she second-guessed saying that.

I frowned at the thought of my secretary not setting something up and made a mental note to address it. "I'm really sorry about that. I had no idea or I would have said to make sure they got you on my books."

My skin itched. The cops were getting closer, but I had to play my cards right. So, I pulled out my wallet and grabbed one of my business cards. With one of the pens from the desk, I wrote my private line on the back and handed it over to the girl.

"Here. That's my private line. If you call that, you'll get me. No Julie gatekeeping the phone and my appointment book."

She stared down at the card in my outstretched hand like it was something precious, or maybe a snake about to strike. Her hand shook as she reached out and clutched it.

"Are you sure?" Her voice sounded so reverent, as if I were offering her something holy instead of a business card.

"I am," I told her with a reassuring smile.

Looking back at the doors, I let out a sigh. "Only problem is, if I'm late for this meeting I have to get to, then I may not even be worth interviewing for your class."

The clerk looked at her with wide eyes, shaking his head. He was smart, maybe too smart.

"Amanda," he hissed.

She straightened her shoulders and motioned for me to follow her. "Jeremiah, we pride ourselves on guest discretion. Especially our high-end guests."

We didn't stick around to hear what Jeremiah was stuttering as we made our way to a side hall and Amanda let me out an emergency exit whose alarm was broken. I slid out the door with a nod of thanks before I walked the two blocks to my car and sank into my seat, closing my eyes when I finally shut the door behind me.

The drive home was quick in the pre-dawn hours, with the light of day just starting to peek out. I'd let my mind drift back to Aiden and the way he'd reacted to me the night before.

It was jarring, to be thinking about something besides my next victim, especially when I had someone on my radar.

I was halfway home when I felt my phone vibrate in my pocket. I pulled it out and swore when I saw Christian's name on my caller ID.

"What?" I bit out as I tried to rein in my frustration. It wasn't his fault I'd had to leave my little bird and it left me feeling all kinds of wrong.

"Wow, someone woke up on the wrong side of the bed this morning," he teased with a chuckle.

I let out a grumble but didn't say anything. If only he knew how wrong he was, because everything had been *right*, or at least it had, until I realized I couldn't kill Aiden and then had to leave.

Part of me knew I should have felt unsatisfied because I hadn't made the kill I'd intended to make the night before. Even though there had been a different body I'd left behind.

But I felt oddly sated. Even though I hadn't killed him, either of them, there had been a thrill in knowing I had Aiden's life in my hands. Briefly, I wondered if it was possible for that to be enough. Maybe not forever, but what if having that sort of power over someone was enough to keep the urge to kill at bay?

I shook my head. It was too early for such introspection. Especially when I had my project foreman on the phone.

"Nothing that has anything to do with my bed is any of your concern, Christian. What did you need, besides to annoy me?"

Last year, I made the mistake of sleeping with the other

man. While I hadn't had an urge to kill him, I definitely shouldn't have listened to the urges telling me it would be a good idea to fuck him. Sure, he'd been willing to do all the dirty and nasty things I wanted, but it also left things a little messy since he worked for me.

"We have a problem at the house on Collins Ave. Need you to come by and figure out what we should do."

I let out a sigh and my head fell back as I let out a groan of frustration. I didn't want to figure out what should be done. That was what I hired people like Christian for, so things could get fixed and resolved while involving me as little as possible.

The anonymity was what worked for me. People didn't need to know who I was. While I had over a dozen shell corporations that handled the financial and legal records of the thirty or so properties I owned, I had little to do with them publicly. This way, if I ever needed to use a property for any of my extracurricular activities, there was no tying me to the property.

While Christian didn't know the sort of man Nathan Turner really was, he did know he preferred to be more of a recluse and live high up in his castle away from people. But as the person who I trusted the most to oversee all the property renovations, he also knew I was the owner of the properties. It might have been careless, having one person know that much about me, but I couldn't bring myself to trust even more people with what I needed done.

Christian didn't ask questions, especially about my personal life, even when he was dying to know something. And he knew even when I was fucking him that it didn't make him entitled to ask questions. Which was why I had let him live.

"Fuck. Give me a half hour to get there." I knew I should have stopped at home first to change so I wouldn't be showing up in the same suit I'd worn the day before, but there wasn't anyone I was going to run into who would have seen me there.

Plus, I needed to deal with whatever it was Christian

needed help with so I could get back home and pour a glass of bourbon and make a plan to get to Duncan.

And find out all I could about Aiden Cooper.

I could already feel the itching starting under my skin and knew it was going to be a hell of a day.

Fuck my life.

6

NATHAN

My fingers drummed a sharp staccato beat on my desk as I stared at the open browser screen, contemplating my next move. Restlessness and uneasiness coursed through me that I wasn't used to dealing with. Too many things started to take root that I didn't know how to process.

Things were planned. I executed those plans, which sometimes ended with me taking the life of another human being. Other times, it resulted in me taking over properties and rehabbing them for various purposes or resell.

But my plans were linear. And things never strayed from the plans.

Except threads seemed to be catching and starting to unravel. Just slight pulls. But if I didn't deal with them soon and get everything back in order, then it would lead to chaos. The very fabric of my thread, my sanity, would be undone. And that wouldn't be good for anyone.

By all accounts, Aiden should be dead. It had been a risk, leaving him alive. Just because he didn't recognize me at the hotel, didn't mean he never would. Not to mention, he'd been on my list too long to be left alive. Eventually, my brain wouldn't be able to handle the fact he continued to breathe.

I'd already allowed him to break my ritual. He's already upended my life into chaos.

But he'd moved and I'd had to let him go. And now, fate had brought him back to me. Except, he felt different than all the others did. Like fate had different plans for him, for me, for us. The need to claim him and make him mine was still there. It just was *different*.

Part of me wanted to insert myself into his life. To become invaluable, make him crave me, depend on me, *need me*. Because fuck knew I needed him.

My head turned to look at my phone, but I refused to go through the pictures again. I'd already memorized them. But the pull to look at the one I knew I shouldn't have taken was strong, too strong.

I didn't know what had possessed me to take the photo of Aiden asleep in that bed. He was on his stomach, his perfect ass up in the air as though it were an offering to me. The blanket had been thrown down, barely covering one bitable cheek.

The truth was, I hadn't wanted to leave him. I'd felt an urge to crawl back into bed and wrap him back up in my arms, and that wasn't me. So, the photo was the best I could do so that I could keep him with me.

But that was a lie. And I knew it. Because my little bird was under my skin. And he was mine and I wouldn't let him go. Couldn't let him go. I'd find a way to get to him and make him mine, whether he liked it or not.

Though, I'd prefer it if he did like it.

Except, he was a cop.

I blew out a breath.

That made things a hell of a lot more difficult for what I had planned.

Tearing my eyes away from the phone, I looked back at the

computer screen that continued to mock me. The cursor blinked, daring me to type in my search query. My leg bounced as I typed in the name of the hotel I'd been at the night before and pressed enter.

I couldn't breathe as I waited for the results to load. But as I scrolled through, there wasn't a lot to be found. I clicked at the top of the news section and let out a sigh of relief to see that while there were articles about the man I'd killed, they were only about his disappearance.

My head fell back against my chair as the tension drained from my body. I still had to worry about Duncan. My brain wouldn't let me let him go, especially considering I'd let Aiden live. And that would make things more complicated with my little bird, to have two people disappear or be murdered who were connected to the hotel where we had met.

But a disappearance? People disappeared all the time. They were unhappy with their lives, jobs, relationships and just left without a word. Of course, there were times when people like me came around and something happened to them and no one knew.

I wasn't stupid enough to believe that no one would ever find the young man I'd killed. Especially considering the hotel had been crawling with cops and I'd let Aiden distract me, which meant I didn't get a chance to get back to him and move him before morning.

Duncan had been too much on my mind, and my plan for him. He'd distracted me that I hadn't even considered that the hotel would realize they had a staff member missing or that he would have family who would miss him and file a police report. Let alone take the time needed to map out the security cameras and their angles in the corridors. For all I knew, they could have caught me with him and then I'd really be fucked.

The itch, the overwhelming, consuming need to slide my knife through flesh hit me like a freight train. I wasn't sure if it was because I hadn't taken out my intended target the night before or because so many things seemed to be spiraling out of my control.

I needed to find a way to rein it all in or things could end very badly for the people around me. People I had no intention of hurting.

But, for now, I did have a name on my list who could sate the beast within me.

After ignoring my phone for so long, when the text tone went off, it made me jump in surprise. I sucked in a breath and let out a low chuckle as I picked it up. As soon as I read the message, I let out a groan and wished I'd decided to ignore it.

CHRISTIAN

When are you going to spill on the new guy?

Fuck. Why did I ever tell Christian anything? I still didn't know what had possessed me to tell him I'd hooked up with someone the night before. It was none of his business.

But I knew why. He'd started to get clingy. To hint about picking up where we'd left off and that was never going to happen. And I'd been desperate to find a way to let him down that didn't involve a knife to his gut.

There's nothing for you to know.

You have a job to do, so do it. I expect a full report on the zoning for the condos by the end of the week.

I hoped he got the hint and left well enough alone. He was decent enough of a friend, I supposed. Not that I had much experience in that department. Even if I thought Christian wasn't trying to get in my pants and had a genuine interest in where things with Aiden were going, I didn't think I could give him any information.

Mostly because I had no idea myself. He had me all up in knots, though. That much I knew.

Fucking *Daddy*.

I leaned back in my chair and looked up at the ceiling, searching for answers when I wasn't even sure what the questions were. I had no idea what had possessed me the night before. I'd never been into any sort of Daddy kink or age play before. I still didn't think I would be into any age play. But something about being my little bird's Daddy, it sent a shiver down my spine.

With a shake of my head, I dispelled the memories from the night before and got back to the work I needed to focus on. I hadn't been in the right headspace when I'd killed the guy at the hotel and I needed to know if I should be worried or not. Especially considering I fucked a cop right after.

After shutting my computer down, I grabbed my syringe, bindings, and a blade. On the way out the door, I set the automation on my home security to engage and lock up, along with setting a sporadic light automation so it would seem as though someone was home and moving throughout the house.

One could never be too careful, especially when they were a serial killer.

Getting into my car, I set my GPS to Duncan's house, where I knew he'd be for the night. When I pulled up, I was happy to see the living room light was on and the television was flickering. I couldn't see him from where I was at. The couch looked empty, but he must be in there somewhere.

I settled in, pulling the binoculars from the glovebox, and waited for the perfect moment. My mind wandered as I waited for Duncan to come back into the room, wondering how Aiden felt about stakeouts. A lot of cops didn't like them because they were boring, but I didn't mind sitting and watching my prey. It gave me proper time to learn about them and plan my next move.

With a grimace, I couldn't help but hope Aiden was not a snacker. I hated having food in my car. It made the car so unclean and unsightly. Not to mention, then you risked leaving evidence behind when you had Twinkie crumbs that you'd bitten into, being left next to the dead body you left on the kitchen floor.

Movement in the window caught my eye, drawing my attention back to Duncan's house. I picked up the binoculars and watched him pace back and forth in front of the couch with his phone pressed against his ear. His face was scrunched and his fist was balled at his side, like he was stressed.

A low, possessive growl rumbled in my chest as I wondered who he was talking to. I might not have any further interest in him sexually after finding my little bird, but he was still *mine*. Yet, whoever he was talking to seemed to be someone he was intimately familiar with, enough at least to have what appeared to be a distressing phone conversation with.

I wondered if it was about the missing hotel employee. Briefly, I wondered if it was about me. How I'd shown up at the hotel, at the wedding he'd been bartending at, but then had completely dismissed him and flirted with and took another man back his room to fuck.

Normal people got upset over things like that, didn't they?

That seemed plausible, but I didn't think he would be that upset about not getting to sleep with me, considering how often we'd skirted the topic in the past. Maybe he was feeling as possessive over me as I was of him.

Or, it had nothing to do with me and I was being a narcissistic asshole.

It was a toss-up, really.

Duncan's shouting got louder, though I couldn't make out any actual words. A new plan formulated in my mind as I he fell back onto his couch, a look of defeat marring his beautiful face. He wiped his hand over his eyes and I couldn't tell if he was crying or not, but I wouldn't be surprised.

He stayed there, on the couch for a long while, not moving. I didn't think he was watching the TV by the way he stared off into space. At one point, I thought he looked straight at me, but he moved his head before I had time to panic about being caught watching him.

Eventually, he turned the lights off and left the room, walking somewhere I couldn't see him anymore. A few minutes later, a light turned on upstairs in what looked like the bathroom. He moved around, getting ready for bed, I assumed. After a few minutes, he passed by the window, but then paused and moved back. He stared out for a moment before moving on and turning off the light behind him.

No other lights were visible after, but I assumed he went to bed.

I sat there, still as a statue, staring at the house. My gaze skittered toward the neighbors' houses every once in a while, looking for any movement that would indicate they were aware someone was watching, but everything was still and silent.

An hour later, I opened the car door and slid into the night, ready to meet my prey. At his back door, it was easy to pick the lock from muscle memory. I'd done it enough times and knew I didn't have an alarm system to worry about.

That was bad for Duncan but good for me.

A low creak announced my arrival as I opened the door, but there was no sound from within the house to indicate it had disturbed the owner. I slipped inside, slowly closing the door behind me with a soft click, making sure to lock it.

The stairs were ahead on my right and Duncan's bedroom was on the second floor, down the hall, third floor on the left. I wasn't sure why a single man needed such a big house. But then again, I wasn't one to talk as his whole house would fit in my downstairs.

I crept up the stairs and into his room, syringe ready as I stood over him. My heart raced with the sweetness of anticipation as his eyes flung open as the needle pierced his skin.

Duncan's hand swung up to grab my wrist, but by that point, it was too late. I'd already injected the fast-acting drug into his system. He barely got to squeeze my hand and expel a stuttered breath before his body went limp.

With a smile, I reached up and swept the hair out of his face, caressing my thumb across his cheekbone. There was fear in his eyes as he stared back at me, locked in his body, unable to move or fight back.

In a way, I knew how he felt. There was a monster inside me that kept me trapped and unable to move, forced to do its bidding. But I knew he wouldn't see it the same. They never did. I'd tried to talk to one of my previous victims, thinking maybe I could finally forge some sort of connection with someone. It didn't work out very well. Left me with more questions than answers.

That had been the second time I'd lost control and gone on a spree where I didn't remember what had happened after. Then, later, I found myself in my bathroom, washing the blood off my skin and clothes.

I shuddered at the memory, my eyes meeting Duncan's. That wasn't something I wanted to repeat ever again. Not when I had my little bird to think about. I had to keep him safe.

He was my priority now. Whether he knew it or not.

With a sigh, I scooped Duncan into my arms and carried him into the bathroom. He tried to squirm, but the paralytic was too strong.

"I'm sorry. I wish I could have prepared things before I brought you in here, but I didn't want to risk waking you up." I set him gently on the cold tile floor, leaning propped up against the sink.

He made a sound deep within his chest and despite the fact he couldn't speak, I knew what he was asking.

"You should be thanking Aiden. If things hadn't worked out the way they did yesterday, this would have been you last night." I grimaced. "And it would have been much less pleasant for you then."

Not that it would be a piece of cake for him, but with the way things had turned out, I thought he would definitely appreciate the less painful end he had to look forward to than I had initially planned.

A single tear snuck down his cheek, but I was unmoved as I stared down at the scared man before me. I turned my back to him, knowing he wasn't going anywhere, and went to the bathtub and started to fill it up with hot water.

My only regret was I couldn't force him to write a confession to the murder of the man I'd killed the night before. If I could have killed two birds with one stone, that would have taken a lot of pressure off my shoulders. But I hoped maybe there would be enough suspicion of the timing of his apparent suicide with the disappearance, and then murder, of the man the police would start putting two and two together.

It was a long shot. But if I could ingrain myself in Aiden's life like I hoped, then he would get to know me and I could make him fall in love with me. That would leave him with no reason to suspect me to be the killer I really was.

With a sigh, I turned off the water when it was high enough. I hated leaving things to chance, but I didn't have a choice in this instance. Too many things had already gone wrong and I needed to clean up my mess and hope for the best.

My fingers didn't linger as I quickly undressed Duncan before placing him in the tub. I admired his effort to struggle against me and live. The fight always made the kills more exciting and got my blood pumping, even if they were fruitless in the end.

The small blade was in my back pocket and I wrapped his fingers around it, then my hand around his fist. I caught his gaze and held it, watching tears stream down his face in earnest now as I guided his hands to slit his wrists. After placing one arm in the water and one arm on the lip of the tub, I took a step back to watch the blood drain from him.

He stared up at me, unmoving. His eyes were pleading with me to help him. But there would be no help for him.

A satisfied smile spread across my face as a contentment settled deep in my body, wrapping itself around me like a familiar blanket. It cocooned me in its warmth. This was what I had needed.

"Thank you," I whispered to Duncan as I watched his eyes drift closed as he succumbed to the blood loss.

Unable to stay any longer, I slipped from the room and quietly left through the back door.

I had a little bird I needed to find and claim.

7

AIDEN

My body still ached with the memory of Nate, even days later. I couldn't remember the last time someone had fucked me that well. Had *owned* me that completely.

In the shower, I stood under the spray with a smile on my face and a lump in my chest.

Part of me hadn't been surprised he'd snuck out before I woke up the next morning. But I was more surprised he hadn't left a note with his name and number or anything. I was sure there had been a spark, and that he'd felt it too.

Not that I expected him to want to be my Daddy for real, and God, I couldn't believe the reaction that word had pulled from deep within me. I'd never called a man that in bed, or out of it. But the way he'd whispered the word in my ear, coaxing me to call him that. A shiver ran through my body at the memory, a yearning for more.

Unable to stop myself, I put one hand on the cool tile and the other slid down my wet body until I reached my aching cock. A gasp escaped my lips as I tightened my fist around myself and gave one slow tug, working my half hard dick to full mast.

"Fuck." I shuddered as I continued to stroke myself until I was panting. The memory of Nate's lips and hands on my body drove me wild. A live wire could have been put in the shower and I didn't think I'd get worked up as fast.

He was intoxicating. Breathtaking. Dangerous.

I didn't usually go for the type, being a homicide detective. My kind of guy was usually the safer bet, more reserved and easygoing. Like Duncan.

But fuck. Nate.

Daddy.

My fist moved faster, twisting over the head, working in the pre-cum over my shaft that leaked out. With a grunt of satisfaction, my head fell back as I pumped my hips into the tight circle made by my fingers.

Thoughts of the way Nate had worked me open and fucked me hard and fast, worked my body like no one else ever had, filled my head as I fucked my hand hard and fast, needing to spill my release.

He ruined me in one single night, with one fuck, for any other man.

"Oh, God, yes, Daddy." I came hard in my hand, my vision blacking out around the edges. My breath came out in short pants as the water cooled on my back.

I quickly washed and rinsed away any evidence of my shame. I'd never made myself come so hard before. Not over a guy who I was never going to see again, who had made it clear when he left without a word that he wanted nothing to do with me.

Fuck. My. Life.

It was fine. Everything was fine. I could go about my life. Move on and forget him.

A heavy sigh settled into my chest without my consent as I

pulled my clothes on, barely even noticing what I had pulled out of my closet. I felt like a robot as I got dressed, barely registering my movements.

"Fuck." Just as I was leaving the bedroom, I rushed back into the bathroom and threw open the medicine cabinet. I stared at the pill bottles on the shelf, my throat working, unable to swallow the lump that had formed.

Tears stung my eyes as I cursed Nate, even if it wasn't his fault. Of course he would have had questions about the scars.

I grabbed the bottles and tossed back the pills, hoping it would keep the panic at bay, despite the fact I knew it was unlikely. Things had been worse the last couple days since meeting Nate, since he asked about the scars.

Even though it had been a long time since I'd been a victim, my brain still forgot sometimes.

Closing my eyes, I shook off the thoughts. They didn't do anyone any good, especially me. And it wasn't even like Nate had stuck around to learn anything real about me. Which, yeah, sucked, but it was probably for the best.

Once he learned how much of a basket case I was, he'd leave. Everyone left. Not that I could blame them. No one should have to be saddled with my metric shit ton of baggage.

I glanced up into the mirror as I closed the door and grimaced.

Shouldn't have done that. I looked like shit. Couldn't be helped, though. The nightmares had been worse the last few days. I'd actually been surprised I'd slept through the night with Nate.

Huh.

In the kitchen, I slammed the freezer door closed after I grabbed two waffles and angrily tossed them in the toaster.

Man, he was such an asshole for putting that thought in my head. And then he had the nerve to *leave*.

Fuck him.

No, fuck me. I need Daddy to fuck me until I can't move or think.

I let out a groan as I leaned against the counter, knocking my head against the cabinet. Maybe if I did it enough times, I'd knock some sense into my brain.

The man was gone. It was a one-time thing and I needed to forget him. To forget the impulse to track him down and make him mine for real.

Because that was all my dumpster fire of a life needed, for the man I had a one-night stand with to press charges for me stalking and harassing him.

I grabbed a plate and fork, spinning it in my hands as I thought about ways I could try to find him and possibly make it seem like I ran into him by accident. He gave me his name, so it wouldn't be out of the realm of possibilities to look him up and see what I could find.

No. He left. If he wanted more, he would have stayed. Or left a note. Something.

I sighed as I cut my breakfast and drenched it in syrup. If I couldn't have him, then the sugar high would have to do. Glancing at the clock, I saw that the time had gotten away from me with all my maudlin thoughts, so I shoved the last few bites of food in my mouth and tossed my dishes in the sink.

When I got to my front door, I almost walked out without my keys, badge, and gun. I was on a fucking roll.

"Jesus Christ."

I needed to get it together. I couldn't let a man get to me like that. It was a one-night stand. He'd made no promises or anything, so I needed to stop acting like a high schooler who had been ditched by his prom date.

There were too many people counting on me to do my fucking job for me to act like an asshole.

After taking a few deep breaths, I got my shit together—literally and figuratively—and drove to the precinct, where I hoped it wouldn't be a nonstop day. With Victoria on vacation housesitting and babysitting for her cousin while she was on her honeymoon, that left me on rotation.

It wasn't that I didn't like partnering with the other guys. It was just that they weren't *my* partner. Though, I was usually left on my own, unless I was filling in for someone else who was out sick. It wasn't too bad, just usually boring. We didn't have many active cases, and none that had a lot of active leads, which meant I was stuck playing gopher.

Overall, it wasn't a bad deal.

Except for Enid, our clerk at the front desk who stopped me as soon as I walked in. Of course, nothing escaped her attention. That woman might as well be a police officer for how scary her attention to detail was.

"Well, well, if it isn't our very own Casanova." Her smirk as she leaned over the desk and threw me a wink let me know I wasn't going anywhere without spilling all the beans.

I groaned and looked at the sky, hoping for lightning to strike me dead. That woman was a menace to society, and to my health. There wasn't a party that Enid wasn't the last one to leave, because heaven forbid she miss any of the gossip.

"There's nothing to tell, En." I tried to scoot past her, but she put her arm out to block my path. Unfortunately, I wasn't much bigger than her, and even if I were, I wasn't stupid enough to even try to use intimidation to get past her. She was a beast who would have eaten me for breakfast.

One perfectly sculpted eyebrow rose as she leaned against the desk, hand on her hip. She didn't need to utter a word, just stared at me expectantly, and she knew I'd crack like an egg.

"Seriously? Come on, Enid. This isn't high school." I knew I was whining, but I couldn't help it.

When she didn't budge, I threw my hands in the air in defeat. Her smirk of victory made me want to let out a growl, but I was feeling too off-kilter from the last two days since I'd woken up on my own to be able to pull it off.

"I really don't know what you want." I let out a sigh and ran my hand through my hair. "We met, had sex, he left."

Enid stared at me. Her gaze swept over me like she was looking deep into my soul. "Mmmhmm. Yeah, I'm not buying it, sweetheart. Not the way you're all flushed with embarrassment just thinking about that tall drink of water that you left with."

I shifted on my feet, uncomfortable. She always saw through everyone's bullshit. And while her tone had an edge of teasing, it hit at the emptiness that had been left behind, that I hadn't been able to fill.

"Not sure what to tell you," I snapped. "He was gone before I woke up. So, clearly, whatever you thought you saw, or whatever I thought there was, it wasn't there."

Her face fell, which was even worse than the hard stare she had given me when trying to get all the juicy gossip. I wanted to look away with shame at treating her that way. She didn't deserve my anger. It wasn't her fault that Nate had left, that I'd gone and hoped for more than I'd been offered.

I'd been stupid. And now I had to live with the consequences of that hope.

"Oh, honey." Her arms came up around me, enveloping me in a tight hug as she pulled me against her. I put my head on her shoulder, my arms coming around her waist as I instinctively hugged her back. She was like the mother hen around the station and that was something I could really use, especially considering relationships weren't something I was comfortable talking to my actual mother about.

Actually, it wasn't something I was comfortable talking to most people about.

Maybe Victoria, once in a while.

Sometimes.

But even her, I'd been vague about when it came to Nate. Except to try to casually ask her about him, only to be left with more questions when I discovered that when she asked, her cousin had no idea who he was or what he was doing there.

That should have alarmed me. Like I said, he was dangerous, I could tell it that night. But my heart didn't seem to get the memo.

"It's all right, Enid. It is what it is. And what it was, was an incredible night with a hot guy. So, I'm just going to let it go."

She snorted as she moved back, putting me at arm's length, and looked at me.

Yeah, we both knew that was a lie. But there was no other option than to move on, no matter what I wanted.

"All right. Whatever you say." She put her hands up in surrender and moved aside.

Leaning in, I gave her a kiss on the cheek. "Thanks, Enid. I'm sorry for snapping."

She slapped my arm and shooed me back toward my desk. "Oh you. Don't you get fresh. You get in there and get to work. You'll find yourself a man who deserves you, Aiden. And if that man was a fool enough to leave you without giving you his number, then he's not the one who deserves you."

I shoved my hands in my pockets and took a step back, beyond her desk, and gave a sheepish shrug, not sure if I really believed her words. But I knew better than to dispute them to her face.

Escaping her pitying gaze, I made my way over to my desk. Thankfully, most of the other detectives at the station who had been at the wedding had already cleared out by the time I'd made a fool of myself and left with Nate. Another small miracle was the fact they hadn't heard through the Enid grapevine about my hookup.

When I made it to my desk without anyone else stopping me, I let out a sigh of relief and dropped into my chair. The empty desk next to mine shot a pang of loneliness through my heart that echoed the ache left by Nate's departure.

Shaking my head, I told myself I wasn't going to be distracted by thoughts of Nate or Victoria. I had a job to do and I was going to do it. Needing a distraction, I pulled up my emails and calendar to see if there were any updates since I'd last been in, but nothing.

A nudge against my chair had me turning to see who was behind me. I smiled when I saw Clemmons leaning up against the empty desk at my back.

"Hey, stranger. What's shakin'?" I offered him a fist bump and a smile. It had been too long since we'd hung out, but the look on his face said he wasn't there for a social visit and I quickly sat up straight in my seat, eager to see what I could help with.

Anything to distract me from the thoughts tumbling around in my brain.

Clemmons eyed me for a moment, looking like he wanted to say something, but then shook his head. My stomach clenched, wondering if maybe the office gossip had gotten around after all.

Instead, he let out a whistle as he pulled his phone out of his pocket and flicked through it. "Man. We got a doozy of a missing persons case. Pretty sure it's going to end up being a homicide, but we aren't sure if it's going to end up being something for you or not. The guy is connected out the ass to the mob."

I fell back against my chair, surprised. The fucking mob. We didn't have much mob activity in the area, though it wasn't completely unheard of. But that wasn't my department.

Thank God.

"Yeah, Thomas Loretti, distant cousin to an out-of-state mob boss. I know, fuck me, right? He's twenty-four. Disappeared from work at the Westport, where he works in the kitchen, on Saturday night. Never came home and his girlfriend called the police when work said he wasn't there either."

Jesus. The fucking Lorettis. I knew who they were. Everyone did, even if they didn't run territory in these parts.

"Anyway. You and Coleman were at the Westport for her cousin's wedding the other day. So, I was hoping you wouldn't mind looking at something and telling me if this guy looks familiar?" The puppy dog look wasn't necessary, but it got the laugh out of me that I was sure he was aiming for.

I rolled my eyes and motioned for me to hand it over. When he placed his phone in my hand, I zoomed in on the kid, who looked like he couldn't have been more than twenty and tried to think back to anything that had happened prior to meeting Nate.

"Sorry, Jim. He doesn't look familiar. But there were so many people coming in and out of the room all day, setting things up. I wasn't really paying much attention to who was flying by." I frowned at the photo, hoping he was just gone off on a job doing something for his *Family* that maybe the people connected to him here didn't know about. Or maybe he ran off to escape from that life.

He nodded as he took his phone back. "Yeah, I figured it was a long shot. But you know how it is. Gotta ask all the potential witnesses all the questions."

Boy did I ever. It was grueling work being a cop, but someone had to do it or there would be no justice in the world.

"Yeah, man. I get it. Send the pic over to Vic, if you haven't already. But I'm not sure if she'll be much help. She wasn't hanging around the ballroom like a muck like I was before the reception." I laughed at myself. Jim joined in, giving me a punch to the shoulder.

He sat on the desk, and we shot the shit for a few minutes, until Freesha walked over and pushed him away from her desk. "Get your smelly ass away from my desk."

I leaned over and fist-bumped her. "Morning, Free. How are the little ones this morning?"

She glared at me over her decaf coffee and I threw a grin at her, knowing I was putting my life in my hands when it came to Detective Freesha St. Cloud. The woman was eight months pregnant with twins and refused to go on maternity leave until it was absolutely necessary. She hated the fact she was forced to desk duty. But with Victoria on vacation, I hoped it meant we got to spend some quality time together before she went on leave with the babies.

"They're assholes." Despite her curt words, the loving way she rubbed her growing stomach softened the meaning. I didn't have kids of my own, wasn't sure if that was in the cards for me and not just because I was gay, but I could see the bond forming between Free and the babies in real time and it was a beautiful thing.

I snickered, ribbing Clemmons with my elbow as he came to stand next to my desk. "Yeah, yeah. You and Josh are lucky to be having those little ones. And look at this way. While you both wanted two kids, at least you got it out of the way in one shot."

The slap to my arm let me know that maybe it wasn't such a good thing. Then again, the way she snorted said she at least partly agreed with me.

I turned back to my computer and the cursor blinked over the search box, mocking me. It wasn't stalking and obsessing over a one-night stand if I was looking him up over a case. There was always a slim chance he might have seen the guy Jim was looking for.

My fingers stilled over the keys as I wrestled over whether or not I should look Nate up in the system. It wouldn't take much. But the chances of him seeing anything, especially since he had come in so late, were pretty slim. And I knew my reasoning for looking him up would have been purely selfish, and chances were, he'd see right through my flimsy excuse.

Did I want to confront him and embarrass myself more than I already had?

Hell to the fucking no.

Clemmons' phone went off, breaking the good mood, and he went on alert as he answered it. His face went white as he got up and took a few steps away to get some privacy. His gaze shot to me, with what seemed to be a lot of agreeing noises and whispered curses.

Freesha looked over at me as she settled into her chair with a grimace. I was sure I had a matching look. Whatever was going on with Jim's call, it wasn't good, judging by the looks he kept throwing my way.

I could only imagine it had to do with the Loretti case. Fuck my life. That probably meant they found a body.

Shit. The last thing I wanted to deal with was the fucking mob. Chances of being assigned the case were slim, though, considering I could be a potential witness. So, perhaps the gods were on my side. But from the way Jim was looking at me as he hung up the phone, it didn't look like I was getting out of going to the crime scene with him.

I wasn't sure if it was my lucky day or my living nightmare.

8

NATHAN

I thought with Duncan out of the way, I'd feel more settled, but I was as restless as ever. And it was all *his* fault.

Detective Aiden Cooper.

He'd been all I had been able to think about the last week. Even while I was killing Duncan, Aiden had consumed my thoughts. That had never happened before. I thought I had purged my soul of him, but he was there, clinging to me like a scent I couldn't scrub away.

Unlike my other obsessions, I had to be more careful when I observed him. He was more vigilant and aware of his surroundings. My little bird knew when a predator was near and knew how to defend himself, thanks to his experience on the force.

But I was a monster he didn't expect to creep out of the shadows of the night. Even if I was the one he craved.

Watching him, I could tell his thoughts were just as consumed with his desire for me as mine were filled with him. Knowing he yearned for me just as badly as I needed him didn't make it any easier for me. If anything, it made it more difficult.

There were still too many risks I needed to consider.

The scanner had alerted me that morning of the body I'd dumped being discovered. I wasn't sure what had taken them so long to discover it, but the fact it took until it arrived in the dump made me question the skills of the police force. Then again, I'd been killing in the city for quite some time without being caught, so I already knew they were questionable at best.

Not that I would ever question my little bird. I knew he wasn't a part of Thomas' case since he'd only just been discovered. That wasn't on him.

I sat in my car, down the street from his house, and waited for him to come home. While his house was nowhere near as vast as my own, it let me know he had done quite well for himself, despite a spotty past shrouded in mystery.

My mind wandered. Thoughts of Aiden in my house, laid bare before me in every room. I wondered what he would think of home, if he would be comfortable there or if he'd think it was an obnoxious monstrosity.

Christian was the only man I'd ever slept with who had seen my real home, and he'd been unable to hide his scrutiny of the place before his own mask had taken over his face and he pretended he thought it was nice. Though I didn't know what he thought was wrong with it.

I didn't understand the human instinct to lie about how they felt about such mundane things. It was one of the reasons I couldn't bring myself to date. I couldn't relate to people. There wasn't that innate need to bond and form attachments and have a family.

Christian had been the closest I'd come to a relationship and that had ended amicably enough, though it was still awkward between us, considering he still tried to push things in a romantic direction. I should have known not to mix business with pleasure because it left me in the uncomfortable predicament where I might need to kill the person I needed the most in my business.

Because I couldn't handle people in my life. In my space.

It wasn't conducive to the serial killer lifestyle.

So, the thought of wanting someone in my home, in my space, was new. But I yearned for him to be there. To greet him after a hard day of work and to take care of him.

Even if he was a cop.

Definitely someone who was *not* conducive to the serial killer lifestyle.

Aiden had me spinning around like a top and I had no idea where I was going to land. It was dangerous, not just for me, but for my little bird as well. He had no idea the inferno he was playing with and how close he was to being burned.

I sat back in my seat, one hand thrumming against the steering wheel to a beat that only played in my head, and wondered how his day had been today. Even though I knew this wouldn't be even close to the first time he'd have gone to a crime scene, there was an ache in my chest that made me need to see him. Knowing he was coming home from one of *my* victims, it made all the difference in the world.

Would he know? Could some primal part of his brain sense me there?

However unlikely, a possessive part of me hoped he felt me. The rational part of me, however, not so much.

The small glass figurine in my hands caught the light from the street a few yards down. It glimmered and shone, though nowhere near as bright as Aiden. Its delicate glass structure reminded me of him, though there was a strength he also possessed, even if others around him underestimated it, just like the casual observer would with the little glass figure of the bird in my hand.

When I'd tried to find the perfect gift for him and I'd seen the bird that had been in mid-flight, I knew that was just right for him. It was just like him, ready to spread his wings and take off, but he'd always come back to me.

My nerves tingled as I contemplated whether or not I should actually leave it for him to find. I hoped he would appreciate my gift, especially after his first day back to work without his partner. He'd have to know it was from me.

Would it scare him? Thrill him?

The fabric of my tailored suit pants got tight as my cock thickened at the thought of him working himself open and pleasuring himself until he passed out, crying out my name as he came.

Again.

It was a power I never knew I'd be drunk on. But I found myself craving every part of him. I needed him, to possess him, to own him.

My hand reached down and rubbed along my aching cock, head tipping back. I was losing time to leave my present, if I was going to do it. But the need to find some relief was too great. Even if it would have been even better if Aiden were the one bringing it to me.

With a willpower that had to have been granted by the gods themselves, I stilled my hand and relaxed the fist that had clenched around the bird figurine. My heart clenched as I carefully looked it over, but just as I expected, it was more durable than one would expect.

Heaving a heavy sigh, I glanced at the clock and knew I was pushing my luck, so I hurried out of the car and made my way down the street. I was careful to keep my head down and the collar of my coat up in order to help obscure my face from any nosy neighbors. In hindsight, despite the fact I had brought my older sedan, I probably should have dressed down after work before I stopped by so I'd fit in better with the neighborhood.

But it was too late, considering I was already there and half a block from his house.

I was surprised by the number of live plants he had on the porch in pots and planter boxes, especially for a single man who worked so much. The thought of someone stopping by to help him take care of his plants or his house sent a spike of jealousy through me. No one should be helping him with things except me.

My shoulders sagged. But that wasn't my job. Not really. At least not until I was able to properly meet him and insert myself into his life. Judging by the state of things, I needed to do that sooner rather than later before someone else got it into their head they could encroach onto my territory.

Looking around the porch, I tried to find the perfect place to leave my gift for him. I didn't want it to be hidden, yet I didn't want it to be too obvious either. When I saw the bird feeder on a shelf with a plotted plant, it seemed like the perfect place.

Just as I placed the delicate figure on the ledge, the unmistakable roar of an engine cut through the night air. With a final glance around the porch, I took the steps two at a time as I made my way down and slid back into the car.

Taillights came down the street as I sat there, breathless, sliding down low in my seat, despite the distance between myself and his house. When his car pulled into the drive, it slowed and then slid into the garage.

My heart raced for a few minutes as the house remained dark, before a single light went on from what looked like the back of the house, barely casting a soft glow for me to see from where I watched. I needed to get closer, but it was too risky. Every fiber in my being ached to be close to him and the distance between us burned like a flame eating me alive.

I wondered if he felt it. The ache of our separation. But I knew the answer. I saw it in the line of his shoulders as he trudged through the house, slunk through the grocery store, and dragged himself along at work.

A growl tore through my chest, and I wished I could have seen how he looked right after getting back from examining something so intimately that was *mine*, just like he was. They were both a part of me and my mind screamed to take him, possess him, own him. To claim him.

But I had to play my cards right. Rushing in and claiming him wouldn't get me anywhere except maybe in a jail cell or a body bag. And that would leave my little bird all alone. Unprotected.

Which was unacceptable.

The front door opened and I perked up, caution thrown to the wind. I pressed forward as he stepped outside. Despite the chill in the air, he didn't have a jacket on. He seemed lost as he ran his fingers through his hair, looking around the porch.

I clocked it, the moment he found the figurine on the shelf. His body froze before going completely lax. I couldn't see him pick it up, but I could tell he had it in one hand and a beer bottle in the other as he settled on the porch swing.

He drew his knees up, wrapping his arms around them, and stared at the bird figure. I could imagine the look on his face, but there was something about the tension in his body that had me drawing in a sharp breath.

Something was definitely wrong. That wasn't my confident little bird who could take on the world without a thought. I knew the scene he had to have come across with Thomas' body couldn't have been pleasant, but what was it that had him looking so weary? What had caused the tears I could just barely see traces of that streaked down his face?

My fingers itched to run through his hair and soothe him. I wanted to hold him in my arms and tell him it was all right, that I would have him and keep him safe. But that was just a fantasy. One I wouldn't be able to indulge in.

The shrill sound of my phone cut through the stillness of the night, ripping a snarl from deep within me.

Christian.

Of fucking course.

He was becoming a thorn in my side. If he didn't watch himself, he'd end up on a list he didn't want to be on.

I took a deep breath, needing to calm myself before I answered the call.

"What?" So much for calming myself.

There was silence on the other end for a moment and I had to look at the screen to make sure we were actually connected.

"Umm. Boss?"

I'd never heard the other man sound so frazzled, so undone. Not even when I had been splitting him in two with my cock. It instantly put me on alert. "What's wrong?"

Christian drew in a deep breath. I could hear him trying to steady himself before he answered my question. "There's a problem over at the North Shore development."

I slumped back in my seat, my eyes seeking out Aiden again. Another fucking problem I didn't need.

"What is it this time? A delayed shipment? The wrong tile?" Despite my flippant words, something niggled in my lizard brain. Christian wouldn't be this unsettled over something so minor and trivial. He'd get it fixed.

No. This had to be serious.

"Um. No, sir. It's on fire."

9

AIDEN

My leg shook as I glared at the small piece of glass on my desk. I wasn't even sure what possessed me to bring it to work with me, let alone display it on my desk for anyone to see. It was like waving a red flag in front of a bull. It was as good as giving an open invitation to ask questions to the rest of my colleagues.

So far, no one had said anything, but in a room full of detectives, it was only a matter of time. Especially once Victoria got back. And the clock was ticking down on my reprieve from her insightful eye. The fact that her cousin had no idea who Nate was still twisted my gut. And the fact that I was almost certain he was the one who had left the small bird figure should have alarmed me.

For the life of me, I couldn't figure out why it didn't.

But the idea that maybe he was thinking of me just as much as I was thinking of him made a fire ignite deep in my belly.

I reached out and ran my fingers along the cool, smooth surface of the wing. There was a grace, a freedom, to the bird that I never felt about myself.

As soon as I'd seen it sitting on my porch, it was like a punch to the gut.

Little bird.

That was what he called me. And this felt like it was left like a token of his affection.

My body folded over my desk, head falling onto my hands as my elbows rested on top of my desk. I should have been concerned about how he knew who I was. Where I lived. How he'd gotten it onto my porch without me knowing or my cameras catching him. Instead, all I felt was heat blooming in my chest at the feeling that *Daddy* had been thinking of me and had wanted me to know and left me a present.

Jesus Christ.

What the fuck was wrong with me?

I was a homicide detective. A cop who had investigated countless murders that had started out just like this. Yet there I was, begging to be some random man's sacrificial lamb just because he had paid me an ounce of attention.

Could I have been any more pathetic?

The whole situation screamed walking red flag, from the moment he'd sat down. But I lapped the attention up like a puppy dog just waiting for an ounce of praise from his master.

Or Daddy.

"Well, helloooo, stranger," a familiar voice mocked from behind me, right before Victoria's arms locked around my shoulders.

I pushed back my crisis and suppressed the groan. The last thing I needed was for her to smell blood in the water and try to figure out what was going wrong in my life now.

Putting on my best smile, I let out a chuckle as I twisted in my chair and turned to give her a proper hug. Damn, I realized how much I'd missed her as my arms tightened around her. Part of me wanted to unload my burdens onto her because I knew she'd be more than willing to offer me some advice, but at the same time, I felt foolish.

"Welcome back!" I ducked my head, unable to meet her gaze, even though I was glad to have my partner back where she belonged. Not that we hadn't texted and video chatted while she was off.

She beamed, her smile growing even bigger than I imagined it could. Who would imagine a week off just to babysit would rejuvenate someone like that?

I was almost awed by the change in her. She was almost like a whole new person.

"Thank you, thank you. I had a great time and I can't believe it's already been a week and I have to be back here looking at your ugly mug." Victoria let out a laugh and I rolled my eyes at her.

"Gee, thanks, Vic. I definitely feel the love."

I bit my lip and went to ask for her opinion, but I stopped myself before anything could come out. The way she eyed me, I wasn't fooling her, but she gave me the space I needed as she settled back into her desk. When I went to open my mouth, I thought better of it once again and snapped my mouth closed.

There was no reason to dredge it up. Though, I couldn't help but still feel the sting of rejection that I'd felt the morning after the wedding, when I woke up alone and realized Nate had left without a goodbye or even a note.

Screw him.

Except, I did, and while it was insanely intense, and there had been a few moments where I had questioned whether or not I'd been safe, it was also so fucking good. Sure, he kind of scared me a little and I didn't usually go after the bad boy type, but he couldn't have been all bad.

At least, that was what I kept telling myself.

But my hesitation cost me. And Victoria took the decision

out of my hands on how to broach the subject of my wedding hookup.

"Sooo... when are you going to tell me about your mystery man you snuck away with?"

She plopped down in her chair next to me and leaned forward with her chin resting on her hands. The *give it to me* motion of her hand made me roll my eyes.

Why did everyone I worked with act like they were in high school and as if they were going to die if they didn't get the gossip? And why did it have to be *my* love life they were suddenly so interested in?

"I already told you, there's nothing to tell." I let out a disgruntled huff. She knew I wasn't an over-sharer who had to regale her with my exploits, but I also wasn't usually cagey about the answer, either. I wasn't sure what the *right* answer was.

Wasn't sure of the right anything anymore.

"Still think it's weird, and maybe a little creepy, that he was at a wedding full of cops, but yet he wasn't on the guest list. No one knew who he was, Aiden. No. One."

I pinched the bridge of my nose, breathing steadily, and counted to ten. She meant well. I knew she did. Even if it wasn't already appreciated.

"Technically, it wasn't full of cops when he showed up. Just like three or four."

The look she gave me told me she was unconvinced. My gaze caught on the figure on my desk and my heart gave a weird little flutter. "He was probably a regular hotel guest who just wanted to see if he could sneak into the wedding. Maybe get a free drink or snack. Wedding crashers aren't that uncommon."

She tilted her head, giving it some careful thought, and shrugged. "Maybe you're right. Still. He seemed intense, from the quick glance I'd gotten of him."

I laughed. "Oh yeah. You aren't wrong about that. He's definitely that."

"Oh my! Are you blushing?" Victoria was way too delighted as she leaned over and hissed at me, hands covering her cheeks and eyes wide. Yeah, I didn't normally get too invested in hookups, as few as they were in my life. But she didn't have to be acting like *that*.

With a roll of my eyes, I pushed her away from me, sending her chair skidding back toward her own desk.

"Come on, lover boy. Out with it. I told you that when I saw you, I wanted all the juicy details."

I let out a groan. Really, I should have known better. Victoria was a great detective and she could sniff out bullshit a mile away. Why I thought I could lie to her, I'd never know.

"Not much to tell. We went back to the room. He left the next morning. And that's that."

The skeptical look she threw me spoke volumes, even among her silence. We knew each other long enough, and well enough, that we didn't always need words to communicate. And I hated this was one of those times.

I didn't want to talk about Nate or how he made me feel. Mostly because I didn't know how he made me feel. It had been like there'd been two sides of him that night.

"Yeah, I don't buy that for a second." One eyebrow raised, she waited for me to spill the details.

"And you'd never seen him before the wedding?"

I shook my head, casting aside my own doubts. There had been something familiar about him. But I was sure if I'd met him before, I would have remembered.

She stared at me, her arms crossed and her eyes narrowed. "I don't know if I like this, Aiden. Something doesn't seem right about this guy. Maybe we should look him up."

Chewing on her bottom lip, she turned back to her

computer and booted it up. "What did you say his last name was again?"

I shook my head, shutting her down immediately. "Jesus, Mom. I'm a big boy, and I'm fine. Seriously, there's not much more to tell. We met, we slept together, he left."

As soon as the words left my mouth, I snapped my mouth shut and looked away, unable to meet her eyes.

Of course, Victoria wasn't one to miss anything. "Then why are you blushing brighter than a firetruck?"

Her words struck me dumb. While there were a lot of things to unpack about that night, work wasn't the place to do that. I shifted in my seat, suddenly uncomfortable.

Looking around, I made sure no one was nearby or paying any attention to us. My sudden need for privacy had her perking up and scooting closer.

I swallowed, my throat dry as I almost choked on the confession. "He had me call him Daddy."

"Oh." Victoria sat back, the surprise clear on her face. I was sure she hadn't expected anything like that. I knew I sure as hell hadn't. Not to mention, she probably was surprised I even admitted to something like that. It was way outside the scope of our usual topics. At least, for me. It was nothing for her to talk about stuff like that. But I was more private and didn't usually talk about things like that.

Then again, it wasn't like I usually had those sorts of topics to bring up.

She schooled her expression and leaned her elbows on her knees, face serious as she looked at me. "So, from the way it's got you all flustered, I take it that's something new for you?"

I threw my hands up in defeat. While part of me was annoyed that talking about this was the last thing I wanted to do, I knew I wouldn't have brought it up if I didn't want to talk about it with *someone*. And Victoria was the only one I had who I could talk to about something like this. I shot her a desperate look, hoping she would just drop it, but also hoping she wouldn't.

She wasn't my best friend for nothing. So, of course, she refused to let it go.

The woman had no pity on me. She waited me out until I gave in and offered her an embarrassed nod.

"Okaaaay," she said, drawing in a deep breath. "I mean. You know I'd never kink shame you. And I'm assuming you liked it. So, I'm not seeing the problem?"

A sound of frustration escaped past my lips. "The problem is that he... he... he put *that* idea in my head, had me call him *that*, and then just ghosted me. And now, I'm not sure what I'm supposed to do. Should I find out more about him or do I let it go as a casual one-night thing?"

My fingers tugged at the too-long strands of my hair in frustration. I wasn't used to dating or hookups. So, of course, when I did finally hook up with a guy, he had to make me question everything I thought I liked and wanted. And not just about relationships in general, but about myself. But then he wasn't actually there to help me navigate it.

It made me realize maybe he was one of those guys who only thought it was hot to be called that in bed and weren't up to actually holding the title. Because from what little information I'd gleaned from my late-night self-loathing searches that I refused to admit ever happened, Daddies were supposed to be there to care and support their boys or littles. Not leave them floundering in the midst of an identity crisis.

Fuck.

I really didn't need that in the middle of a work week.

Vic squeezed my arm, grounding me and helping to pull me out of my spiral. "Hey. It's okay. Maybe he's not the guy for you, but there are still lots of guys out there. And even if he isn't the one for you, maybe you were meant to meet him so he could help you discover that part of you. And *that* is why you haven't been able to find Mr. Right yet, because you were looking at the wrong kind of guy."

I tilted my head in consideration. Sure, it was possible. But something in my gut didn't believe that.

It was Nate. He was meant to be my Daddy. The little figurine on my desk was proof of that, even if I couldn't tell Victoria about that. She'd think I was crazy. Worse, she would think *he* was crazy.

Fuck. What if he was?

I shook off the thought, not ready to deal with that rabbit hole just yet.

But I needed to find him. I needed to talk to him and we had to hash this out. There were questions that only Nate could answer. Though, I wasn't sure if it would be a good idea to show my hand and let him know that in one night I might have become just as obsessed with him as he seemingly became with me.

"Cooper! Coleman!" Chief Vasquez's voice boomed from his office, startling me back to reality.

"Yes, Chief?" Victoria asked as she sprinted into his office. I let out a chuckle. It seemed she was eager to get back to solving murders after her week of tedium at her cousin's house.

Though, I didn't know how anyone could consider wrangling a ten-year-old to be tedious. Just the thought of it gave me a headache.

I slowly walked into the room and hooked my thumbs in my belt loops as I leaned against the door. "What do you have for us?"

Chief Alex Vasquez tossed a file folder onto the desk and gave a sneer.

"There's another one. Seems to line up with the other two you have. Not sure if it's connected to the Loretti case or not. You'd have to check with OC for what they have. But from what I can see, there were some similarities."

He let out a huff and my eyes went wide, seeking out Victoria to see her response. For the most part, we'd been able to keep the similarities of the other two victims out of the media's frenzy. The last thing we needed was a panic. But three murders all with the same MO?

Possibly four?

That was going to be harder to keep under wraps.

We potentially had a fucking serial killer on our hands. Of course, we couldn't confirm anything yet, not until we saw the new victim, but from the way Chief was acting, he was pretty sure it was our guy.

"Fucking hell," Victoria said as she leafed through the file.

"Travers and Nash caught it a few hours ago. They just handed me this," he said, indicating the file with the preliminary notes and a few pictures that had been printed out.

I let out a low whistle. From the bruising around the guy's neck and the setting of the scene, he definitely looked like he could be linked to our other two cases.

Fucking hell.

I wasn't sure if I was excited or scared shitless. Serial killer cases could be career-ending or career-making cases. Only time would tell which way the chips would fall for Victoria and me. But I had a feeling nothing was going to be the same after this case was over.

"I need the two of you to get your asses down to the crime scene and see what you can find. Not that I think they missed anything, but you'll be looking for different things—for similarities to the other scenes and victims." He gave us a stern look that clearly said *Don't fuck this up*.

"Unfortunately, the vic is already in the morgue, so you can't see him at the scene to examine him, but I told Jefferies not to touch him until after you were able to stop by and take a look."

"On it, Chief." I nodded at the Chief and ushered a grinning

Victoria out of the office. It wasn't ideal to get handed a case after the body had been moved from the crime scene, but it wasn't the first time we had to deal with a situation like that. There were still procedures we would all still have to follow.

The thought of dealing with my first serial killer had my stomach all in knots. If the press got wind of the possibility, they'd have a field day and there would be panic. That was the last thing we needed.

We needed to maintain control of the situation so we could control the narrative.

"Do you have to look so giddy?" I muttered as I grabbed what I needed from my desk before we set out to the crime scene.

Victoria grinned wider and shrugged. "It's just good to be back."

I let out a long-suffering sigh. Some days, I wondered what I had done in a previous life to be her partner. Other times, I counted my lucky stars that we had been paired together.

For this case, I had a feeling I would need her strength and moxie.

Fucking serial killers.

10

NATHAN

I hated going to The Docks. The place was loud and always so crowded I could hardly move without accosting someone—or being accosted. I didn't like to be touched unless I initiated it, which was rare in a place like this.

Too many people wanted too many things. Especially with the way I dressed in custom-tailored suits and the air of confidence that surrounded me. Apparently, it gave off *Daddy* vibes. But I had no interest in taking care of the needs of another person, not even for a night.

Unless that person was Aiden, apparently.

When I noticed the GPS tracker I'd put on his car had shown he was at The Docks, I thought there had to be a mistake. But twenty minutes later, he was still there.

I couldn't let my boy in a place like that, unprotected. Too many men would think they could touch what didn't belong to them. But it was okay. He'd figure out the rules soon enough. I'd help him.

The bouncer stopped me at the door and collected the cover charge, which was an insane amount. Thankfully, money didn't mean anything, so I handed it over without batting an eye and made my way over to the bar. I glanced around at the barstools, expecting to see him there, but after a quick assessment of the bar and nearby tables, I didn't see him anywhere.

My heart raced and my palms started to sweat. That wasn't something I thought people actually did outside of books or movies. But my nerves were getting the better of me.

Where the hell is he?

Thoughts bombarded me as I tried to figure out what had happened. He could have broken down and I wouldn't have known it. Or maybe he was somewhere nearby and not actually at the club. He could have let a friend borrow the car.

Possibilities were endless.

But I had worked myself into such a frenzy, I wouldn't be able to calm myself until I had seen Aiden with my own two eyes.

After a minute or two of panicking and trying to figure out what my next move was going to be, I was surprised to find him *on* the floor, dancing.

He wasn't much of a dancer, but the guy at his back that he was grinding against didn't seem to have any complaints. He seemed so different at the club than he did anywhere else in his life—more free, more himself.

I scowled. It wasn't jealousy. Really, it wasn't. More like I just didn't like other people touching my things, and Aiden was *mine*.

The guy's hand slid from Aiden's hip and my eyes narrowed more and more the closer his hand got Aiden's crotch. He tried to wiggle away from the man, but the arm he had banded across Aiden's chest held him in place, not allowing him to get free.

I saw red as Aiden continued to struggle against the man and I wondered why he didn't take him down. Sure, he might be smaller than the guy, but I knew how tough he was. He was a decorated police detective. His size be damned.

Honestly, it was one of the things that drew me to him. There was a quiet strength in that compact packaging.

But at the end of the day, it didn't matter why he wasn't defending himself. I would free my little bird. I was his Daddy, whether he knew it or not, whether he wanted it or not. And it was my job to protect him and take care of him.

And that was what I was going to do.

Starting with the asshole getting handsy with my little bird on the dance floor.

I pushed through the densely crowded floor of writhing bodies and made my way to where Aiden and the asshole were *dancing*. When I got next to them, Aiden didn't seem to notice me at first. He was too intent on trying to peacefully extract himself from the situation that the lumberjack of a man next to him seemed to keep him in.

I, on the other hand, didn't have such qualms.

Before I even finished formulating a plan, I moved behind them and grabbed the guy by the throat. I yanked him back against me, and he seemed surprised as he shouted and squirmed for a moment. Then he went stock still, feeling the edge of my blade at his side.

Goal accomplished. His hands were no longer on Aiden.

He spun around to see what was happening. The line between his brows and the frown on his face were easy to read as confusion. It was the tilt of his head as he stared at the scene before him, that I wasn't able to read quite as well.

Over the loud noise of the club, I heard Aiden's confused voice say my name.

"Nate? What are you doing here?" He didn't sound mad, but he also didn't sound exactly happy either. I was sure he would have rather dealt with the towering hulk on his own, but he would learn I was a possessive asshole and that he was mine.

No one was going to get away with touching what was mine, especially if he was unwilling. Hell, even if he was willing.

A growl started deep in my chest. While the asshole pressed against me felt the vibrations, and the pulse in his neck picked up speed, Aiden was none the wiser to all my baser instincts wanting to come out and play.

"Move along, asshole. He isn't interested." I didn't press enough to cut through his clothes or skin, but I did give the blade a slight nudge to remind the guy to behave. "Now, apologize." I shoved him forward, sliding my blade back into my pocket so Aiden wouldn't notice it.

"Sorry, man," the guy stuttered before he darted away, giving me one last wary look.

"What the fuck was that?"

I tore my gaze from the retreating man and looked over at Aiden. My head cocked to the side as I watched him march toward me, his hands on his hips and a scowl on his face. He was angry, but I didn't know why.

"Aiden?" I wasn't used to people reacting to me the way he did. Most people bent over backward to accommodate me and to try to make me happy.

I'd say it felt wrong to have him act that way, but everything about him felt *right*.

"You're mad?" I asked, wanting to understand what was wrong. What I'd done wrong.

I thought I was protecting him.

My little bird let out an exasperated huff and tried to walk away, but I grabbed ahold of his arm. Looking back, I was lucky he didn't turn around and swing. There was a vibration coursing through his body, a tension I didn't like.

"Of course I'm fucking mad." The way he looked at me told me I was missing something that should have been obvious. It was a look I used to get a lot while I was growing up and it hit me like a punch to the gut.

"Oh. I just..." My voice was low, so quiet I wasn't even sure if he heard me as I looked at the ground. Anywhere but at him and what achingly looked like disappointment on his face.

I wasn't used to being unsure. My brain screamed at me to get out of there, to run, to flee. Except, I was the predator not the prey. In that moment, though, I felt small even though I was the one who towered over him by at least half a foot.

He continued to stare at me, but his posture relaxed. I wished I could say the same for myself.

"Seriously, what do you want me to say, Aiden?" I got in his space, partially so he could hear me and there was no misinterpretation, but also because I needed to be near him.

"Nothing," he bit back.

He was being a brat and I didn't know if he was testing the boundaries we hadn't even begun to establish or if it was just who he was. Either way, I knew I needed to be careful with how I reacted to him. One wrong move and this could have all been over before it really began.

"That guy was being a creep. You were clearly uncomfortable. So, I was doing what any good Daddy would, and I came over here to help you."

With fire blazing in his eyes out of nowhere, Aiden pushed me back. "Except you're not. And in case you've forgotten, I'm a cop. So I don't need your help in getting rid of a handsy creep in a club."

My jaw fell open as he ranted at me. With each barb he threw, it found its target and I didn't even know where to begin to defend myself.

Hurt at his words, though I didn't know what else I expected after forcing myself into his life, I stumbled back a few steps away from him, hand outstretched as though he were a venomous snake I was warding off.

"Right. Okay. Clearly misread the situation."

If my victims could see me then, on the verge of a fucking panic attack over a man who didn't want me. I didn't know where the rich, confident man I used to be was, but I wanted him back. Feelings sucked and I wanted them gone.

Zero out of ten, I did not recommend.

"Fuck, Nate," he muttered, hands in his hair, as he stalked off the dance floor, leaving me with no other choice but to follow him. For the first time in my life, I felt uncomfortable in my skin, for an entirely different reason. I wasn't used to dealing with people, with feelings.

And Aiden was stirring up a lot of them that I didn't know what to do with.

He stormed up to the bar and ordered two shots. I thought at first he ordered one for each of us, but he downed the first and then the other right after. Before he could even reach into his wallet, I had my card out and handed it to the bartender.

"Should I reopen my tab or is that all you need?"

He glared at me for a moment and then let out a deep breath as he braced his hands on the bar and leaned back as he contemplated his choices.

"Can we get two waters? Then I'm good."

I nodded to the bartender to let her know we'd take the waters and be on our way. When she handed them over, I opened Aiden's and handed it over to him, then took a sip from mine as I watched him. "Of course, anything you need."

He let out a sardonic laugh that left me more confused than ever.

"Talk to me, little bird." My voice was soft but commanding, dare I say, almost pleading.

He chugged his water and watched me, as though he were studying me.

"Why do you call me that?" he asked.

I was pretty sure he asked me that night we slept together, too, but I couldn't remember if I gave him an answer or not. Looking away, I shrugged. There weren't adequate words to make him understand. Especially if I wanted to try to keep him in my life.

Which opened up a whole other can of worms and unanswerable questions.

The frustration was easy to read on his face, but there wasn't anything I could do about it. I couldn't give him the answers he wanted, even if I had been inclined to tell him the truth.

"Fuck it," he said, chugging his water before he grabbed my hand and dragged me away from the bar.

11

AIDEN

It was a night full of bad decisions. And it didn't look like it was going to get any better.

All I had wanted was to unwind. To go to my favorite club, drink, and maybe find someone to take me home with them so I could forget all the bullshit I'd had to deal with during the day.

To make me forget about *him*. The man who had me call him *Daddy* and then disappeared from my life without a word.

As expected, I hadn't been on the dance floor long when strong hands gripped me from behind as I swayed to the beat of the music. While I wasn't the best dancer, and most of the time didn't actually like to dance, I could sway and grind with the best of them. Not even caring about who was behind me, I closed my eyes and let the music and the feel of someone else being close to me wash over me.

The feel of their hands was all wrong, though. Even though they were big and obviously strong, just the way I liked them. But they didn't hold me the way I wanted to be held.

Like *Nate* touched me when we had been locked together. For once, I thought he was different.

Of course, it had to be fucking *him* who thought he had to come to my rescue, not that I needed to be rescued. I was more than capable of taking down a drunk handsy asshole who thought he had a right to touch what wasn't his.

And it made me so fucking *angry*. I didn't even know why. But it made me want to punch him in his perfect face.

To keep from doing something stupid, like assaulting him for no real fucking reason, I stormed off. Pushing past the other patrons, I made my way to the bar and put my hands on the smooth bar top, taking in a few steadying breaths.

When I glanced back, I wasn't sure if I was happy or even angrier to see that he had followed me.

God, it was endearing yet agonizingly frustrating. He looked like a lost puppy trying to figure out why he was being called a bad dog. I rolled my eyes and turned back to the bartender, who had come around to see if I needed anything.

Boy, did I ever.

The worst part of the situation was I didn't even know why I was pissed at him. Sure, he had left and didn't leave me his number, but he hadn't been obligated to do that. We hadn't made any promises.

But so many things about that night *seemed* like a promise. A promise of more. Which was my own stupid fault because he never actually explicitly made any of those promises. It was all just shit I read too much into.

Like always.

"Two tequilas, please."

He just made me feel… off-kilter. I was a bundle of nerves as I had opposing urges warring within me—one part of me telling me to fall to his feet and never let him go and another part telling me to run as far away as I could. The man was a walking red flag and there I was, a man who definitely should have known better, wanting to free-fall into the danger zone.

It was maddening and I wasn't sure what the right move

was. Based on the fact he just helped me with the drunk gropey asshole, I didn't think I had anything to be afraid of with him, but I couldn't be sure. All I knew was that warning bells were going off, especially with the look he'd had in his eyes when he'd had the dude by the throat, but I was content to ignore that given the situation.

And that scared the hell out of me.

"Should I reopen my tab or is that all you need?" Nate's amused voice was like honey soothing over my frayed nerves as he handed his card to the bartender after I downed both shots.

I'd needed the shots to calm myself, not just from Nate's sudden appearance but also from the way the asshole had me shaken when he got all handsy. But I didn't want to think about either of those things anymore.

Definitely didn't want to admit to the second one.

Nate nudged me, and I remembered he'd asked me a question. Shit, he'd been serious about the tab? I didn't want to take advantage of him, at least not in that way. But I thought we could both use water, even though I didn't know how much Nate had to drink before he found me on the dance floor.

"Of course, anything you need," he said, sounding so sincere. I scoffed, unsure if I could believe his words. They were easy to believe when he was there, but then he left so easily. And then I'd be left with nothing again.

Better not to get used to anything when nothing about him was permanent. He was just a hookup. And then he happened to be at the same club and stopped an asshole from going too far. That was all it was.

No need to read into the fact that he was at a gay club, considering I knew for a fact he was into men. But part of me had wanted him to be there because of me, as impossible as it was.

He let out a sigh as I drowned myself in the water.

"Talk to me, little bird." Again, he looked at me like a kicked puppy and my heart flip-flopped in my chest.

I watched him carefully as I took another sip of my water. The confusion and desperation were plain to see. Something told me he wasn't used to dealing with whatever emotions I was eliciting in him. I wasn't sure if I liked that or not.

Either way, I was screwed because I definitely didn't like the emotions he was eliciting in me.

Liar.

"Why do you call me that?" I asked, unable to help myself. But he didn't answer me. Instead, he looked away as if he couldn't look at me while I was asking such a question. It annoyed me. Mostly because he wouldn't give an answer and because it sparked *something* I couldn't pinpoint.

"Fuck it," I muttered before I downed the rest of my water and grabbed Nate's hand and dragged him to the bathroom. I was already on the express train to Bad Idea Land when it came to Nate, so why bother playing it safe?

When we got inside, I slammed the door shut and shoved him in a stall and locked the door. He looked shocked at my display of aggression, but I was done playing by his rules. Done playing it safe.

Within seconds, his mouth was on mine, devouring me like a man who had his first taste of water in days. He had me pinned against the door of the stall, a thick thigh between my legs, rubbing against my throbbing cock as he drove me to the edge of madness. I let out a low, dirty moan at the way his hands lit up my body as they grazed along my arms and sides until he reached the edge of my shirt and pulled it up so he could attack first one and then my other nipple with his lips, teeth, and tongue.

I keened at the feel of him, at the way he made me feel. He'd be mine forever, if it were up to me.

"Nate. Jesus, please," I begged, though I wasn't sure what

for. I needed him more than I needed anything else at that moment. There had been a pressure building up inside me since I woke that morning with an empty bed, and he was the only one who could give me the relief I desperately craved.

"Needy little bird," he said with a chuckle as he kissed his way up my neck before biting my ear and eliciting a new set of fireworks that sparked inside me.

I let out a sound of agreement. "Your needy little bird."

He pulled back for a second, looking at my face. I wasn't sure what he was looking for and it made me feel uncomfortable. Looking away, I bit my lip, but his hand came up and cupped my cheek. He turned me back to look at him. "Eyes on me."

"Fuck, Nate—"

He cut me off with a *tsk*.

"Is that what you call me?" He leaned in and growled next to my ear.

My knees went weak. I couldn't. Not again. I couldn't let him get in my head like that and take it away. It was too much, too difficult the last time.

"No, Daddy." The words were out of my mouth without my permission. I bit my lip to keep back the moan of what that word did to me.

Fuck, I really was a needy little bird. But I had no idea when that happened.

"Good boy. Don't worry, I know how to make you fly." Nate dropped down to the dingy floor and the look he gave me as he unbuttoned my pants was pure sin. I didn't even know how he had enough room to maneuver between myself and the toilet in the stall, but I wasn't going to complain.

"Fuuuck." My head fell back, but I had nowhere to brace myself as we were crammed into the small stall. Knowing anyone could hear us at any point sent a spark of excitement through my body. It was wrong, but it felt so right with Nate. He made everything feel right.

A small part of my brain was still operational and knew how dangerous this was. I was a cop, for fuck's sake. I shouldn't be getting blown in the men's room of a gay club by a guy I had a one-night stand with, who had me call him Daddy.

Jesus Christ. I was a walking fucking cliché.

And I didn't fucking care one damn bit.

Brown eyes stared back at me as Nate ran his hands up and down my thighs, easing the tension out of me, helping me to relax. I hadn't even noticed until that moment that my entire body was trembling.

Desire or nerves, I wasn't sure. Maybe both.

Without saying a word, or taking his eyes off me, Nate tugged my pants and underwear down and immediately sucked my aching cock to the back of his throat. His hands gripped my ass tight enough that I knew I'd have bruises for days as he swallowed around my sensitive cock head.

"Fuck, Daddy, that feels so good." My hands flew to his hair, clutching tight, afraid I'd lose myself if I didn't have some way to keep myself grounded. The way he worked my dick made me see stars. It was the perfect amount of suction and stroking of his tongue along my hard flesh.

He pulled back, grazing his teeth lightly, and I let out a shout as my body bowed forward from the sensation. There was no way I wouldn't be heard if someone were to walk by, or walk in. My dick twitched at the thought. Fuck, I never knew I had an exhibition kink. Nate really was making me discover a whole new side of myself.

"You're going to kill me if you keep doing that," I said with a chuckle.

Something flashed in his eyes and he gave me a wicked grin. "Only if you ask nicely, little bird." Then he was back on me like a man on a mission, and I supposed he was. It was risky, being in the bathroom. We could get caught, so the sooner he could make me come, the better it would be for both of us. Especially since I'd need time to return the favor.

My hand tugged the short strands of his hair and he let out a groan that vibrated throughout my entire body. I was sure I had found heaven in that bathroom stall.

One of Nate's hands moved to my crease and as soon as his finger grazed over my hole with the slightest pressure, I was shouting with my release that he swallowed down like a pro.

He gave me a predatory grin as he popped off my softening dick and stood to claim my mouth in a filthy kiss that left me swooning the moment his tongue demanded entrance.

Even through my haze, I could feel his arousal as our bodies were pressed together, grinding despite the fact my cock had become oversensitive after that mind-shattering orgasm. I still wanted him, needed him.

I reached for his pants, but one of his large hands grabbed my wrist and held it still as he shook his head. I pulled back, giving him a questioning look, but he just leaned forward and gave me another kiss. This time, it was much softer and somehow felt more intimate than anything else we'd shared.

I opened my mouth to ask him what was wrong, when he shocked the hell out of me.

"Come for dinner with me, little bird. Let me take you on the type of proper date you deserve."

12

NATHAN

I didn't know what had possessed me to ask Aiden out on a date. I didn't date. Ever. Not once, and there were good reasons for that. Reasons Aiden would never know.

But now I'd put myself in a situation where I'd be expected to put on a performance and act like a normal person. To act like his *Daddy* and I wasn't sure if I could do that.

Fuck.

But I'd do what I could. I'd protect him any way and every way that I could. Starting with not letting him drive, and since he'd seemed apprehensive about our late-night date, I ordered a ride-share before we left the bathroom.

Because I could be a fucking gentleman.

As we waited for the ride-share, we leaned against the outside of the club wall. I watched him fidget with his phone, obviously nervous. Looking down at my own phone, I saw that the driver was still a couple minutes away.

"If you don't want to go, please don't feel obligated."

His head popped up, eyes wide with surprise.

"Oh. Um. No. I don't. Feel obligated." He looked back at his phone, lower lip caught between his teeth. The look of concentration on his face was adorable, like he was trying to solve a problem. I wondered if that was what he looked like at work, when he was trying to make the evidence of his cases fit and catch killers.

Killers like me. Fuck. I really shouldn't have asked him out. I shouldn't have slept with him in the first place.

What the fuck is wrong with me?

I stared at him and part of me wished I had killed him in the hotel room that night. Or I should have taken him and had some fun with the kill. But the thought made me sick.

Because he was mine. But the war still raged inside whether the claim I staked should be him as my victim or my boy.

All I knew was that I needed him. More than I needed anything else in this world. But I'd never had to worry about *feelings* before, not like this.

"Wait." He hesitated a moment. Like he wasn't sure he wanted to ask what he was thinking. "Did *you* feel obligated to ask me out?"

Wait. What?

Now, I was the one who was confused. Did he really think that? After all that?

"No?" How the hell had so many of our wires gotten crossed?

I let out a sigh that turned the night air white and pulled him against me. My fingers danced along his spine, in what I hoped was a soothing manner, as I wrapped my other arm around his waist and held on tight.

Nothing ever felt as right as having him pressed against me. Not even the blood of my victims cooling on my skin, and that was a fucking heady feeling that was better than any high I'd ever experienced.

"I'm right where I want to be, little bird."

The way he melted against me, at my words, made something melt within me. A warm, gooey feeling in my chest that bloomed as he looked up at me under impossibly long lashes. His eyes full of trust for a man who never should have let me touch him, let alone given him an ounce of trust.

But I knew, in that moment, I'd do everything in my power to earn that trust every day. Even when he didn't know how hard I had to work at it.

I leaned down, my lips grazing his, just as headlights bathed us in warm light.

Aiden laughed as he pulled away, craning his neck at the approaching vehicle. "Is this us?"

Grumbling, I looked up the information in the app and herded my little bird into the car once I confirmed it was our ride. Since it was late, there weren't many options for dinner, but thankfully, he didn't seem picky and his eyes lit up when I suggested burgers from his favorite place.

I wasn't sure if it was because there was so much alcohol in his system that the greasy food sounded good or if he was excited about the prospect of us having something in common. He'd never known it was from me stalking him and watching him stop at the same place at least twice a week on his lunch while he was working.

Thinking of how much takeout he ate made me frown. It wasn't very healthy, and I wondered if I could convince him to at least get some salads to go with it once in a while, and maybe some fruit. I didn't want something to happen to my little bird because he didn't take care of his health.

And it was my job to take care of him now, since I was his Daddy.

It was a terrifying notion that made me a little dizzy. A half-cocked thought that was out of my mouth before my brain could filter it. As I looked at him, snuggled in my arms, I couldn't regret it, though. Not when I had him.

Thankfully, the drive was short. I wasn't sure how much Aiden had to drink before the two shots at the bar, but in the ten-minute car ride, he'd nodded off and curled into me. The way he tucked himself under my arm made my heart thud in my chest. He had me wrapped so completely around his little finger, that I realized with a start that I'd do anything for him.

Which was very dangerous. For both of us.

"Wake up, little bird. We're here." The car slowed to a stop as the driver pulled into the parking lot. It was mostly empty, thankfully, so there shouldn't be too much of a wait for me to get my little bird fed.

His head slowly lifted from my shoulder, eyes glassy in that way they get from waking when you've just fallen asleep but had already gone in deep. I chuckled as I unbuckled and opened the door.

"Come on, baby. You need to eat. Out."

He grumbled as he slid across the seat, his cheeks burning red, clearly embarrassed. I wasn't sure why. But it was a cute look that I knew I'd never get tired of seeing.

I closed the door behind him and led him into the diner. He blinked a few times, the lights too bright for his sensitive eyes. As the hostess sat us at a table, he looked around, assessing the room.

When the hostess asked for our drink order, I asked if we could just start off with two waters. With a smile and a nod, she placed our menus on the table and left us to wait for our waitress.

"For as much as I love this place, I don't think I've ever seen the inside of this place beyond the hostess stand at the front." He gave a soft chuckle as he sat down.

"Oh? How come?" That surprised me. I knew he was busy with work a lot, but I assumed he would have had other dates here, considering how much he loved the place.

He shrugged and looked at the menu as though it were the most interesting thing in the world. "I dunno. Guess I never really saw the point in coming here and eating alone."

Huh. So he really didn't bring dates here? Or Victoria? That didn't make sense, especially since he loved the place so much.

"Why alone? Surely you could bring any number of friends or dates here." He had friends, unlike me. So I couldn't understand why he seemed so lonely. But the uncomfortable look that flashed across his face had me pulling back from that line of questioning.

"Umm… I…" He refused to look at me, his eyes focused on the menu that I wasn't sure he was actually looking at. Not that he needed to. He got the same heart attack burger every damn time.

"Sorry, that's none of my business." I cut him off before he felt the need to explain himself to me. There was no need for that. Not yet. Not ever.

Despite my overwhelming desire to know every little thing about him, I never wanted to make him feel uncomfortable. I wanted to be his safe space. And if that wasn't a kick in the pants, I didn't know what was. Because I wasn't safe. But I would be, for him.

The awkward moment was broken by the waitress coming over with our drink order that the hostess had taken and getting our dinner order. Without thinking, I ordered for both of us and as she walked away, Aiden stared at me, mouth open.

I tried to read his expression, but it was so guarded. The way his forehead was scrunched, it was obvious he was trying to figure something out. Hated to tell him, but I wasn't a puzzle anyone could solve.

My stomach sank as I realized I had probably already ruined my chances of getting a second date, and we hadn't even gotten our food yet. I didn't even know what I'd done.

"You ordered for me?" It wasn't an accusation, but it also was more than just a statement.

Oh.

Leaning back in my chair, I folded my hands in front of me and studied him. "I did. Does that bother you?"

The way he squirmed in his seat was a clear indicator of how much it wasn't a problem. But the look on his face told a different story. I wasn't sure which one to believe.

"No," he said slowly, as he let out a breath. "But you ordered my specific burger that I get every time. Down to my customizations."

My hand froze with my glass halfway to my mouth.

Fuck, fuck, fuck. Did I? I did, didn't I?

Like a deer in headlights, I stared across the table at him. A cop. He literally could have arrested me right then and there for stalking and had a solid case because that man had the strangest burger order.

I was so fucking screwed.

"I, umm, I can explain." Yeah. Sure, I could. But the explanation wasn't going to be any better than anything he could come up with on his own.

His face shuttered. Fuck. I hated that.

"Just like I'm sure you can explain the bird figurine you left on my porch." He ran his fingers through his hair and choked out a brittle laugh.

"Aiden." I tried to figure out something to say, but there was nothing. Nothing could make any of it better. I wasn't equipped for this. I should have just left him alone and I was going to pay the price for my greed.

"I—" He held up his hand to silence me and I snapped my mouth shut. It was fine. I didn't really have anything to say anyway. Not really. Platitudes. Excuses.

From across the table, his wet eyes met mine. "Is showing up at the same club I was at, at the same time I was there, also something you can *explain*?"

I tried to swallow past the lump in my throat, but I felt like I couldn't breathe. There wasn't enough air in the room. Everything I had worked toward, I was about to lose it all because of one stupid mistake.

Isn't that what brings down all serial killers?

My breathing was ragged, fists clenched tight on the table.

I had to fight every instinct because I wouldn't fight *him*.

The scraping of his chair jerked me back to reality. But instead of coming toward me with cuffs in his hands, he stalked off, away from our table. I wasn't sure where he was going, but there was a war raging inside of me. One part of me urged me to run, to flee, to survive. The other part of me screamed to go after him, to protect him. There weren't even any dangers nearby. But the urge to protect him would always be there, and it would always win.

Resigned, I stood and went to take a step, but he spun back toward me.

"No. You sit back down until... Fuck. Just sit back down." There was fire in his eyes. Worse, under that a hurt I had caused, and I was sure I wouldn't get the chance to fix it. But fuck, I would if he gave me even half a chance.

I put my hands up in defeat without a word. He eyed me as I sat back down and waited for him to decide my fate.

When he walked out of the room, I still had the opportunity to flee, to activate one of my escape plans. But the thought of leaving him behind was worse than any punishment he could come up with.

My hands on the table, I sat back and waited for my little bird to come back with his judgment.

13

AIDEN

Fuck my life. I hated when Victoria was right. I should have let her look him up like she had begged me to. She was never going to let me forget this.

I resisted the urge to look back at the table where I'd left Nate, as I stormed away. There were only a few people in the diner and I refused to meet any of their eyes as I passed their tables in my attempt to make my escape.

But where was I really planning on going?

Up ahead, there was a sign for the restrooms, so I veered to the left and hid in the men's room, making a beeline for the sink. I hadn't even known I was shaking until my fingers tried to grab ahold of the sink and slipped the first time.

Shit. I needed to pull myself together.

I looked in the mirror and didn't recognize the wild man who stared back at me. My eyes were too wide and my pupils were blown, with a glassy sheen that spoke of way too much alcohol and nowhere near enough food. No wonder Nate was adamant about feeding me.

Nate.

My stomach turned and I darted into the stall just in time to drop to my knees and purge everything into the toilet. I wasn't usually a sloppy drunk. My nights didn't end with me hugging the toilet, with my head hung in shame. I knew how to hold my liquor.

What I didn't know how to handle was the realization that the guy I fucked was a stalker. Honestly, it shouldn't have been a surprise, and it wasn't, not really, not after finding the little figure. But it still hit me like a punch to the gut to realize just how wrong I had been about him.

Because the voice in my head had warned me that things went way beyond just normal stalking. That he was dangerous and if I wasn't careful, I would get burned, but I hadn't cared. I'd wanted him and I didn't care about the signs or the red flags. In fact, I'd intentionally disregarded them and chosen not to look into him despite knowing I should, and the pressure from Victoria to do so.

Bile rose up my throat and I spat it into the bowl, gagging on the foul taste.

I couldn't go back out there. There was no way I could face him, not when I didn't know what he was capable of, what he wanted.

A flash of anger shot through me. I gritted my teeth and slammed my fist against the wall of the stall before I pushed myself to my feet.

Fuck. Him.

There was no way I'd let him make me feel small or powerless. Not like he did at the club. That had to be his game, but I refused to play. I wouldn't cower or beg.

I was a fucking cop and I didn't need anyone to protect me. He should have done his homework before he set his sights on me, but it was a mistake that was going to cost him.

Making my way back to the sink, I was a little unsteady on my feet from the violent puking. Plus, I'd already been starving when we'd gotten to the diner. My stomach was even more in knots after emptying itself in the toilet. Though I wasn't sure I'd be able to eat anything. Especially not with him.

I washed my hands, sheer determination keeping me upright as I walked to the door and threw away the paper towels on my way out.

Doubt crept in as I made my way back to the table. I wasn't sure if I hoped he was there or if he had left. There were still so many unanswered questions I had, but I wasn't even sure if I cared about the *why* either way.

What he did was fucked up and inexcusable. Letting him explain would just be giving him a chance to make me doubt myself, to make me forgive him. And I couldn't do that. I *wouldn't* do that.

I was surprised when I rounded the corner and saw him still sitting there. His head was down, shoulders hunched, with his hands folded on the table in front of him. He looked like a man waiting for his execution.

Fuck.

This was not the night to be dealing with all the shit that Nate was throwing on my plate. I didn't want to deal with it after all the drinking I'd done, even if at that point I'd thrown it all up.

I grimaced at the aftertaste left in my mouth. At least I didn't have to worry about a kiss goodnight.

Steeling my resolve, I sat back down. Confusion nudged its way into the maelstrom of emotions swirling inside me when he didn't look up.

Was he ignoring me? Did he not even care?

Before I could say anything, the waitress came back over and placed our burgers on the table in front of us.

"Can I get you anything else?" She looked between us, like she wanted to say something but looked nervous. I wondered what Nate had said to her while I was gone. Maybe I shouldn't have gone back to the table. But it was too late. I was already there.

Surprised he hadn't taken the initiative, I glanced up at Nate, but he still refused to look at me. There was something about seeing him sitting there, lip tucked between his teeth, as though it was the only way he could keep himself from answering, where he seemed like a shell of himself, that sent a pang through me.

No! Stay strong.

"No, thank you." I offered her a tense smile and she turned and left without another word, leaving me alone with all my bad decisions.

I leaned against the seat, staring down at the burger that usually had me salivating. But the thought of eating it made me want to run back to the bathroom and throw up again.

"You were stalking me." It wasn't a question because I didn't need to ask. There was enough circumstantial evidence to know without him admitting it. But if I had any doubts, the way he flinched at the words was proof enough.

He didn't say anything to confirm or deny, though. Smart on his end. But annoying as fuck for me. I knew why he wouldn't want to answer my questions. As a cop, if he said anything incriminating, I could arrest him. But I wasn't interested in that. I just wanted answers.

"Hmph. And here I thought you said you were going to explain. Was that just another lie?" There was a bitterness to the words that I couldn't keep at bay. But it got the reaction I wanted from him.

He peeked up at me, glaring. "Nothing was a lie."

"Bullshit." I pushed away the plate of food and crossed my arms before leaning down on the table. Our gazes locked and I wouldn't let him look away.

Nate let out a huff. I didn't like the way his body had gone all rigid. It felt *wrong*.

"Who are you?"

The question seemed to throw him off. His brow furrowed, confusion clear across his face. "I already told you. Nathan Tu—"

I shook my head. "No. I want you to tell me *who* you are."

His teeth gnawed at his lower lip and his apprehension seemed to grow the longer we sat there looking at each other.

"I don't know what that means. I-I am telling you."

My mouth opened to try and explain what I meant, but as unease rolled through him as he struggled with such a simple question, my heart ached for the way he seemed to flounder and be completely lost over such a simple question. But I was also curious, and I wanted to see what his answer was.

I waved my hand in a gesture to let him continue and sat back.

He took a breath, rubbing his hands on his thighs. His gaze shot toward me from under his lashes for a moment before he went back to looking at the table, as if he couldn't bear to look at me.

"I'm a land developer. I buy land and businesses that are neglected and revitalize them into something new, ideally something that benefits the community, but I'll admit, it doesn't seem to always work out that way. I like learning new things, but it's usually from books because I'm not very good with people."

I let out a sharp whistle.

"Wow. Okay. I'll admit, I wasn't expecting the job." With a chuckle, I leaned forward and offered him a soft smile.

My eyes raked over him, noticing the little things. The way his outfit was perfectly tailored, even though it was more on the casual side. That told me it was expensive, designer, not something bought from a big chain store. So, he obviously was good at his job and did well for himself. So, despite his claims of not being good with people, he probably didn't have a hard time finding people for hookups.

Which begged the question, why was he fixated on me?

"Did you follow me to the club?"

Wide eyes shot up to mine before they quickly glanced back down as he worked through the question. The gears were practically turning at light speed as he tried to figure out the best answer, before he finally swallowed hard before sitting back in his seat. His fingers flexed slightly against the table, and I wondered if it was a tell of a truth or a lie. Something to tuck away to figure out later.

"Yes."

Oh. The admission stunned me. I opened my mouth to respond, but I wasn't sure what to say to that. Everything I'd prepared had been in anticipation of a denial. Begrudgingly, I had to give him some respect for not trying to bullshit me.

"Why?" That was the one thing I couldn't figure out. If he knew my name and where I lived, then he could have just as easily gotten the information on where I worked or even my phone number. So, why didn't he just approach me or text me?

He had to know it was creepy either way.

For the first time, he seemed uncomfortable as he shifted in his seat. "Because I wanted to see you. But I didn't think I should. I thought I could stay away, that it would be best for you."

"Why?" I felt like a broken record, but I didn't understand. And I didn't like the fact that he took the choice away from me, but then barged into my life anyway.

A heavy sigh left his body, like he was explaining something simple to a child who was acting stupid. I was starting to get annoyed.

"Most people don't actually like me once they get to know me. I thought I'd be doing you a favor." He picked up his glass and chugged the rest of the water that was still in it before he set it down. The silence stretched on for an uncomfortable amount of time, but he stared at the ice as he shuffled the glass from hand to hand.

"You do know stalking is illegal, right? And it's not too smart when you decide to do it to a cop." What I wouldn't tell him, was the way his attention made me feel all warm and fuzzy inside. Like he cared enough to watch over me and protect me. Which was ridiculous, because I was a cop and could protect myself.

He nodded and his Adam's apple bobbed, his eyes not leaving his hands. His mouth opened and closed a couple times, as though he were trying to figure out his next move, or to work up the courage to ask his next question.

"I suppose this is the end of our first and last date?" His eyes flickered up to my face for a moment before darting back down. "And that I'm under arrest."

I'd barely heard the last part, as he spoke so low, but the dejection in his voice was obvious, even if the words hadn't been at first. As the words took root and my brain processed what he was assuming, my heart lurched.

Fuck. No. I said I'm not forgiving him.

"Shut up and eat your burger." I had no idea what I was doing, and it was probably something I was going to regret, but as I pulled my plate toward me and bit into my own burger, ignoring the way he stared at me with wide, uncertain eyes, I told my doubts to go fuck themselves.

14

NATHAN

I felt like I was crawling out of my skin. Not even stalking an asshole who had gotten on my bad side and put himself on the top of my list made me feel any better about being away from my little bird.

It had been three days since I'd seen Aiden at the club and then had our disastrous dinner date. Part of me was still convinced he was going to change his mind. That he would show up on my doorstep at any moment to arrest me.

We hadn't seen each other since we left the diner, where he had insisted we take separate ride-shares home. It had killed me, but I understood he needed his space. And I was willing to give it to him. For the moment. We had moved on to texting, but it wasn't the same as being with him in person.

I'd never felt like this over anyone, like I *needed* them or even wanted them. He was like an infection that got in my system and I couldn't get him out. But in a good way.

Maybe.

I still hadn't decided.

The fact was, I'd never been on a real date before, but I hadn't wanted him to know. But maybe I should have, especially with the whole stalking debacle. Logically, I knew the mechanics of what a date should look like—and yeah, the blowjob should have been how it ended, rather than how it started.

Sitting back in my truck, I closed my eyes and tried to imagine what Aiden was doing. It had been hard, but ever since he realized I'd been watching him, I had promised him I would stop. It was the hardest promise I'd ever made. And keeping it was even harder.

Of course, he wouldn't know if I broke it, but I wanted to earn his trust and keep it. I couldn't risk it, not at this point. There was too much at stake.

The way he eventually started smiling at me, sending me bashful looks from under those gorgeous eyelashes throughout the evening, it gave me hope that perhaps I could find a way to redeem myself, even if I didn't really deserve it. But he'd never know that. Not if I had anything to do with it.

Talking and trying to get to know someone had never been my strong suit, so I wasn't sure what I was supposed to ask Aiden during our date turned interrogation turned maybe-date. The stilted silences let me know he was just as unsure as I was. But it didn't make me feel better. I wanted to get to know him, but I didn't have any experience to fall back on.

The blare of a horn from down the street brought me back to what I was supposed to be doing. I shook my head to try to clear away my thoughts of Aiden, but he was never far away.

When I saw the vehicle had nothing to do with the man I was after, I picked up my phone and scrolled through my messages with Aiden, trying to think of something to say. I was desperate to know more about him, but social etiquette had never been my forte. I had never quite figured out how to relate to people or seem interested in their lives.

He carried most of the conversation, even when it wasn't him demanding answers regarding my *extracurricular activities*, and told me about his favorite movies and music. I was surprised when he had even asked about mine in return. Though he was slightly appalled when I said I didn't watch much television or listen to a lot of music. So I scrambled to think of an artist I'd listened to and by the look on his face, I was sure it was at least a decade too old.

That was why I had been texting him since I'd woken up the following morning, asking him stuff from a list of questions the internet told me were good things to ask a potential partner when first getting to know them. The problem was, I already knew Aiden, at least the important parts. He just wasn't aware of how much I already knew.

My phone buzzed, and I looked down with a goofy smile at his outrage over what he liked to describe as my lack of culture. I thought he was being a bit dramatic, but I'd never tell him that, especially since I was glad he was talking to me at all.

AIDEN

I can't believe you've never seen it. It's iconic, man! They start off all cute and furry and then they change into little monsters that want to destroy and kill. lol.

We have to fix this one day.

Sure. Just tell me when and I'm all yours.

I let out a sigh as the man I'd been waiting for decided to make his appearance at that moment, exiting from an apartment building too nice for the likes of him.

His timing took me away from my little bird. Seemed like he really knew how to piss me off.

The man seemed to be in a hurry as he got in a late model truck and took off down the street, barely taking the time to even check for oncoming traffic before he'd pulled out into the street.

It only took a few moments for me to get the car into gear and round the corner to catch up to Clint Davenport. I knew thinking about Aiden would distract me and I couldn't afford a distraction when I was stalking my prey. That was how mistakes were made and people got caught.

And I had no intention of ever getting caught.

Especially when I had my little bird to think about and protect.

AIDEN

Do you have any brothers or sisters? Nieces and/or nephews?

No, I'm an only child. No real family left, since my parents are gone.

Apparently, I had no willpower when it came to this man.

What I couldn't tell him was that my parents had been too afraid to have any other kids after they realized I wasn't like other children. I never did find out if it was because they were afraid they'd be like me or if they were afraid I'd hurt them.

Either way, it was probably the right call on their part.

One of the few right things they did.

My foot tapped on the floor, a strange sense of anxiety shooting through me as I tried to decide if I should leave it at that or tell him more. It was almost too easy to talk to him and tell him what I was thinking.

It was dangerous.

Because while my parents had been good people, as far as I could tell, their fear of me had made my life isolating. I didn't have friends or learn how to mask most of my behaviors and idiosyncrasies until I was older. It made things difficult for me as a child.

Though, it made being gay easy. I didn't have to worry about passing on any genetic predispositions to a child. And I never thought I would have a long-term partner that I would want to have a child with to worry about surrogacy and which of us would be the donor.

But I found that Aiden made me think about a lot of impossible things.

AIDEN

Oh, that sucks. I'm sorry. What happened?

Forget that. You don't have to answer that, if you don't want to.

It's fine.

They were in a car accident. Hit by a drunk driver when I was 24.

AIDEN

Did they catch the guy?

The police were never able to find him.

Of course, I didn't explain that the police would never be able to find him because I found him first. I may not have many feelings, or feel things the way other people do, but a part of me had still cared that they were my parents and that some asshole had taken them from me.

They'd been my shield against society, and the law, and once they were gone, there had been a lot of hard lessons I'd had to learn on my own about how to use my family's name and money to keep myself out of trouble.

It hadn't always been easy, but I had always been resourceful and I'd do whatever I had to do in order to keep myself out of prison.

Or worse.

I didn't want him asking too many questions about my family. It wasn't that I wanted to hide who I was, but it wasn't something I wanted to get into. Considering I'd given Aiden my real name at the wedding, he could have easily looked me up. I was surprised he didn't. Part of me wanted to ask why, but I also didn't think I should press my luck.

Then again, he could have been doing what I had been doing, and asking questions he already knew the answers to. Maybe he had even been trying to catch me in a lie.

Or he wanted to ignore all his instincts when it came to me, same as I was doing for him.

From a block away, I watched as Clint slipped through the doorway into his run-down house that had seen better days. The porch sagged under his weight and I wondered how he hadn't gone through any of the rotted boards yet. I'd rummaged around the inside a couple times already, and I knew it didn't fare much better than the outside.

The cockroaches were right at home.

I waited back a few minutes before I wandered to the vacant house across the street and snuck into the backyard to minimize my risk of being seen. It had been condemned months ago, so I snatched it up through one of my shell companies when it went up for auction. Eventually, it would be one of my renovation projects, but for the time being, it was the perfect place to set up surveillance on my next victim.

Most of the house remained as-is from the purchase. One of the few exceptions was I had a generator hooked up to supply power to the wall of monitors I set up in one of the upstairs back bedrooms that I turned into an office. That was where I could sit to be close while monitoring Clint.

Just in case he got any funny ideas.

AIDEN

So... tell me more about your job as a developer.

I let out a sigh. Answering questions about myself had always been hard. Mainly as I tried to figure out what answer it was that people were looking for. But I had to be careful with my lies to Aiden. He'd already shown me that.

Not to mention, there was a weird, uncomfortable feeling in my chest every time I did it.

That was something I refused to look at too closely.

Well, I already told you I'm a land developer. I buy cheap properties that no one else wants and I renovate them or do what I need to in order to change their zoning, then I sell them for a lot of money.

Pretty boring, actually. But the money is good and I get to travel when I feel like in order to check out properties.

AIDEN

Do you like it?

I sat back in the chair as I stared down at the phone clutched in my hands. It tapped nervously against the small desk against the wall with the screens, and I frowned as I considered his question.

No one had ever asked me that question before. *I'd* never asked myself that question before. There was a convenience to it and it afforded me a very comfortable lifestyle. Plus, it was what my father had done, to some degree.

It's a job. I enjoy it probably as much as I would enjoy anything else. But it definitely has its perks.

Having multiple shell corporations to buy up land came in handy. I had various safe houses set up around the city and even outside the city limits, where there were off the books—as all my residential properties were because nothing would ever be traced back to me—and usually had either a room or two, or the basement, outfitted for habitation in case I needed somewhere to lie low.

Then there were places like the one across from Clint where they were monitoring stations. Some of those even came in handy for the kill. And the best part was then they'd shuffle through the hands of a few of my other unofficial corporations before they finally landed with *me* and then be slated for remodel. It was a surefire way to keep my hands clean, relatively speaking, and make sure all the evidence was destroyed and cleaned up.

I glanced up at the monitors in time to spot Clint hastily exiting his house.

Shit.

I need to go to a meeting now, little bird. But I will call you when I get home, okay?

AIDEN:

Sure. I need to get back to work too.

Talk to you later.

It didn't escape my attention that twice we had talked about my job and we had yet to talk about his. Not since the wedding reception. I wondered if I was supposed to bring it up.

Would it be too on the nose? I'd looked him up, of course I had, and he was a damn good detective with an impressive record. Not that he'd ever be able to catch me.

But it made me wonder if he was suspicious of me at all. Given that he knew I'd been stalking him, I had to assume he must have caught at least a red flag or two. But he never mentioned anything after his initial confrontation. It almost made me even more uncomfortable.

I let out a sigh as I snuck through a few backyards to get to the car I had stashed a block in the opposite direction of where I'd come from when I'd followed Clint back to his house.

Part of me knew it would be easier if I killed Aiden, but I'd already established I couldn't do it. He was the only one who had ever escaped through my fingertips.

Not that he went very far, as I still had him in my grasp. Just in a different way than I intended.

It was why I found myself sliding into my car and following the man who dared to put his hands on what was mine.

15

AIDEN

If someone looked up *stupid* in the dictionary, they'd find a picture of me. The definition would be of a man in his early thirties who was desperate enough when it came to his love life that he threw caution to the wind, ignored a parade of red flags, and was infatuated with a man who admitted to stalking him.

I rolled over in bed and threw my arm over my eyes, wishing I could block out the sun, and the doubts. A week had passed since Nate had followed me to the club and then taken me out to dinner.

A week since I'd found out the man I'd slept with and had continued to fantasize about being my Daddy for real, had continued to stalk me after we went our separate ways.

While I might have been an idiot and still been attracted to him, I wasn't a complete moron and still at least acknowledged I was putting myself in a dangerous situation. One I damn well knew better than to do.

The problem? I couldn't find it in myself to care. Something about him drew me in like a moth to a flame. I knew I was going to get burned, but I couldn't help it.

My hand rubbed down my face as I tried to figure out what the fuck I was doing. It wasn't me. I wasn't a risk taker. My life was about order. Law and order. I was a police officer, a homicide detective. Yet, there I was, waking up hard as nails and horny as hell, wishing Nate were there to fuck me into my mattress.

I let out a soft moan as my hand continued down my body to my chest, and tugged on my taut nipple. A sharp hiss escaped from my lips as I gave it a sudden twist, my hips bucking as my cock sought friction it wouldn't find.

The last thing I should do was tease myself, but then again, I didn't have anywhere else to be. I had all day that I could lie in bed and think about how my Daddy could use me and make me come over and over.

But before I could get any further, reality crashed down on me as my phone rang. With a groan, I diverted my hand's destination and reached over and answered just before it went to voicemail.

"Hey, Ma." Shit. I needed to get myself under control. Last thing I needed was my mother asking questions because she was concerned that something was wrong. Hell would freeze over before I explained that I was just horny and had been about to masturbate.

No fucking thanks.

"Oh, so you are still alive. Good. I haven't heard from you in so long, I was starting to wonder." Her dry response left me cringing from the guilt she managed to lob onto me from the other side of the city.

"Shit. Ma. Don't do that." I wiped my hand over my face and rubbed my temples, hoping to relieve some of the tension that already started to build up from the conversation.

It wasn't as though my parents didn't have a good reason to worry. But it had been the center of *everything* for over fifteen years.

Everyone told me to move on. But how could I, when my mother still did shit like that?

With a sigh, she offered an apology. "You know your father and I worry about you, Aiden. And with that job of yours. I just... I wish you would have chosen something that was safer."

It was an argument we'd been having since she found out I joined the Academy.

"You know why I do what I do, Ma."

I sat up and got out of bed. That conversation required me to have a lot more armor covering me than the sheet that had been draped over me while I'd been sleeping. Not to mention, it was weird to talk to my mother while I was naked.

"Doesn't make it any easier." The weariness in her voice made me pause as I rummaged through my dresser for a pair of sweats and a T-shirt to pull on. While the reminder that I'd gone missing when I was seventeen and returned several weeks later with no memory of what had happened to me while I'd been gone still weighed heavily on all of us as a family, it wasn't usually something that actively distressed Ma anymore.

Something was definitely wrong.

"You're right," I said, my voice soft as I thought back to that time. "It doesn't make it easier. But it gives me a sense of purpose to get answers for people who are no longer able to fight for them anymore."

"I know." And she did. None of this was new information.

"What's this really about?"

In the bathroom, I splashed some cold water on my face and quickly swiped my toothbrush through my mouth a few times while I waited for my mother to be able to compose herself enough to formulate her answer.

That was one thing I got from her. No one could rush me when it came to answering a question, no matter how impatient they were. It was why torture would never work on me.

At least, I didn't think it would, given the scars I returned home with.

Mom made a huffing noise from the other end of the phone before finally letting out a sigh of defeat. "Your sister and Victoria both told me you've started to date someone new. I'm just wondering why I heard it from them and not from my only son, that's all."

All the air in my lungs got caught in my throat. I couldn't breathe.

What. The. Fuck?

I had no idea why either one of them would tell her that at this stage, let alone how Alyssa even knew about Nate.

"Run that by me again." I had to have heard that wrong. Right?

She let out a chuckle. Anytime she could catch me off guard, she thought it was a riot.

Yeah. Real funny, Ma.

"Why the fuck are they gossiping about my freaking love life? To *you*?"

The way she cackled on the other end made me feel like I missed some vital piece of information in the conversation somewhere. "Apparently, the two of them get together once a month for some sort of girls thing where they have drinks and gossip. Your name came up, and Victoria was telling her about some new man in your life."

She *hmmphed*, obviously upset at having been left out of the gossip as I groaned at having been dragged into the gossip.

"There's nothing to tell right now. We went out for one dinner. That's all. I like him, but I'm not sure if it's actually going to go anywhere." I wasn't going to tell her I knew it was mutual, or that he'd been *enthusiastic* in his pursuit of me.

On one hand, I didn't want to encourage her, but also, with my history, I didn't want to concern her with something that was probably harmless.

There was some shuffling around on the other end of the phone and I could tell Ma was getting comfortable. Oh boy. I was in trouble.

"But you like him?"

"It doesn't matter," I muttered. "I'm not sure it's going to go anywhere. He's nice, but we're just... different."

"Different?" She said the word like it was a foreign concept, as I made my way to the kitchen and started pulling out ingredients to make some breakfast.

I let out a sigh. There was no easy way to get out of this. She was like a dog with a damn bone. Or a fucking bloodhound.

"It was one date. Don't make it into more than it was." Hopefully, I sounded more confident and stern than I felt. But by the sound she made, I wasn't sure she agreed with me.

"Hmm. Well, to hear Victoria talk about it, she just made it seem like *more*, that's all." There was no missing the hopeful tone in her voice. And it made me feel like an asshole.

I didn't answer her for a moment, putting the phone on speaker and leaving it on the counter so I could concentrate on scrambling my eggs. Because, a gourmet cook, I was not. I'd be lucky if they were not black or rubbery, and edible by the time I got done torturing them on the stove.

Sighing, I bit the bullet as I poured the egg and milk mixture into the heated pan. "Ma. You know I love you. And I know there is a guy out there for me, and I know I'll find him. Eventually. I'm just not sure Nate is the one."

Out of the corner of my eye, I spotted the spatula in my sink full of dishes and hurried to wash it so I could flip the eggs before they could burn.

"Well, if he's a nice guy and he treats you right, then I think you deserve that, even if he isn't *the one*. You should still let yourself enjoy it while it lasts."

The innuendo could have been spotted from the moon. And that was a huge pile of *nope*. No way was I standing there, listening to my mother talk about my sex life, or make implications about it.

My cheeks heated, thinking about the things Nate and I had gotten up to, about the way I called him Daddy, or how much I loved the way he got rough when he fucked me, holding me down, his hand on my throat. Somehow, I didn't think my mother would be making jokes if she knew the truth.

"Please, just drop it." I scraped at the eggs a little harder than necessary, but I'd rather take out my frustration on them than Ma, who I knew meant well.

The silence on the other end made my heart drop. I didn't mean to upset her. I just didn't want her to expect more from my situationship with Nate, because I wasn't even sure what to expect from it. Besides a mess.

An ashy smell pulled my attention back to the task at hand. With a start, I looked back at the stove and yelped when I realized a thick, gray smoke wafted up from the frying pan.

Shit!

I grabbed the pan and turned the burner off as I dashed toward the sink.

"Hold on, Ma!" I shouted toward the phone as I dropped the pan in the basin and turned on the water.

She chuckled knowingly. "Burn your breakfast again?"

A low grumble emanated from my chest as I tried to figure out why I was so fucking bad at cooking. It was a devastating character flaw, knowing I could burn water. Unfortunately, it was as embarrassing as it was true.

My mind drifted to Nate and how he promised to cook for me one night. In his house. Because that was apparently something he did. I let out a groan, realizing he probably was well aware of my lack of culinary skills. I almost didn't want to know how good of a cook he was.

I turned off the water and scooped up the phone off the counter, bringing it back to my ear. "Sorry about that."

"Why don't you finish dealing with your science experiment and then come on over and I'll cook you breakfast?" She said the words with delight, as though they weren't a trap. If I went over there, I'd have no way to escape the questions she had about Nate.

Just as I opened my mouth to come up with some sort of excuse, my doorbell rang. Flustered, I rolled my eyes and wondered who else was trying to invade my peace on my day off.

Getting ready to tell Vic off for barging in, plus gossiping with my mother and sister, I flung the door open. But the words died on my lips.

My gaze traveled down his impressive body, taking in the tight Henley, and I wondered why he wasn't wearing a jacket. But damn, those jeans really showcased his thighs.

A throat clearing had my gaze shooting back up to Nate's face. His smirk nearly drove me to my knees. The amusement was clear as day; the asshole knew the effect he had on me, which made it totally unfair.

"Nate? What are you doing here?"

Was that even my voice? Why did I sound so breathless? I didn't understand how it could make me feel that way. No one else had ever gotten to me the way he did.

His brow crinkled before he leaned in and sniffed. "Is there a fire? Is something wrong? Do I need to call 9-1-1?"

I barked out a laugh at his distress, but my hand flew to my mouth to stifle the chuckles. It wasn't funny and I didn't like to see him distressed or worried about me.

"No. It's fine. I just burned my eggs." I bit my lip and looked down at the welcome mat under his feet, not wanting to meet his eyes as I admitted that out loud, despite the fact I was pretty sure he already knew how awful I was in the kitchen.

He tutted at me with a slow smile. "Oh, little bird. What ever am I going to do with you?"

"Did you say Nate?" The words in my ear slammed me back to reality. Shit. I forgot I still had Ma on the phone.

"I'm going to have to take a raincheck, Ma."

"Pssh. Nonsense. You bring that boy over with you for breakfast. I'll see you in twenty."

The line went dead and I glanced up at Nate in horror. I wasn't sure which of us looked more uneasy at the impromptu invite to my parents' house for Sunday breakfast, but he was definitely the first to recover.

"Apparently, I'm not the only one who had the idea of asking you to breakfast this morning?" He glanced around, unable to look me in the eye. I wasn't sure what happened to the confident man I'd come to know, but there was definitely something spooking him.

I was pretty sure it was the whole *meeting the parents way too soon* fiasco that he'd found himself in. But there was a warning bell going off in my head that was signaling danger ahead.

"You don't have to come. Trust me, I know it's way too soon for subjecting you to my Ma." I let out a brittle laugh that felt too forced and by the strained smile, it wasn't fooling him either.

Somewhere, we had taken a turn, and I wasn't sure where things had gone off course or how to get us back on track. Or if I should even *want* to get us back on track.

A worried look flitted across his eyes as he studied my face. "What do *you* want, little bird?"

16

NATHAN

I walked up to the front door with a pit in my stomach. Everything about the situation was *wrong*. I shouldn't have been there.

Whatever demon had possessed me to follow Aiden's lead, I should have cast it out, hunted it down and then killed it. Because that was what I did, what I was good at. I didn't know how to be a normal person, how to be someone's boyfriend. I didn't do the whole meeting the parents thing.

My footsteps faltered as Aiden took a few steps ahead of me and went to knock on the door. He turned back and looked at me with a frown. In fact, he'd been looking at me with a lot of worried glanced the whole way to his parents' house.

I didn't like it.

"You don't have to be here." His voice was soft and steady, the words laced with understanding. He knew a little about my past, what happened with my parents. I hated that he mistook my apprehension for something else, but it was less dangerous for him to think that it was an old hurt over having lost my parents so tragically.

"I drove," I reminded him. "I would never abandon you."

My little bird rolled his eyes and gave me a soft, indulgent smile. "They're my parents. I'd be fine. It's not like you'd be leaving me in the middle of the desert with no way to get back to civilization."

I pulled him close, wrapping one arm around his waist, and cupped his cheek. Staring into his eyes, I gave him a soft peck, aware we were in the middle of a well-populated neighborhood where there were most likely nosy neighbors peeping through their curtains.

Leaning in, I brought my lips to his ear and whispered softly, "They may be your parents, but I'm your Daddy."

His breath hitched and a satisfied smile spread across my face as he pulled back and watched me. I booped his nose before lacing our fingers together and tugged him to turn around. "Come on, baby. Let's do this."

Aiden nodded, his eyes glassy as he practically tripped over himself to get back to the door. His mother must have been one of the nosy women at the window, watching from behind a curtain, because we hadn't even gotten back to the door yet, and it opened to reveal a smiling woman in casual loungewear, with an apron.

"Oh, good! You made it!" Her smile seemed sincere enough, though I was never a good judge, but Aiden instantly relaxed at my side, so it set me at ease.

"Hey, Ma." When he went to move forward, his hand slipped from mine, but he gave it an extra squeeze before he let go and moved into his mother's tight embrace.

I'd never been one who needed affection or reassurance about anything. But something in my heart surged over the way Aiden had taken that extra moment for me. It grounded me in a way I'd never needed before.

"And you must be Nathan." My brow quirked, realizing that must have been one of the things he'd been furiously texting to his mother as I drove us over to his parents'. He hadn't been very discreet about texting her, despite the fact that he kept saying it was *nothing*. I'd wondered what he was warning her about, and it had left a bit of a sour taste in my mouth.

My gaze roamed over to him, and he just smirked. Cheeky little bird.

"I am. Thank you for the invitation, Mrs. Cooper. Though, it wasn't necessary." Even I knew my words were stiff and uncertain as I held my hand out for a handshake. But I couldn't help it. This was way beyond out of the stratosphere of my realm of comfort.

His mother looked at my hand with a frown, and for a moment, I thought she was going to refuse. And for another terrible second, I thought she might hug me. She looked back at Aiden, but he held her gaze firmly, but I couldn't decipher their silent communication.

When she turned back to me, her smile was as warm and pleasant as could be. But I thought it was as much a mask as mine.

"Please, call me Ellie." She reached out and shook my hand, but only held it for a moment before dropping it.

Turning toward the door, she waved us inside. "Well, let's get out of the cold. Breakfast is waiting."

Aiden watched her go before he turned and looked back at me with a pensive expression. "Are you okay?"

I cocked my head to the side as I walked up to him and put my arm around his shoulder and led him into the house. "Of course. Why wouldn't I be?"

The truth was, I was so far from okay, but I could never tell him that. He wouldn't understand. But I would smile and do whatever I had to in order to get through breakfast with his parents, because it was important to him, because he wanted me there.

And apparently, I'd do anything for Aiden.

Including forcing his parents to dine with a monster.

He shrugged as he kicked off his shoes inside the front door, and I followed his lead. "I don't know. You seem… tense."

I let out a breath and my gaze wandered down the hall to where his mother had disappeared. "I suppose I am. I'm sorry. Just, I've told you I don't date, so I've never really done the whole meeting the parents thing until now. It was just… easier."

Confused, he slipped his hands into mine. "Easier?"

My thumbs stroked his hands. "Yeah. Easier. To not think about what I'd lost. What I didn't have anymore."

Realization dawned on him and he took a step back. "Shit. I mean, I knew… You'd told me. But… I'm sorry."

"Hey, hey. No." I pulled him against me, wrapping my arms around him. He trembled against my body and I felt like the biggest asshole in the world. "You didn't do anything wrong, Aiden. I could have said no to coming here. I meant what I said, about wanting to take care of you and to give you everything you need and want."

"Not at your expense, though." The wobble in his voice nearly broke my heart. "It shouldn't hurt you."

"Oh, sweet boy." I breathed the words against his tear-stained cheek, wishing I could take all of it back. It wasn't worth his pain. "It's a long-healed scar. Just one I've never had to look at before. I'm okay. I promise."

Like the spider monkey I knew he was, he pulled himself up and wrapped his legs around my hips and clung to me, with his head on my shoulder.

"Daddy," he whined, burying his head in my neck.

A soft intake drew my attention to the other end of the hall. My head slowly turned toward the sound as my boy went still as a statue in my arms. There wasn't even a soft breath panting against my neck. A low vibration shook him, one I would have barely noticed, if I hadn't had him wrapped so tight against me.

His mother stared, wide-eyed. Neither of us broke eye contact for a long moment. Until Aiden dropped from my arms.

I reached for him as he turned and walked stiffly away, evading my silent plea. Without a backward glance, he darted out the front door like the devil was chasing him. The heavy door slammed behind him, making me wince.

"Sorry. I didn't mean to interrupt." Ellie seemed uneasy as she looked away, wringing her hands together.

I could feel my mask slipping, the image of my little bird embarrassed and terrified as he fled from his own mother. He was mine to protect, to cherish, and I'd already failed him. Against his *mother*.

My eyes narrowed as I took in her flushed appearance and the way she wouldn't look at me. Her eyes kept darting back toward where I assumed the kitchen was, like she was hoping for her husband to come and save her from this awkward situation.

While I understood that the whole Daddy thing was a kink and that most people didn't like it flashed around and that seeing it was awkward, I didn't have the capabilities to understand *why* it was awkward. I wasn't wired that way.

To me, I just wanted to take care of my little bird, to be there for him, provide for him, guide him, protect him. That made me his Daddy. It just was. It was a fact, like the sky is blue.

But normal people didn't see it that way. So, as his Daddy, I knew it was up to me to fix it somehow, though God knew I was the last person who should have been sent to deal with something emotional like what Aiden was going through. But it was part of taking care of him, and I'd do it.

"There is *nothing* wrong about what you just saw or heard." I crossed my arms and leaned back against the wall, daring her to contradict me. The last thing I wanted was to be the cause of a rift between Aiden and his parents, or the cause of an unfortunate accident. He deserved better than that.

At least she had the decency to look embarrassed.

"I know that." While her words may have tried to convince me, her tone didn't sound so sure.

I glanced toward the door, knowing my car was locked and that meant my little bird was out in the cold. My hand rooted around my pocket for the keys as I cast another glance toward his mother, who looked like she had finally begun to realize the damage she had inflicted on her son.

Her shoulders straightened as she looked me in the eye. After taking a deep breath, her bottom lip wobbled, but it did little to move me.

"I'm sorry. I didn't mean to embarrass or upset him. I just didn't expect..." Her words trailed off with a sigh. "We don't talk, not really. Not about important things. And I guess I can't blame him for not talking to me about something like *that*. It just came as a bit of a shock that he was into that sort of thing."

She offered me a sad smile as she bit her lip before glancing back at the door. "But as long as he's happy, and being safe, and whatever he is doing is consensual... Well, then, who am I to tell him what he can or cannot do?"

I stared at her, unsure if she meant it, but hoped for Aiden's sake that she did. His family meant the world to him.

"But I'm glad he has someone who cares about him, looks out for him."

"I'll always look out for him." It was a promise I could keep, even if there came a day he thought he could get rid of me.

Like a balloon with a hole, she deflated before my eyes. Her shoulders sagged and she leaned against the wall. With a nod, she looked away, obviously fighting back tears. "I'm not sure how much he's told you, and I won't go into details because it's not for me to decide what he wants someone to know. But he went through hell when he was younger. And he deserves someone now, who will take care of him. Even if he thinks he doesn't need it."

I opened my mouth to say something but quickly closed it.

There was nothing I could tell that woman that would make any of what he went through better. And just like she didn't want to betray what he went through, it wasn't any of her business, the things we had talked about, the things we'd gone through.

"Well, I better go check on him."

Ellie nodded, straightening up from the wall, and started to leave. But before she left, she turned back to me. "Tell him I'll keep breakfast warm until he's ready to come back in."

I studied her for a moment and wondered if she truly thought he would come back in or if she was fooling herself. But I didn't know enough about their relationship to comment. "I will. But understand, if he wants to leave, then I'm taking him home. He's my first priority over breakfast."

She nodded. "I wouldn't expect anything less."

It felt like a trap as I walked out the door. My heart sank as I found him pacing next to the car with his arms wrapped around himself, shivering. He stopped when he saw me, but he didn't come to me or lift his head to look at me, and that wouldn't do.

"Little bird?" My voice was soft as I approached him, careful and slow despite the way my brain screamed at me to pull him close and claim him and never let him go.

The last thing I wanted was to spook him.

When I stood in front of him, I reached out and lifted his face with a finger tucked under his chin. His tears had frozen to his cheeks, causing the skin to get irritated and red as the ice crystals clung to his chilled flesh. My palms framed his face, thumbs caressing his cheeks in an effort to warm them even a little.

"I'm so fucking embarrassed." There was a devastation to his voice that I didn't understand. "Why... Of *course* she would have to walk in at that moment."

Aiden pulled out of my arms and began pacing next to the car again.

"Baby, I know you're upset. And if you want to go home, then that's where I'll take you, but your mom would like it if we go back in and have that breakfast."

His mouth hung open and he stared at me like I had just told him I murdered a baby, which was ridiculous. Even I wouldn't do that.

"Are you serious? You expect me to go back in there? *Now*?"

My hands went to his shoulders, squeezing for just a moment.

"I don't expect you to do anything, especially if it's something you don't want to do." I moved back a couple inches so I could look into his eyes, study him and try to tell what he was really thinking.

"How am I supposed to face her? Ever?" His hand raked through his hair, gripping the strands tightly as he tried to release some of the agitation he was feeling.

Aiden's voice went soft as he looked back up at his childhood home, a place that had once been a sanctuary of safety. That had all been ripped away in one careless moment and my heart went out for him, even if I couldn't draw on my own experiences of understanding.

"She knows. She heard... What I called you. That you... I..." He shook his head.

I tilted my head as he sagged against the car in defeat. An unfamiliar tightness clutched at my chest.

"Aiden." His name came out carefully, controlled, and the tone had his head whipping up, wide eyes meeting mine.

"I understand that you felt embarrassed at the moment, your mom knowing something you consider to be intimate." I looked down at my clutched hands, my eyes furrowed. It was a nervous habit, but I didn't have those. But my boy brought out a lot of things in me that I wasn't used to dealing with.

With a sigh, I straightened my shoulders and looked at him head-on, giving him the attention he deserved. I also needed to see his reaction to what I was about to ask. "But the way you're acting, it's as though you're... ashamed."

He flinched at my words, but no denial came. The silence stretched for a long moment before he heaved a sigh.

"Can you please just take me home, Nate?"

17

NATHAN

My little bird flew the coop and I felt like he took my heart with him. Before him, I wouldn't have even thought it was possible, that I could love or give my heart to someone. But I had, and then he ran from me, taking with him most of the pieces, only leaving behind enough to keep me alive.

I still hadn't been able to grab Clint, and it pissed me off. Part of me wondered if I was able to offer him up as a sacrifice and present him as an offering to Aiden, if he would find his way back to me. Though, I also knew the likelihood of it being for the reason I wanted it to be, would be slim. More than likely, it would be with suspicion as to why the guy I manhandled at the club suddenly showed up dead and mutilated.

"You'd think he'd have some empathy, right?" Leaning down, I stared at the man tied to the chair as he struggled against the ropes that had his hands and feet bound together. "But no, it's been radio silence. Won't return my calls or my texts."

My hand grabbed the man's chin, pulling him closer. "That's a little rude, don't you think? I tell him I want to lay the world at his feet, but his mother hears him call me Daddy one time and he thinks he can run from me? After I promised to give him everything?"

I gripped the knife that dangled at my side. The anger burned through my veins like a fire I couldn't extinguish.

Confusion. Betrayal. Hurt.

When I had dropped Aiden back at his house and he asked if he could have a raincheck for breakfast, I hadn't wanted to leave him. Every instinct had screamed at me not to leave him alone. And they'd been right.

My boy had shut me out. I didn't know how to care about people, and this was why it was useless. Pointless.

He didn't want me now that he thought it was something shameful. Being with a man was fine, he knew his parents accepted that, but he didn't know how to accept that they could accept him wanting, *needing* a Daddy.

Because he thought he was supposed to be the one in control, the one to provide and protect. He didn't understand it didn't have to work that way. That he could be strong and still be vulnerable.

I stared at Jared Mackay and sneered as he screamed behind the gag I had shoved in his mouth. Usually, I enjoyed listening to the screams and pleading of my victims, but none of it brought me joy since my little bird ran away from me. After a few hours of his incessant sniveling, I'd needed to drown out his cries.

Briefly, I wondered if my monster would still be sated if I no longer found the wonder and satisfaction that I used to.

"How did someone I've only known for such a short time get so embedded under my skin? He shouldn't mean that much to me in such a short amount of time. Yet, I find that losing him has meant losing a part of myself."

My gaze wandered up to meet Jared's.

"Have you ever had someone in your life like that?" I cocked my head and considered him but dismissed the notion. Most likely, he was just as alone as I was. Otherwise, he wouldn't have been seeking out the *company* of young boys and girls.

Baring my teeth, I thought about ripping his throat out and bathing in his blood. I might have needed to satisfy a monster, but even I had rules and wouldn't go after children, and certainly not for the things he was after. There were worse monsters than me out there, and he was proof of that.

After two days of keeping that piece of scum tied in one of my empty warehouses, it was time to take out the trash.

"Well, Jared, thanks for sticking around and listening." I stood and walked behind him, my blade gripped tightly in my hand, arm outstretched. His muffled screams did nothing as he tried to move away, as I knew he had nowhere to go, no way to escape.

I raised the blade and brought it up to his throat, no desire for my usual flair, no drive to draw it out. All I wanted was to get it over with and go home, even though I'd be alone. Feeling nothing, no rush of euphoria or bliss filling the emptiness inside, I drew the blade across his throat and let the blood spray.

Jared's blood dripped down his body and pooled onto the plastic sheeting I had lined on the floor, the sheeting on the wall catching the arterial spray. If I were an artist, I would have called it a masterpiece, but I wasn't that vain.

His body twitched and convulsed as the last dregs of life left him with a pathetic gurgle.

My head fell forward, as though I were praying, except there was no God I believed in. No higher power could exist and have created me the way I was, have allowed me to become the man I was, or other men to be like me, or worse.

No God would have given me a glimpse of heaven with my little bird, just to snatch it away.

I wiped my blade off on Jared's shoulder and turned to

make my way to where I had stashed my clean-up supplies, when a faint noise caught my attention from the other side of the warehouse. My head whipped around, gaze seeking where the noise could have come from. No one else should have been there.

The warehouse was mostly empty except for a few large machines left by the previous owners of the building. Everything that could be easily discarded, I had already had cleared out. Which left very little room for an intruder to hide.

My hand slipped into the waistband of my pants and slowly withdrew my gun, trying to conceal the movement from whoever was there. Acting as nonchalant as possible, I went over to where I had my supplies and rooted around, casting furtive glances around the vast space from the new angle. But I was still unable to see anything.

Either they were moving with me to remain undetected, or they were very good at hiding.

Frustrated, I drew in a deep breath and tried to center myself and remain calm. It wouldn't do any good to charge into a situation unprepared. I didn't know who was there or if they were armed.

Fuck. What if it's the police? Worse, what if it's Aiden*?*

No. I couldn't let myself panic. The likelihood that he would have been able to figure out my little secret from the few times we were together was slim. It was a big leap from stalking to being a serial killer.

Wasn't it? Honestly, I wasn't sure, but I hoped so.

Making it seem as though I were leaving, I headed for the big heavy doors. The hairs on the back of my neck stood, letting me know I was being watched, which was interesting considering it was the first indicator I'd had since I'd dragged Jared into the warehouse two days ago that there was any danger lurking.

When I got to the doors, instead of opening them and leaving, I slammed my palm against the switch on the wall, flooding the open space with bright light and activating the machines that I knew were still hooked up. Anyone who broke in would have assumed an abandoned building would have no electricity. But they wouldn't have known it wasn't exactly abandoned.

There was a flash of movement on the other end of the warehouse, behind one of the large machines. It was almost obscured, if not for the dark clothing that had allowed the intruder to initially blend in. But now it made the unmistakable figure of a man stand out against the brightly lit room.

"Stop right there." My voice was steady and commanding, and I raised the gun to point at the retreating man, who froze instantly at the sound of the hammer cocking.

I slowly made my way toward him, watching as he stood rigid, slowly raising his hands above his head to show he was unarmed. His heavy panting gave away his fear and finally kick-started the predator in me to want to hunt and claim.

The trembling figure slowly turned, keeping his head down, still obscured by the hood of the sweatshirt he was wearing. "Please, sir."

My eyes narrowed, breath catching at the words. There was something familiar that gripped around my heart and squeezed. I let my head fall to the side as I studied him. His stance was rigid, but the pose was submissive.

There was something that tugged and poked at the edges of my memory.

"Give me one good reason why I shouldn't shoot you where you stand." I wasn't sure why I hadn't done it already. Any other time, I would have without question, but something held me back.

His head snapped up and wide, fearful green eyes bore into mine.

Fuck.

Shit. Shit. Shit.

"Jesus Christ, Christian. What the fuck are you doing here?" I lowered the gun, lunged forward, and grabbed his arm. He tried to shake me off and back away, but after a moment, he fell to his knees, head bowed.

The perfect submissive.

But not *my* submissive.

No matter how much I knew he still wished it were true.

Though, maybe not anymore, depending on how much he had just witnessed. And he left me with a dilemma I never thought I'd be faced with, whether or not I needed to kill someone I knew for discovering my secret. Because I never thought I'd care enough about someone to think twice about killing them.

While I might not want a relationship with Christian like I did with Aiden, I did find that a part of me cared about what happened to him. He had become one of the very few people who I could count on one hand that I ever gave a fuck about.

And I didn't like it.

I released his arm and tucked the gun back in its holster. "Why are you here? You must have followed me? Why?"

Christian looked up at me, tears in his eyes, but he didn't shed them. He knew they didn't work on me. "I'm sorry, Nathan. I... You had me worried."

He shook his head and looked away. Except, his gaze landed on Jared's dead body and his face paled. "Oh, God."

My hand cupped his chin and forced him to look up at me. "He can't help you, Christian. No one can."

The whimper he let out went straight to my cock. But he wasn't prey, wasn't a victim. Christian was a friend. A war raged in my mind as to what I was supposed to do about him. He knew too much, but for once, I didn't have the driving need to kill someone, even for self-preservation.

"Why were you worried?" I couldn't think of anything that

would have caused him to tail me to the warehouse and stay long enough to watch me commit a murder. Then again, once he was inside, it would have been difficult to get out without being seen.

He pulled his head out of my grasp and shut his eyes as he let his head fall, unable to look at me. "You've made reckless decisions. Put off business meetings, left the office early or showed up late. Normally, you're calm and collected, but you've been snapping at everyone. Unprofessional and brash."

When he finally looked at me, there was a wounded look in his eyes that tugged at a part of my heart I thought would never feel for another person. It wasn't like how Aiden made me feel, and it wasn't how my victims made me feel either. I didn't like it. There were too many new sensations and feelings overtaking my body recently and it was overwhelming.

I couldn't do this, not now, not with him.

When I opened my mouth to protest, nothing came out.

But that couldn't have been true, could it? I prided myself on treating my employees with respect and dignity, even when they got under my skin, which was rare.

"You lock yourself away, Nathan. I can't get you to talk about it. Instead, you just sit tucked away in your office, brooding. Or you leave for hours with no one able to get a hold of you."

Christian heaved a sigh and finally looked back up at me, shoulders held back, spine straight. "You've been an asshole the last week," he said with a scoff. "But, at least now I know you're somewhat human and have feelings, and that it's all about a boy."

His bravado left him as quickly as he found it. Sucking in a breath, he tried to swallow but choked, the tears finally leaking out of the corner of his eyes.

"A boy you would apparently kill for, or because of... or fuck, I have no idea."

I could see him beginning to unravel and I had no idea how

to fix any of this. There was no guidebook on how to come out as a serial killer to your friend.

Maybe I should write one. It would probably be a best seller. In fiction, of course.

"Shit. You should have just *asked*, Christian, instead of following me." Now, he'd created a much bigger mess, one I wasn't sure how I was going to clean up.

A brittle laugh escaped from his dry throat. "I tried. You were so wrapped up in whatever all the fuck *this* is, that you didn't want to hear what anyone had to say, not even me. Hell, maybe especially not me, if you were so wrapped up in losing whoever it was that you were seeing that I didn't even know about."

Jealousy didn't look good on him, but I couldn't blame him. I had left him out of the loop. But I knew he was still wrapped up and interested in what we had and I hadn't wanted to lead him on or make feel bad. I second-guessed that decision once I had him face-to-face with one of my victims, thinking it might have been better to have had him to confide in, to talk to him about my problems with Aiden.

"I'm sorry that I shut you out, Christian. It wasn't fair, especially since you have always been the only one in my life I could talk to about these things."

"Not everything." His gaze darted back over to Jared and he grimaced. The disgust was written across his face but so was the acceptance of his fate.

I bit my bottom lip, again wrestling with the decision I was being forced into. With a shake of my head, I looked toward the ceiling, as though there were going to be some divine intervention giving me guidance. "I *really* wish you didn't follow me, Christian. This was something I never wanted to be faced with."

"Sorry," he said with a cocky grin I knew he didn't feel.

Sighing, I looked over at where I still had Jared's cooling body. "Get up and come help me, asshole."

His eyes went wide, his throat working hard to swallow as he stared at me in shock. "I'm sorry, what?"

I couldn't blame him. After all, I had been the one who had told him to help me cover up a murder and I still was surprised that I hadn't just killed him and chosen self-preservation.

Sighing, I ran my hand through my hair and stared him down. "The way I see it, you have two options. Option one, you join Jared over there. Option two, you never speak about what you saw here today and you do exactly what I say and you get to keep breathing. I know which one I would pick, but the choice is yours, Christian."

His face paled as his eyes darted between me and the dead body.

"Fuck."

I didn't move or say anything as I let him work out the options for himself. He was a smart man and I had no doubt he'd make the right choice. I just needed to let him think things through.

There was a tremor in his shoulders, but he stood tall as his gaze met mine. "What do you want me to do?"

18

AIDEN

I stared down at another dead body and cursed my luck. What had once seemed like a golden opportunity to make a name for myself to solve a serial killer case, had turned into a nightmare.

Nearly two weeks had passed since the disastrous breakfast at my parents' house with Nate. And I knew I had overreacted, but by the time I realized that maybe it wasn't as big of a deal as I'd made it out to be, I'd been even more embarrassed over the way I'd acted. How did I expect him to want to deal with me and my shit when I pulled a stunt like that and pushed him away?

Even if he had been prepared to be my Daddy, that didn't mean he wanted to deal with someone who acted like a child.

"Who found him?" I glared over at the beat cop who had just come back over after throwing up his breakfast. Death was messy. I understood that. But if he was going to make it in this profession, he needed to get a stronger stomach or he wouldn't make it very far.

He nodded at the man who was looking around the park, uneasy. "Early morning jogger. Says he likes to go off trail through the park and he stumbled upon him. Said it wasn't the first time he found someone naked in the park, but it *was* the first time they were dead."

I bet.

My gaze wandered back over to the man with a new purpose. Most witnesses who *stumbled* upon a murder victim usually had something to do with the crime. But the man's sweat looked like it could be from actual exercise. But that didn't mean he didn't set up the victim beforehand.

"What else do we know?" I leaned down and noted the wounds on the body. They were the same as the other victims. Deep, narrow slashes all over the body along with superficial cuts that wouldn't have contributed to the death. And there, under the ribcage, were the deeper wounds I'd been looking for.

I knew a long, jagged blade had been stabbed right to the hilt over and over into the soft flesh.

A shudder wracked through my body before I shook myself, refusing to let the past drag me down. The last thing I needed was to be the talk of the precinct, or worse, the entire police force.

Of course, when I needed Victoria to be by my side to divert attention, she was giving me a wide berth, something about needing an attitude adjustment. My gaze flickered over and caught her flirting with the EMT on scene, who stood by, with nothing to do, since there was no live victim to transport anywhere.

"The vic is Jared Mackay and the witness is Christian Carter, a local realtor."

"Hmph. All right. I don't want anyone to touch the body except the coroner. Keep back anyone who tries to come near the scene. I'm going to go talk to the witness."

Despite not looking thrilled at being left to babysit the dead body, the officer didn't argue with me, which I was glad.

I didn't have it in me to get on him about doing his fucking job.

I walked over to where the jogger was standing with one of the other beat cops who had been first on scene.

"Angie," I said, greeting her with a half-hearted smile.

"Hey, Coop. Tough one, huh?" She shook her head as she glanced toward where the body was tossed carelessly by whoever had killed him.

With a glance back, I was happy to see her partner had a little bit of color back, and not of the green variety. "Yeah, then again, they're never easy, no matter how many you go through."

The last thing I was going to do, would be to indicate it might be the work of a serial killer, not even to another cop. Especially in front of a stranger, a civilian.

"Mr. Carter," Angie started, "this is Detective Cooper. He's one of the lead detectives who will be working on the case and will need to ask you some questions."

The man nodded and turned to me with a shuddering breath. "Of course. Whatever you need."

"Thanks, Angie. Can you stay on the perimeter? Keep note of anyone who comes near, especially if they act suspicious?" I glanced toward the small gathering a few hundred feet away. It wasn't anything that would be hard to contain, but these sickos liked to come back to the scene of their crimes. And I wanted to know who all was poking around my crime scene.

"You got it, Coop." With a smile, she left and went back to her partner. It looked like they exchanged some heated words before she walked off and greeted Doctor Timmons, the coroner, as he arrived on scene.

My gaze went back to the witness, who looked at me like he was less than impressed. I wasn't sure why, but it pissed me off for some reason.

"So, Mr. Carter, I'm going to record this conversation on my phone, if that's all right with you?"

He frowned for a moment before he nodded. "Yeah, sure. That's fine, I guess."

"Great. Thank you. So, can you tell me how you happened to come across the victim this morning?" There was already something suspicious about the man who stood before me. I wasn't quite sure what it was, just some gut instinct.

He looked around the dense trees that surrounded us and shuddered. "I like coming out early, before there are a lot of other joggers in the park. Usually, I am pretty adventurous, hiking and climbing. You know?"

Our eyes held, and there was no reason to think he was lying, but there was something else, another meaning that seemed hidden under his words. There was one thing I knew for sure, and it was that he wasn't being completely honest with me. And I wondered what he had to lie about, when it came to such an innocent question.

"Right. So, you were feeling adventurous this morning?" Something ugly twisted in my gut at the insinuation.

He smirked, as though he could sense my discomfort and reveled in it. "I was. So, as I often do, I started to go off path and hike around after I completed a few miles of my run. But I didn't get very far, maybe twenty minutes or so, and I stumbled upon..."

The words trailed off and his hands waved in front of him, gesturing toward the dead body he had discovered.

"Was anyone else around? Did you see anyone before or after you discovered the body?" I shuffled back and forth on my feet, agitated at how little I was getting out of him. But most witnesses didn't actually witness very much.

He shook his head. "No, there were a few people walking near the North Entrance when I got here this morning. But they were long gone by the time I went into the woods. I don't remember seeing anyone around for a bit before then. Definitely no one else in the woods."

I nodded as I typed some notes on my phone.

"Okay. Thank you for that, Mr. Carter."

"Did you touch him or anything around him when you found him, Mr. Carter?"

His brow furrowed as he thought back on the memory.

"I-I don't think so. But honestly, it all happened so fast and I hadn't realized it was anything I was going to need to have to think back on and remember. At first, I thought he might be someone who was homeless or maybe hurt. But then..." His gaze drifted back to the man. There was a sorrow in his eyes that couldn't be faked. No matter what lies he was telling, he was sorry the man was dead.

"When I moved around him, and got to his front, I saw... well, you see what he looks like." His eyes met mine again and they were wet with unshed tears. "It was awful. I don't think I'd ever seen anything so terrifying in my life."

He began to shake, the last few of his words unsteady. Afraid he was going into shock, I motioned for one of the paramedics to come over. Victoria trailed behind with him. Nice of her to join our investigation after all.

"Hey, Zeke," I whispered, when he got closer. "Can you make sure Mr. Carter is all right?"

Zeke glanced over at where our witness stood, shaking, and he grimaced as he offered me a fist bump. "Of course."

"When forensics gets here, his hands will have to be checked for evidence. Maybe his clothes too. They'll make that determination. But I'm worried about shock."

He gave me a soft smile over his shoulder as he turned to head over to deal with his patient, since he was finally needed on site. "You got it, boss. We'll take good care of him and make sure everything is taken care of."

"Thanks, man."

I turned back to my partner, bitch face on full display.

"What?" She crossed her arms over her chest, giving me a glare in return.

Shaking my head, I made my way back to the car. "We're supposed to be working a case here, Vic, not flirting with EMTs."

She huffed and I could hear her following behind me as she stomped on the leaves and branches that littered the ground. "Oh, that's rich. Like you haven't flirted with Zeke at crime scenes."

My back stiffened. She had me there. The man was *fine*. But I never let flirting with him keep me from actually doing my job.

"You're just salty because you broke up with your boy toy. Or, were *you* the boy...toy?" I ignored her callous laugh and slid into the driver's seat, slamming the door. My breathing was heavy, heart pounding in my ears, and I had half a mind to leave her ass stranded.

I gripped the steering wheel like my life depended on it. Anything to keep from throwing the car in drive and peeling away without her. Not that she wouldn't deserve it. That had been a low blow to bring up my breakup with Nate, if you could even call it that.

But I never thought Victoria would use something I told her in confidence against me. It had been really difficult to open up and tell her about what happened at my parents' house. To admit to how I called Nate *Daddy*, and that I liked it.

The longer it took her to get in, the more I wanted to leave her. When I glanced over and saw her standing next to the door, with her hand ready to open it, I wondered what had stopped her.

"You coming, or what?" I needed to get the fuck out of there. Away from her, but I would never tell her that.

Everything had been crumbling since I watched Nate drive

away that morning. I couldn't breathe. And I didn't know what to do.

That was a lie. I did. But I didn't know how I could go back and fix it, because I couldn't. It was done. We were done. I'd broken us. All over something so stupid. My own insecurities and hang-ups.

And the worst part was, Ma fucking loved him and couldn't wait to see him again.

So, fuck my life. Because I was fucking screwed.

And this goddamn killer.

I shook my head as Victoria finally, *fucking finally* got in the car.

She looked out her window as I sped away, back toward the station. We were in a holding pattern now. Had to wait for forensics and the coroner to give us their reports. There hadn't been anything the witness could give us that could help. Not that I had expected there to be, but it sucked either way.

Victoria turned toward me, taking a deep breath. "Hey," she said softly. "I'm sorry I've been such a bitch."

I snorted. "Yeah, you have. But so have I."

She gave me a half smile and nodded. "Yeah, but you have a reason. I haven't been a good friend about it, and I should be."

With a sigh, I turned into my spot in the precinct parking lot. "Yeah, you should have. But I haven't been a very good friend either. Because it's obvious you're going through something, too. And I haven't been there for you either. So, that changes now. Whatever it is, I want you to know you can talk to me."

She didn't say anything for a minute, just looked out her window before she turned and launched herself into my arms. "Whoa, whoa. It's okay, Vic."

I wrapped my arms around her, holding her tight and petting her hair. She scared me, acting that way, but I wasn't going to press, if she wasn't ready to talk about it.

After a few minutes, she pulled back and wiped a stray tear from her eye, which sent a spike of panic through me. "Vic?"

"I'm okay." She gave me a watery smile and punched my arm. There was my girl.

"You sure?" I wasn't convinced, but I'd accept whatever answer she gave.

She bit her lip and looked down at her lap, twisting her fingers together. "Yeah. I will be, and so will you."

I let out a heavy sigh and glanced out my window, unable to look her in the eye. "Yeah… I will be. I know I will."

We sat there in an uncomfortable silence for another minute or two before she opened her door and got out of the car. When I hesitated, not turning off the engine, she leaned down. "You coming?"

My jaw flexed as I tried to find the words to answer her. "Naw. I'll see you later."

I willed her to close the door and walk away, and finally, she did. My hands shook as I pulled out of the parking lot and hit the call button on my phone and waited with bated breath.

19

AIDEN

I hit the call button on my phone and waited as it rang. And rang. My gut twisted, sure the call was about to go to voicemail.

"Hello?"

My shoulders sagged in relief, knowing he'd answered, even if it seemed to be reluctantly. But a new fear overtook me as I choked out a single word that had haunted my dreams. "Daddy..."

The pause on the other end was worse than any nightmare that had plagued me in the last fifteen years. For a horrifying moment, I wondered if he was going to hang up without talking to me. Or worse, maybe he already *had* hung up and I had just been too slow to realize he was no longer on the line.

"Little bird."

Those two words, whispered like a tentative prayer through the phone, had my knees going weak. I clung to the dresser. In hindsight, I probably should have sat down before I tried calling Nate. Because I knew whether he was ready to forgive me or not, it wouldn't be an easy conversation.

"I, um, I was hoping we could... talk."

God, why was I so nervous? I was sure that if nothing else, Nate would give me the opportunity to say what I wanted to say. He would listen and he would be willing to talk. Even if he wasn't willing to take me back.

The thought was like a stab in the heart. I didn't want to be without Nate. Without my Daddy. In such a short time he had somehow become my everything and it terrified me. Perhaps it should have been a sign that I should have walked away then, but I was weak. I wouldn't walk away unless my Daddy told me I had to forget about him.

Please don't say we are over for good, Daddy.

"Of course." He sounded too reserved, too cautious for my liking. I wanted my warm, teasing Daddy, the one who seemed to always know what I needed to feel better. Who was always willing to give me what I needed.

I rubbed my sternum, trying to ease the tightness that squeezed around my heart.

"Do you want to come over? Or...?" I didn't know what other option would be the *or*, but I figured I should give him an out from having to see me, if he didn't want to. It was something we could do over the phone if he was going to let me down easy. Or even somewhere that was neutral ground, I supposed, if he didn't want to be somewhere with a bed where we could just be tempted to fuck and pretend our problems didn't exist.

He didn't say anything for a moment and I gave him the time he needed to consider my question without pressuring him. Even though I wanted to scream at him to say *something*, or more accurately, to say that he needed me just as much as I needed him and that he'd been dying without me and he'd be right over.

"I am just in the middle of wrapping something up. But I could maybe meet you for dinner, if you are free."

A little bit of the wind left my sails at the way he hadn't seemed to be in a rush to fix things or talk, but I decided to look at the positive. At least he wanted to see me and talk and he didn't just brush me off. He would have been well within his rights to tell me to get fucked after I ghosted him.

"Sure. That sounds great." I tried to force a smile, even though he couldn't see me. Anything to hide the disappointment in my voice. "Just text me like an hour or so before you're planning to pick me up so that I can be ready, okay?"

Unfortunately, I didn't think I'd need to be as prepared for this date—*is it even a date?*—as our other dates, so I probably wouldn't even need the hour. But better safe than sorry.

"Will do." He paused for a moment, muttering something I didn't catch under his breath. "I need to go now. But I will text you when I am able to, so you can start getting ready."

I had barely been able to get out an, "Okay," when he'd hung up.

My shoulders slumped as I made my way to the bed with shaky legs that I wasn't convinced would be able to carry me the few feet. I wasn't sure if that conversation could be counted as a win or not. On one hand, he'd answered and agreed to talk to me, but he'd also been distracted and short with me. Not that I felt I deserved his undivided attention after the shit I must have put him through.

When everything had gone down, I'd only thought about how it had made *me* feel. I hadn't taken into consideration how Nate must have felt, meeting my parents for the first time, and having that secret exposed. Then, on top of it, I bolted and left him to deal with *my* parents.

I'd been such an asshole.

Plus, it wasn't as though he hadn't tried to reach out to me. I was the one who ignored his calls and texts until he finally told me that he was giving me the space I needed but that he would be there when I decided I was ready.

Except, I hadn't gotten that impression from the phone call we'd just had.

What if I'd waited too long? Maybe he'd found someone else?

Oh God, what if he did find someone else? Maybe someone who wasn't embarrassed by their relationship and didn't bolt at the first public mention of him being their Daddy.

But I wasn't embarrassed about him being my Daddy, was I?

I glanced back down at my phone, shuffling it back and forth between my sweating palms. My brows furrowed as I considered the question that had been plaguing my mind since the drive home that seemed to take hours from my parents' house.

Turning around, I crawled up the bed and curled into a tight ball of misery. There was nothing I could do to change the past and I wasn't sure I deserved to have a future with Nate. No matter how much I needed him, craved him.

A few tears slipped down my cheeks and I wiped them away, angry that I let a man reduce me to something so weak.

Vulnerability isn't weakness.

Huffing out a sigh, I shoved the voice to the back of my mind and swallowed the tears. They didn't do any good. Not now. Not anymore. I'd cried enough for him when I first started to ignore him. And I had no reason to cry, considering it was all my fault. *I* was the one who stopped answering his calls and texts, so I had no one to blame for my misery except myself.

It was just easier to try to find some reason to blame him.

But I didn't want to be angry. Especially when I had finally swallowed my pride and contacted him. I just had to hope he'd listen and try to understand. That he would give me another chance to prove I wasn't an asshole and that I was worth his time and the effort.

Fuck.

None of this was doing me any good. And I didn't have anything else planned for the day, so I dragged myself back out of bed and into the bathroom. I turned on the water for the shower, as hot as I could stand it, and while I waited for it to heat up, I went to the medicine cabinet over the sink and grabbed my meds.

I fucking hated taking them. But they helped. Most of the time.

Swallowing the pills, I looked in the mirror and cursed the puffiness in my eyes. With a shake of my head, I turned away and got undressed and slid into the shower with a hiss as the water heated my chilled skin.

While I debated with myself on whether or not I should jerk off, I washed my hair. All I could think about was how I wanted my Daddy to fuck me and take me apart, to own me and ruin me for all other men. But if there was even the slightest chance things would go my way, I wasn't sure I wanted to have already come.

I wasn't supposed to come unless Daddy said I could.

My eyes traveled down to my dick as the water rinsed my hair and I frowned.

Not even a twitch.

Dammit. I was so in my head over all the shit, that even when I was thinking about getting fucked, I didn't get hard.

But I guessed that answered whether or not I was jerking off in the shower, since my dick wasn't on board with the suggestion.

Sighing, I grabbed the soap and made quick work of washing and rinsing my body. The shower was no longer the relaxing activity I had hoped it would be, that would help me get my mind off of all thoughts that wouldn't leave me alone.

I let out a frustrated growl as I turned the water off and reached for the towel to dry off. Nothing was going right and I couldn't figure out how to get it all back on track.

The thought crossed my mind that Daddy would be able to help, that was what he was there for and good at, but a bitter laugh escaped my lips because I wasn't sure he would.

Not anymore.

I stepped out of the bathroom, towel loosely wrapped around my hips, and stopped dead in my tracks.

"What are you doing here?" I hadn't meant for it to sound like an accusation, but the way his eyebrow quirked up as he leaned back on his hands, lounging on my bed as if he had every right to be there, made my heart flutter.

He stood with a smirk and his eyes glinted as he took in my appearance. "I thought I'd surprise you. Didn't think I'd be the one getting the surprise."

My mouth opened and closed a few times as confusion clouded my mind. There were too many thoughts bombarding my mind, not to mention horniness at his sudden closeness. "How did you get in here?"

Nate chuckled and trailed a finger down my arm, leaving goose bumps in its wake.

"I'm serious." I took a step back. At first, I'd been annoyed at myself for that being the first thing out of my mouth. But I had a damn good alarm system. I was a cop, for fuck's sake. He couldn't go breaking into my house.

Except, it wasn't the first time.

I eyed him warily as I sidestepped him, adrenaline spiking.

"Where do you think you're doing, little bird?" He watched me with the eyes of a predator and I was so fucked that it made my dick hard. I wanted to run, but I also wanted him to catch me.

"You said you were busy. Why did you brush me off if you were just going to come over?"

He folded his arms over his chest, his lips pursed in a thin line. "You mean like you brushed me off since we left your parents' house?"

I cringed, knowing he was right. No matter how much I regretted it, that didn't change the facts.

My shoulders slumped. "I'm sorry. I shouldn't have done that."

Defeated, I walked over to the bed and plopped down. "I've been miserable without you. Every day, I wanted to call or text."

"But you didn't."

I let my head hang in shame.

"I didn't." The words were barely a whisper. "I got so wrapped up in my head, worrying about what other people—what my parents—would think of me, of us, that I couldn't deal with it. I didn't want to think about it."

Out of the corner of my eye, I saw Nate lean against the wall. He didn't look happy and my heart sank. I'd fucked everything up and I was going to lose the one man who I could have loved for the rest of my life.

Shit.

I didn't know when the hell that had happened, but the realization had tears streaming down my face. Biting my lip, I tore my gaze away from him, afraid he'd see the truth in my face.

"The truth is, I've never been with anyone like you, never had a *Daddy*. And all of it, I think it scared me. How much I liked it, wanted it, needed it... you. That I became terrified I'd lose you.

My breath hitched and I wished my pills would kick in faster or I was going to have a full-fledged panic attack on Nate. And that was the last thing I wanted him to deal with.

Taking a deep breath, I closed my eyes and tried to focus on anything else. "You never answered me. What happened to whatever you were busy with?"

Nate grunted. "I left an associate to take care of it. It's fine."

I looked up, biting my lip. "What about us? Are we?"

20

NATHAN

Aiden scampered back on the bed away from me as I glared down at my boy and I wanted to be angry. Everything in me wanted to turn around and walk away and forget about him. To leave him and never think about him again because I knew it was what I should do.

Except that was a lie.

More than anything, I wanted to fall at his feet and chase away the sadness and banish his demons. But I was his demon, the cause of his sadness. So, maybe I *should* have just left him, but I was a selfish asshole.

Where do you think you're going, boy?

But I didn't trust myself to say anything at the moment, so I turned and went to his dresser. Taking my time, I rustled through his drawers. Behind me, there were several noises of protests coming from him, but I ignored them. When I found what I was looking for, I turned back and marched over toward him.

I motioned with my free hand for him to stand. He cautiously stood, shaking in nothing but his flimsy towel.

With a sigh, I set down the clothes I picked out, except for the soft cotton boxers. I looked up, raising an eyebrow. He flushed and raised first one foot and then the other, to allow me to put the underwear on him. Before I pulled them up over his hips, I tugged off the towel, but I ignored his cock that had sprung to life and was begging for attention.

But that wasn't what he needed at the moment, even if he begged to differ.

Truth be told, I wasn't exactly sure what I was doing either. But I knew he was freezing and I was supposed to take care of him. So, that meant I couldn't let him stay in the towel any longer.

Once the boxers were in place, I gave him a soft kiss on one hip and then the other.

A slow smile spread across my lips, sure that the shiver that ran through his body wasn't just because he was cold that time.

I reached behind him and grabbed the soft, fuzzy bottoms I'd pulled from the drawer. He hated to admit it, but he loved the feel of the fleece against his skin, the way it was soft and warm.

He made a choked humming noise that was half a question, but I ignored it.

When the pants were on, I smoothed my hands up and down his legs, rubbing the material against his skin. Aiden sighed and leaned against me, as though he were a balloon that lost all of his air. But that was okay. I'd hold him up if he needed me to.

Aiden looked up at me, sleepy and happy despite the fact he still was shivering without a shirt on. But I would remedy that. I quickly grabbed the soft flannel shirt and tugged it on. I buttoned it all the way up to his neck and the chuckle he let out made my heart soar.

It was a sound I wanted to hear from him for the rest of my life.

The only thing that mattered was keeping my boy happy.

Not that it would be difficult to accomplish, but my life was... complicated. And I knew if he ever found out the mountain of secrets I kept from him, it would be over in a heartbeat.

Leaning down, I kissed his nose and the smile he gave me almost broke me.

He was so soft and open. A flash of fear shot through me at how I almost opened this sweet boy up all the way, had his insides on the outside as he showed me everything he was.

My thumb swept over his cheekbone as our eyes locked.

"Why do you suddenly look so serious, Daddy?" He bit his lip and averted his gaze, as though he were afraid he had done something wrong.

But then his gaze snagged on the outfit I'd dressed him in and he frowned. He looked up at me, confused. "I thought we were going to go out for dinner? Why am I dressed down like this if we're going out?"

His pout was so fucking adorable that I couldn't help but lean down and steal a kiss. I knew I shouldn't have done it. There was still too much we needed to discuss.

Do we, though? He's my little bird and I'm his Daddy. Can't it just be that simple and we forget all the bullshit?

I swept him up in my arms and he gave a startled laugh. Grinning, I carried him out of the bedroom and down the hall until we got to the living room. Once we got there, I gently placed him on the couch and bundled him up in one of the fuzzy blankets on the back of the couch.

"We can still do that later if you want. But, for now, I can make you lunch. And then we can have an early dessert between meals." I threw him a wink over my shoulder on the way to the kitchen and he blushed before looking down at his hands, pulling the blanket tighter around him.

"Umm... I'm not sure what all I have as far as groceries go. I need to go to the stores."

Turning, I gave him a stern look and wagged a finger at him.

"I noticed. But, you happen to be in luck, because I went to the store and picked up some essentials before I came over."

His cheeks heated even more and he couldn't meet my eyes. Good.

I didn't like embarrassing him, but it wasn't acceptable that he didn't take care of himself. Even if he was proving the point that he needed a Daddy.

"Not like I can do much good with cooking, anyway."

Sighing, I shook my head. He had a point. He was a disaster in the kitchen. But there were a lot of things he could make himself to eat that didn't involve almost burning his house down.

"Menace," I muttered affectionately.

I got to work making some sandwiches. They weren't anything fancy, just a couple BLTs and some fresh cut up fruit. But judging from the contents of his fridge, it was a gourmet meal for him.

The smile that spread across my face as I saw my boy all bundled up on the couch warmed my heart, but also made me...sad. He looked miserable and I never wanted him to be anything but happy and full of light.

He took his plate with a tentative smile and I couldn't help but lean down and steal another kiss from him. Anything to ease the tension radiating from his body. "Relax, little bird. Daddy's right here."

I ran my finger down his cheek and my heart thudded against my ribs at the way he leaned into the touch.

His eyes were big and brimming with tears as he looked up at me.

"I missed you, Daddy." He practically choked on the words as he shoved his plate to the cushion next to him and threw himself onto my lap.

My arms wrapped around him, and I leaned forward to put my own plate on the table. The food could wait, but Aiden couldn't. He would always be the most important thing in my life.

It should have scared me, knowing someone else held so much power over me. Especially a *cop*. It could all come crashing down so easily. But none of that mattered. He was worth it.

He wiggled in my lap and my hands flexed against his hips. His hands trailed up my arms until he reached my shoulders and the shy, almost tentative touch sent sparks through my system. I wanted to claim him, ruin him, bury myself in him. But I also wanted to make sure I gave him everything he needed, so I let him set the pace and sit in the driver's seat for once.

"Take what you need, little bird. I'm yours." My words were soft as I licked at the soft shell of his ear, eliciting the most delicious moan.

When his hips rocked forward, sliding his hard cock over my own aching erection, I let out a hiss. Before I even knew he was moving, his lips crashed against mine in a hungry kiss. It was full of teeth and tongue, and want and need. It was beautiful and glorious to see him unravel for me.

"Mine," I growled as I bit his lower lip and tugged on it.

He continued to rut against me, chasing his pleasure, but he didn't seem to be in a hurry to move things past where we were.

"You want to come in Daddy's lap, baby?"

Aiden couldn't even get an answer out besides a low, keening whine. His face was utter perfection, mouth slack and eyes blown so wide they were black. His back arched as he moved against me.

My fingers squeezed bruises into his hips, marking him as mine.

He was beautiful.

Perfect.

Mine.

But I needed more. I tugged the front of his sweats and boxers down, and he hissed as the air cooled the overheated flesh of his aching dick. He humped the air, looking for the delicious friction to help bring him the release he needed. I wasn't going to make it that easy for him, though.

I held him in place with one hand as I fished my own leaking cock out of the pants I'd changed into before I had come over to his place, and I wrapped my hand around both of us.

Aiden dug his fingers into the back of my neck as he let out a hiss, bucking his hips wildly as he fucked my fist.

A low groan tore from my chest at the way it felt to have him pressed against my needy dick, wrapped tight in my fist. I wished I had thought to grab some lube, but we were both leaking so much, it almost wasn't necessary, there was almost no burn.

I had to stop myself from throwing my head back because I wanted to watch my boy fall apart in my lap. He was perfection personified as he took what he wanted from me. I'd let him take everything, if he wanted it. He could have it all.

"That's it, little bird. Take what you need. Let Daddy make you feel good."

My words sent a shiver through his body and he clung even tighter to me, his knees tightening against my sides. I'd live forever in that moment if I could, with him staring down at me like I was his everything. Because in that moment, I could pretend I'd earned that look.

I pulled his head down and my tongue plundered his mouth as my fist worked over our cocks, catching the pearls of pre-cum at the tips and smearing them down the sides. He groaned in my mouth, before pulling back and bucking wildly into my fist.

"Shit. Oh, God. Fuck, Daddy..."

My free hand trailed down his shoulder and pecs to his

nipple and I tweaked it through his shirt. I should have stripped him, but I'd been too wild and hadn't been thinking straight with a horny Aiden in my lap. I would have loved to tease that nub while I made him scream my name, while seeing the expanse of glistening, naked flesh on display for me.

"Come for me, little bird. Come for Daddy. Give it to me."

He shouted as he rutted into my fist, shuddering as his release splashed onto both of our clothes that neither of us had bothered to shed before we had gotten started. Not that I cared. I'd carry his cum on my clothes with me forever.

I fell right behind him, my cum mixing with his as his mouth found mine, our tongues tangling together as he went limp above me. I stroked us a few more times, and I smirked as Aiden let out a pitiful whine from being oversensitive. After one final stroke, I took pity on him and let go, but I didn't release him from the lazy kisses we were still trading.

"Hi," he whispered, cheeks pink from exertion and a bit of embarrassment.

"Hello, yourself." I chuckled as I leaned up and gave him another quick peck on the lips.

He snuggled in, obviously not ready to move and I wrapped my arms around him, willing to let him lie there for as long as he wanted.

"I really am sorry about the way I acted after we left my parents' house," he said with a sigh. "I just didn't know what to think or do. Or what you would think."

There were a lot of things I could have said, and wanted to say, but none of that really mattered.

"You would have known what I was thinking if you had talked to me, instead of shutting me out. But if you still want to know, I think your parents are great people and they love you and just want you to be happy. And that's all I want too."

Fuck. I hadn't meant to say that out loud. I really shouldn't have.

Aiden looked up at me with tears in his eyes. "I'm really sorry, Daddy."

"I know, baby. I know." I squeezed him to me and kissed his hair. My hands ran up and down his back, rubbing soothing patterns all along his spine, or at least, I hoped they were.

"Come on. We need to get up. My dirty boy got us all filthy and now we need to wash up and clean our clothes or we'll be all sticky." I gave him a reprimanding look, but the chuckle he gave me let me know it didn't hit its mark.

Instead, it hit somewhere deep inside my chest.

21

NATHAN

The snow fell softly as I bundled my little bird into his coat and ushered him to the door. I'd had some worry about the weather, but the forecast had said there should only be a few flurries in the morning leading into the afternoon and taper off before most people sat down to eat.

"Are you sure about this, Nate? Maybe we should just stay home." Aiden stopped and turned around in my arms, casting a wary glance up at the overcast sky. When he looked back at me, and his gaze caught mine, I leaned in and pressed my forehead against his.

I wanted to give him whatever he wanted, but I also didn't want to let him hide. He still had a lot of anxiety over what had happened the last time we went to his parents' house and the idea of going back there with me played heavily on his nerves. It wouldn't do anyone any good to put things off.

Not that I particularly wanted the first official meeting with his parents to end up being this farce of a holiday meal. Though, as I gazed at Aiden's face, no matter how anxious he was, I couldn't deny that this year I had plenty to be thankful for.

He grimaced and walked out the door, stopping to stare ahead. I nearly bumped into him as I walked behind him and pulled the door closed.

"Aiden?" I wasn't sure what had stopped him and I scanned the street, but I didn't see any potential threats.

The look he gave me as he turned around was... confusing. A lot was going on there and I wasn't sure how to read it.

"Is that your car?" He almost choked on the last word. Which, I guess the suped up SUV could barely be classified as a *car*.

I chuckled and kissed his head, grabbing the keys out of his hand and turning back to look at the door.

"Baby. It's Thanksgiving. This is *your* family's holiday. We can do whatever you want to do, but I *know* that you want to spend the holiday with your parents and your sister. But tell me now, am I locking the door or are we going back inside?" I looked over at the car, already loaded up with the goodies we were taking with us, before I turned back to him, waiting him out.

As I stared into his eyes, a thought struck me that chilled me worse than the snow swirling around us ever could. "Little bird? Do you want to go to your parents' alone?"

His head snapped up, eyes wide and his forehead creased as he stared at me as though I'd spoken in tongues and couldn't quite decipher what I'd said.

"I mean, we've only been back together for a week, so if it's too soon for you to want to bring me around, I'd understand."

Aiden launched himself at me, covering my mouth with his hand. "Don't be silly. Of course I want you to come to my parents' house with me. This is our do-over. Our opportunity to do it right this time."

He sagged against me for a moment, like a deflated balloon that lost all of its air. I wasn't sure what was up with him, but I could tell something was bothering him. And since we had a little bit of a drive, I hoped I could get it out of him before we got there so we could settle it and not have an uncomfortable meal.

He leaned back and chewed his bottom lip, until I reached up and tugged it free. I leaned in, pulling him close to me, nuzzling against his ear. "Now, now, little bird. We've already discussed this. I'm the only one allowed to give you pleasure *or* pain."

A soft gasp ripped from deep within his chest as his head shot up, eyes glazed. Maybe it had been a little mean to tease him, but it was better than him being in his head, needlessly worrying about how his parents were potentially silently judging the fact that I was his Daddy.

Little did he know, he had much bigger worries when it came to me with his parents. But hopefully, no one would ever be the wiser about those fears he should have been focusing on.

I booped his nose and smirked at his obvious arousal. "Later. First, we need to get through dinner with your family, baby. Now, let's go before we're late."

Aiden groaned and stomped toward the SUV, but he didn't put up a fight, despite his petulance. I smiled and shook my head at his antics. I loved how he had a bit of a bratty side. He made my hand itch to punish him and I wondered if he'd be into that.

It still amazed me how things had worked out.

Getting in the SUV, I quickly turned it on and cranked up the heat, knowing he got cold easily. He eagerly leaned forward, holding his hands up to the vents, and cast me a grateful smile. "Thanks, Daddy."

I brushed a stray lock of his hair aside and my heart slammed into my ribcage as the depths of my feelings for him overwhelmed me. Staring into his eyes, I wondered how he had managed to captivate me so completely. "Of course, little bird."

We made our way to his parents' house in a comfortable silence, and my hand found its way to his knee. My fingers gently stroked him through his jeans, attempting to soothe his unease. He stared out the window, still with an anxious look on his face, and sighed.

But I didn't stop. I'd never stop offering comfort to my little bird when he needed it.

"You don't have to worry about your parents. You know that. Right? They love you and just want you to be happy."

He let out a slow breath and turned to look at me, and the expression on his face made me second-guess everything. I glanced back at the road before my attention wandered back to him. "Aiden? You are happy…right?"

I didn't know what I'd do if he said no. There was a whole life I'd never thought I'd have, or even want, but that I had started to envision with him. If he said he didn't want that, it might actually destroy me.

"What?" He looked at me in shock, mouth hanging open. "Of course I'm happy! No, fuck. Why would you even say that?"

I shrugged. It wasn't like I was a relationship expert. He knew about my inexperience. "Just checking."

He wiggled in his seat as he turned to fully face me. It was distracting, and difficult to keep my attention on the road, but somehow I managed.

"I'm sorry, Daddy. I'm just all in my head. Of course I'm happy. You make me so happy." A smile lit up his face as he leaned against the seat and watched me drive.

A new worry wiggled its way into his brain as his smile slowly morphed into a frown, the line deepening between his eyes. When he finally spoke, his voice came out a soft whisper. "*You're* happy, right, Daddy?"

Worry was one thing, but at the sound of distress in my little bird's voice, I quickly pulled into an empty lot. The building looked long abandoned, so we wouldn't be disturbed.

My breathing was ragged, as though I were breathing through a sponge or something was obstructing it. The idea that he thought I wasn't happy was unfathomable. There was worry in his eyes as he glanced around the overgrown lot, biting his lip.

"Daddy?" A low growl ripped from my throat at the tremor in my boy's voice.

I yanked the seat belt off and flung myself across the console, tugging him against me. My lips crashed against him, his breath caught in his chest in surprise. But it was only a moment before his hands were on the back of my head, clutching into fists in my hair as he held me like he planned to never let go.

Fuck. He better mean it because I was never going to let him go.

Teeth clashed as we kissed in a frenzy, hands roaming over each other's bodies, mapping each other like we were works of art we were just discovering for the first time.

"You make me the happiest I've ever been, sweetheart." I breathed the words into his mouth, quiet as though afraid that saying them too loud would shatter the perfect moment. That if they were too real, it would all be over. Because it could be over in the snap of a finger if he ever discovered the truth.

But I'd do anything to keep that from happening. To keep him forever. And the thought scared the shit out of me.

"I love you, little bird." I hadn't meant to say it, but once the words were out, I couldn't take them back. Didn't want to take them back.

He pulled away, eyes wide as he stared at me in wonder. "You... you... you love me?"

For a moment, a swell of panic threatened to rise. Had I pushed too far, too fast? But as I looked into his face, all I saw was the eager and hopeful little bird I'd fallen for, staring back at me. In his eyes, I saw all of my feelings reflected back at me and my heart soared.

"Of course I do," I whispered as I slid my palm around his head and into his hair. "How could I not? I knew from the first time I saw you, that you were meant to be mine, no matter what."

Tears threatened to spill as he craned his neck up and captured my lips in a searing kiss that left its claim on my soul. "I love you too, Daddy."

Pulling back, I smiled at him and cupped his cheek. If I could have, I would have stayed forever in that moment with him. But as nice as my SUV was, it wasn't made for living in. Plus, I didn't want to disappoint his family by making him late.

Wow. Look at me. Concerned about impressing the parents. I chuckled at the thought, ignoring the unease that rolled through me. Guilt had no place in my world.

I shimmied back into my seat and smiled at the way Aiden was left all flushed and debauched, before putting the car in gear and pulling back onto the road.

The snow had continued to steadily come down while we had stopped, and there was a thin layer on the street, but it wasn't anything my new snow tires couldn't handle. I hoped.

Thankfully, we hadn't been far from his parents' house and in less than fifteen minutes, I turned down their street, with plenty of time to spare before it was time to eat.

What I didn't like, was the way Aiden seemed nervous once again, twisting his fingers in his lap. I didn't want to say anything, but with the way the snow kept coming down, I almost wished he would tell me to turn the car around and that he wanted us to have a low-key Thanksgiving at his house.

"What's wrong?"

He let out a nervous chuckle, his eyes never straying from his window. "Nothing gets by you."

I waited him out. But he didn't have long, not with his

parents' house rapidly approaching. But I slowed the car down to give him the time he needed to put his thoughts together and say what he needed to.

"Okay." He took a deep breath. "So, I might not have actually told my parents that we had broken up."

My eyes widened and I went to say something, but there was nothing to say. I cleared my throat and tried again. "You... didn't tell them that we broke up?"

He shook his head.

"Why not?"

Aiden groaned and threw his head back against the seat. His hands covered his face to hide his embarrassment, but his flush reached down past his neck.

More than anything, I wished I could lean over and unwrap him and see how far down it went.

"Ugh. It was so *stupid*. Ma fucking loved you and there I was. I'd already pushed you away, expecting the worst." The weary sigh he let out made my heart stutter. I hated to think about how he'd been alone during that time, that I couldn't console him and tell him it was all right. Couldn't hold him and comfort him.

"It's only natural." Or so I assumed.

He shook his head. "Maybe. But even if they had reacted poorly, it wasn't as though it would have actually changed anything that had happened. I felt like an idiot. And she was so happy to finally see me happy. I didn't know how to tell her I was an idiot and blew it."

I reached over and pried the hand closest to me from his face and kept it clasped tightly in mine. Following the urge to comfort him, despite the fact that the events that had transpired had well passed, I brought his hand to my lips and laid a soft, gentle kiss to his knuckles. "You weren't an idiot. And you didn't ruin anything."

Aiden let out a choked sob and I could feel his eyes on me. "How the fuck are you so perfect?"

His words sent a chill through me. I found I couldn't look at him and kept my eyes focused on the road ahead as we approached his parents' house. "I'm far from perfect."

I pulled into the drive, cutting off any response he might have had. His back went ramrod straight as nerves overtook him again.

"It's fine, little bird. Just breathe."

He nodded as his gaze met mine and he took a deep breath, mentally preparing himself for whatever was to come.

"There you boys are! I was worried about you with the snow!" Ellie was at the door, waving and calling out to us, before we even got out of the car. She bustled over and enveloped Aiden in a warm hug before giving me a quick embrace as well.

"Happy Thanksgiving, Ellie." I smiled at her as she leaned back and took one of Aiden's hands in both of hers. It made me happy to see her still be so accepting of him.

Not that I'd had any doubts. She'd told me that morning after he'd run off, that it wasn't any business of hers what our relationship was like, as long as we were safe and it was consensual—and that he was happy. He just hadn't given me the opportunity to convince him that she had meant it.

Staring at them, I knew I wanted to protect what they had. No matter the cost.

"You two go on in," I urged them, shooing them along. "I'll get all the goodies and bring them along."

Aiden looked like he was going to argue. He didn't like not carrying his weight. No matter how many times I told him it was mine to carry, that I was Daddy.

He glanced back at the house, no doubt longing for the warmth. "Are you sure? I can help."

The chattering of his teeth said otherwise.

I gripped his chin and gave him a quick, chaste kiss—we had an audience, after all. "I can already see you shaking under all those layers, little bird. Now, be a good boy and go on inside."

The next shiver was for a completely different reason and I gave him a wink as he scowled at me. But he let his mom loop her arm through his and lead him back to the house, so that was all that mattered.

We hadn't packed that much stuff in the back of the SUV, but it did require two trips. When I came back in with the pans of dessert I'd baked a few days prior, his dad was sitting in the living room.

He stood from his chair and offered me his hand. "Jeff. Happy Thanksgiving." In his other hand, he held a beer, which he held out and offered. While it wasn't a brand I usually preferred, I had to admit it wasn't bad.

Not that I would turn it down either way.

"You too."

He eyed me as I sat back on the couch, while Aiden and his mom were in the kitchen chatting, waiting for his sister to arrive.

I wasn't sure what he was looking for, but I hoped he didn't find me lacking.

"Sorry we didn't get to meet last time you boys were here."

I wasn't sure what to make of his grimace, if it was over the thought of his son being kinky the *Daddy* thing in particular. My teeth ground together to keep from saying anything that would embarrass Aiden even more.

A few minutes later, there was a commotion at the front door.

"Ma? Pops? Is Aiden not here yet?" A woman, who I assumed was Alyssa, called from the front hallway. "Also, who is the pretentious asshole you let park in the driveway? What even is that monstrosity?"

I chuckled as I took a sip of my beer. Jeff offered me an apologetic shrug as I stood, but I waved him off. I was far from offended. More like amused.

"That would be me," I said as I leaned against the doorway. Alyssa startled, midway through taking off her snow boots, with her hand flying to her chest in an effort to steady her racing heart.

With a smile, I walked down the hall, offering her my hand. "Nathan."

"What the fuck, Alyssa?" Aiden barreled around the corner, eyes blazing with fury. It made me feel all warm inside, knowing he was getting angry on my behalf, even if it wasn't necessary.

I offered him an indulgent smile. "It's okay, little bird. I admit, it is a little bit of an extravagant car. But it's great in bad weather. And, since I had precious cargo I was carrying today, I wanted to make sure I was safe as can be."

I threw him a wink as I grasped his hand and tugged him up against my side. He gaped up at me, mouth opening and closing a few times before he let out a huff and settled on just glaring at his sister, who had just watched our little display with a smirk and had begun to fan herself.

"Ya'll are too cute for words. You know that?" She came up and hugged Aiden, rocking him back and forth, before whispering in his ear how happy she was to see him so happy. I heard his partner's name mentioned in there somewhere, but I hadn't heard the context it was said in, so I let it go. For the moment.

Ellie called out a moment later, breaking up their hug. "All right. Is everyone going to stand in the hall, or is anyone going to actually help with dinner?"

Aiden laughed and leaned back. "Coming."

I raised a brow. "No. You go sit and watch the game with

your dad. I will go help Ellie. Alyssa can come help, or play twenty questions, like I know she's probably dying to."

She let out a sharp laugh, like she hadn't been expecting me to be so direct, and Aiden looked back and forth between us, panic-stricken. But I pushed him toward the living room and praised him when he complied. "Good boy."

"I'm so screwed," he muttered as Alyssa laughed again before we headed down to the kitchen.

22

AIDEN

Sweat soaked my body as if I'd run a marathon without ever leaving my bed. I wished it had been from a more pleasant experience. Such a long time had passed since I'd had a nightmare that I thought I was over them.

I wiped a hand over my face and tried to shut out the images that lingered in my mind. Living through the events of my childhood once had been more than enough, even if I didn't remember a good chunk of it. But having the bits I did remember, along with the aftermath, constantly on repeat in my mind while I slept wasn't my idea of a good time.

A low groan escaped my lips as I pushed myself into a sitting position. My head throbbed and felt cotton-y, as though I had a hangover. I frowned, trying to remember the night before. I didn't remember drinking myself into a stupor.

Truth was, I wasn't much of a drinker. A few beers, maybe a shot or two. I didn't over-indulge due to my anti-anxiety medication that kept the panic attacks at bay. Clamoring out of bed, I wondered if I forgot to take my meds before bed and that explained the nightmare and the weird feeling I'd woken up with.

With a shake of my head, I tried to dispel the weird thoughts that had twisted and merged in my sleep. Memories of my childhood plus thoughts of Nate and everything that had been going on with him had sunk their claws into me and refused to let go. I didn't need a shrink to psychoanalyze me with their mumbo jumbo to know that the stress was eating me alive.

As I stumbled to the bathroom and turned on the shower, I wondered if I was ever going to catch a break with this fucking case. For every step closer we got, I felt like I got pushed two steps back. It was beyond frustrating.

Everyone made mistakes, and eventually, this guy had to as well.

I closed my eyes as I stepped under the spray of the shower and let it soothe away some of the stress and wash away the sweat and desperation that clung to my skin.

While I shampooed my hair, memories of Nate drifted through my mind. I still couldn't believe how well he meshed with my family. I didn't date much; too much trauma, I supposed. But the very few people I had introduced to my parents, it hadn't gone well. They'd instantly known they weren't right for me.

But with Nate, they'd liked him right away. Even after that embarrassing first morning.

Thinking about Nate, while naked and in the shower, had my cock twitching in anticipation. Except he wasn't there to offer me any relief. I needed him like an addict needed a fix.

How had I become so dependent, so needy, so *desperate* for him in such a short time?

No man had ever driven me to the point of obsession before, where I felt like I'd die without him by my side, let alone filling my greedy little hole.

I groaned as my hand slid down my body and gripped my

hardening length. But just as I slid my fist up and down in a teasing temp, my phone went off with a text.

"Son of a fucking bitch." It was the first of my days off, so it had better not be work. And anyone else better have a damn good reason for interrupting my time with my hand.

Knowing my sexy shower time was over, I quickly finished washing and turned off the water. As I stepped out, I grabbed the towel and quickly dried before I grabbed my phone off the edge of the sink and my breath caught when I saw the message waiting for me.

NATE

Are you free today? I was thinking maybe we could catch a movie and a bite to eat? Maybe that diner you love so much?

Are you asking me out on a date?

NATE:

Absolutely.

Then, yes. Actually, I am off today. But... I have a feeling you already knew that.

I bit my lip as I stared down at the screen. My eyes drifted around the room, brow furrowed. There was no way he could have known I'd just been thinking of him, right?

He'd admitted to stalking me, but I'd never asked how far it went. Maybe I needed to remedy that. But I didn't think he actually would have gone as far as to break into a police officer's house and what... Bug it? Set up cameras?

No. I shook my head. It had to be a coincidence. He had just been thinking about me at the same time I'd been thinking about him.

Didn't stop me from worrying my lip between my teeth.

NATE

If I knew, I wouldn't have been asking, little bird.

A thrill went through me at the nickname. There was something about it, something *forbidden*. In the back of my mind, there was a whisper of a memory, long forgotten, that stirred when he called me that name. But it didn't elicit fear like the memories of my nightmares.

I'd love to go out on a date with you, Daddy…

Do you want me to meet you at the diner or the theater?

There wasn't a response for a few minutes, so I trudged back into the bedroom and debated what to wear. Ultimately, I settled on a black jockstrap, tight dark wash jeans, and a soft dark gray sweater. I stared at my reflection and ran my fingers through my hair to tame it—and my heart, since Nate still hadn't answered my last text.

I sighed, wondering what I'd done, or said, that had upset him and made him not answer me. My shoulders slumped as I made my way to the kitchen. But as I opened the fridge to find something for breakfast, my heart, or stomach, wasn't interested in eating anymore.

How do I always manage to fuck things up so royally?

Leaning against the open fridge, I let out a frustrated groan and backed away, slamming the door closed. It wasn't fair that I'd finally found a great guy, and I didn't even know what happened, but in the span of a few texts, he ghosted me.

Men fucking sucked. And not in a good way.

I made my way back to the bathroom, yanked open the medicine cabinet, and grabbed my meds, since I had been so wrapped up in Nate earlier that I forgot about them and my head was still feeling all funny. I'd already felt the dark edges of anxiety creeping up on me from not taking my meds on time, letting me know I was in for a hell of a day.

And logically, I knew that was where my anxiety over Nate was coming from. But fuck logic.

Swallowing the two tablets dry, I looked at myself in the foggy mirror and bit back a sharp laugh at the funhouse-like image that stared back at me.

The fucked up, warped image reflected perfectly what I felt on the inside. It was no wonder Nate had realized he could do better than my needy ass and ditched me. I was pathetic. Saved me the embarrassment of ever having to tell him about my past.

My cheeks heated at the thought. It was the biggest reason I didn't date. Letting a man see my scars and having to answer the inevitable questions was just too much. I couldn't handle it. Didn't want to handle it. So far, I'd lucked out and Nate hadn't asked.

Probably should have taken that as a sign he hadn't been serious about me. Men who were serious about relationships tended to want to know why their partners had scars from practically being gutted.

I shuddered and wiped my hand across the mirror as I turned away, unable to look at it any longer. The person looking back didn't even resemble me anymore. But then again, I didn't know who I was most of the time.

Good thing my parents didn't know I had stopped seeing my shrink or they would have been on my ass about that. But fifteen years later, I didn't think she could help me any more than she already had. So, I kept the meds refilled but as far as talking shit out, that hadn't seemed to do me any good for a long time.

Though, I wished I had someone impartial at the moment

to talk to about Nate. Lord knew Vic wasn't impartial, and apparently, my sister was her new cohort.

When my phone *dinged* again, I was tempted to ignore it. Part of me wanted to crawl back into my bed, pull the covers over my head, and go back to sleep for an eternity. Or, at least, long enough to start the day over again. But a second message had me rolling my eyes and hunting down where I had left it.

I found it on the kitchen counter. And I was still half tempted to ignore it, but when I picked it up, the screen lit up and showed me the preview of Nate's message.

NATE

Understood?

Brows furrowed, I swiped my phone open and went into our chat to see what he was talking about. I wasn't prepared for the sucker punch of emotion his words delivered as my eyes went wide as I let them sink in.

NATE

Last time I checked, I was your Daddy, which means it's my job to take care of you.

So I will pick you up in an hour, if you'll be ready.

Understood?

I swallowed thickly, blinking back tears. Maybe I had made him angry, but not for the reason I'd originally thought. But because he wanted to take care of me and I hadn't been allowing him to do that. I just wasn't used to it. Sure, my parents did when I was younger, but that was because they had to.

As an adult, I think we forgot that it was okay to lean on others, to let someone else take care of you. I certainly wasn't in the habit of letting anyone do that. Not that I had anyone lining up and volunteering to do it.

But there Nate was, demanding to be given the job.

My hands shook as I typed my response back.

I understand Daddy. And I'm ready, whenever you want to come pick me up.

After another moment, I sent him another text.

Should I not eat breakfast?

NATE

You didn't eat breakfast yet?

A quick glance at the clock had me realizing it was almost noon and I grimaced.

Oops?

I could practically hear him growl in response, in my head, and it brought a smile to my face.

NATE

I'll be there in fifteen minutes. We will eat and then we can see a matinee. After, we can spend the day however you wish, little bird.

Sounds good, Daddy.

Thank you.

I went back to the bathroom and washed my face, needing to get rid of the evidence of my earlier distress. Worrying Daddy was the last thing I wanted. After another quick look in the mirror, my fingers twitched with a need, but I wasn't sure what Nate would think of the addition.

Feeling brave, I reached back into the medicine cabinet with trembling fingers and pulled out a rarely used bag. I dug around for what I needed, and for a minute, I frowned, thinking maybe I had thrown it out. But then, I cleared away everything and found it sitting at the bottom of the bag, waiting for me.

After taking a deep breath, I leaned forward in the mirror and concentrated on what I was doing, getting into the zone. I was out of practice, but in the end, I thought it looked pretty good. Not overdone, but the light charcoal lines under my eyes were just enough to make them pop.

I bit my lip, eyeing the rest of the contents in the bag. But I wasn't sure if I was brave enough.

A minute later, my phone buzzed with a text from Nate to let me know he was pulling into the drive. I took a deep breath and grabbed the clear, cherry flavored gloss before I could chicken out. Staring in the mirror, I swiped it over my lips and my reflection offered up the first real smile I'd seen in a long time.

My heart pounded in my chest as I walked out the front door, hoping I wasn't making a mistake in showing this part of myself to Nate.

23

NATHAN

Rage.

I had to trample it down as my boy climbed into the passenger seat, refusing to look at me. At first, I thought it was because of our conversation. It made me want to hunt down and kill every person who had ever hurt him, ever made him feel like he wasn't worth the effort. Like he wasn't worth being taken care of.

As his Daddy, *of course* I was going to fucking pick him up and take him out for our date. It had never even occurred to me that people in his past would have expected him to drive himself. This precious boy deserved to be treated like he was special, like a prince.

For as long as he let me, I planned to be that person for him.

But watching him sit next to me, there was something different about him. I just couldn't quite put my finger on it.

I reached over and gently took the seat belt from his trembling fingers, giving them a quick squeeze.

"Here, let me, little bird." The words came out as a soft hush, as though a spell had been cast in the quiet of the car. I clicked the belt in place and smiled as his cheeks flushed.

"Thank you, Daddy," he muttered, eyes focused on his hands that he had dropped to his lap. He went to bite his lip, but stopped himself.

My eyes zeroed in on the movement, always mindful of his lips, but curious as to what had halted his nervous habit. I noticed his lips were shinier than normal, and at first, I just thought it was from him licking them. But I leaned a little closer and got the lightest scent of cherries.

A smile spread across my face as I realized my little bird had put on lip gloss. I hadn't known that was something he liked. The knowledge made me more curious about the way he had his face hidden from me.

I reached out and cupped his chin with my index finger, stopping when his body went rigid. My head cocked to the side as I watched him breathe heavily, in and out, in and out.

"Little bird, please look at me."

He hesitated for a moment, but slowly, he turned his head to face me. His eyes were wide as he met my gaze and I offered him a soft smile. My brave, sweet boy.

My thumb stroked across his cheek, just under his eye. "You look beautiful. Thank you for trusting me. I know it must have been a lot."

He nodded, almost biting his lip again and letting out a groan of frustration. I chuckled at his antics and put the car into gear just as his stomach growled.

"All right, let's get that monster in your belly fed before it bursts through and eats *us*." Aiden let out a laugh, his eyes sparkling, head ducking. I figured it was a job well done, a mission accomplished. Anytime I could make my little bird laugh and look carefree, I would take it as a win.

When we pulled up to the diner a few minutes later, I put up my finger, indicating for him to wait, when he moved to get out of the car. He shot me a confused look, but I got out and made my way over to him, opening the door and leaning down to unbuckle the seat belt for him. His cheeks flamed a brilliant shade of pink, and I wondered if it would be too bold to suggest him wearing more makeup.

I wasn't sure what it was that drew him to it, or why it was something he had seemed to hide up until this point, and the last thing I wanted was to make him uncomfortable, so I didn't say anything. But a piece of my heart did thaw at the shy look he cast my way as I slotted our fingers together and led him into the diner.

Hopefully, this time we would have a much more pleasant experience, without any more secrets being exposed.

While I loved the way his mind worked, I couldn't help but feel a little too seen with how keen his observational skills were. But still, I wouldn't change a thing about him.

There was something special about him that I couldn't help but cherish and want to watch blossom.

"Table for two, please," I told the hostess, with a smile, when we got inside.

She showed us to our table and while he seemed uneasy about the makeup, especially when a few people he seemed to know gave him funny looks, breakfast had gone off mostly without a hitch. Aiden had ignored the other patrons, not even giving them a polite greeting. His focus was solely on me by the end of our meal, and I couldn't say I was upset about that.

"Did you enjoy your pancakes, little bird?" I asked him softly as I drove across town to the theater.

His head lolled in my direction, with a wide grin across his face. I was sad to see the lip gloss was gone from eating, especially when I hadn't even gotten a chance to taste it, but the eyeliner was still there, perfectly casting a slight shadow under his eye.

"I did. Thank you."

I couldn't help but wonder why he always looked so conscious whenever I did something or asked him something like that. But I didn't want to draw attention to it and ruin the mood, so I let it go.

For now.

We continued on in a comfortable silence, and I let him control the music, syncing his streaming service to the radio so he could listen to his music. Again, the way his eyes went wide when I made the suggestion, made me want to go on a rampage and hunt down every man he'd ever dated before me.

I just had to remind myself there would be no one after me. I'd make sure of it.

The movie theater lobby was mostly empty when we got there, since it was early afternoon during the middle of the week, but that was fine. It just meant that we would get the theater to ourselves. I bought tickets for a rom-com I knew he would like, even though I wasn't sure if he'd seen it. But that was okay. Hopefully, we wouldn't be watching much of the movie anyway.

"Popcorn?" I asked as we went through the gate, getting our tickets stamped.

"Hmm? Oh, yeah. Though, I'm not sure if I can eat much more." Aiden patted his belly and gave a laugh.

I gave him a look in return. "Popcorn is a movie date staple, little bird."

He rolled his eyes and wandered off to look at the rest of the goodies while I got the popcorn. While the girl behind the counter was filling up our bucket, I went up to him and put my arm around his shoulder.

"Did you want to get something else, baby?" I whispered in his ear.

When he shook his head, I leaned back and looked at him. His face had lost the carefree look and I didn't like it. It also didn't escape my notice the way his eyes kept sliding to the gummy worms.

Not saying a word, I reached in front of him, grabbed a package, and took them to the counter.

"Daddy," he hissed, looking around as if suddenly remembering we were in public. "I said I didn't want them."

I looked at the bag of worms before holding them up.

"Oh, these? No, they're for me. Low blood sugar," I said with a wink.

Grumbling, he stalked over and grabbed the bag out of my hand, scowling at me. "Mine."

Biting back a smile, I handed my card over to the girl who was patiently waiting for our antics to be over, before I pressed a kiss to his temple. "All yours, little bird."

I gathered up our drinks and popcorn and ushered him to the theater, where we sat in the back. There were a few other groups in there with us, in sets of two and three, but I paid them no mind as I set our drinks in the holders and the popcorn on the seat next to me.

When Aiden settled into his seat, I tugged him in against my side, with his head on my shoulder. He let out a content sigh, and I wondered when the last time was that he had just let himself relax. Especially with someone else.

"Thank you, Daddy." His words were quiet, and I almost missed them with the way his head was buried in my neck.

I squeezed his neck and he sat back to look at me just as the lights started to dim.

By the time the previews were over and the movie had started, his arms were wrapped around my neck and I was leaving love bites all along his jaw.

"We... we need, fuck. We need to stop, Daddy." His words were breathy as he panted, practically moaning as I bit at the hinge of his jaw.

"Hmmm. Do we? I don't see anyone complaining." I licked a

strip up his neck and reveled in the way he shuddered under me.

His eyes met mine and the way he tried to look stern was adorable. "Yes. I'm an officer of the law. I can't get caught in the back of a movie theater like this."

With a sigh, I disentangled myself from him because he was right. And the last thing I wanted was to make his life even more difficult than I already had.

I booped his nose, enjoying the shocked look on his face. "You win, little bird."

Reaching over, I grabbed his bag of gummy worms and snorted at the betrayed look on his face. "Open up, little bird. Let Daddy bird feed you."

While it was corny as hell, it made him chuckle, so that was all I cared about. And, of course, he promptly listened. His lush pink lips opened for me, wrapping around my fingers as I fed him the worm.

I leaned down and gave him a kiss, biting off a piece of the worm. "You're trouble, little bird."

"I know." He smirked and snuggled back into my side as we sat through the rest of the movie, even though we had no idea what was going on. But it didn't matter. All I cared about was spending time with him and that he enjoyed our time together.

When we walked out of the theater, I didn't want to let him go, or leave quite yet. Plus, downtown painted a pretty picture with the snow on the ground from a few days back and the sun bright in the sky.

"I was wondering if you'd care to go for a walk?" My shoulder bumped his as we meandered around the front of the building.

He looked around and nodded. "Sure. That seems like it could be a good idea."

"Cool."

As we walked around the downtown area, looking at all the

storefronts that had started to put out their Christmas displays, Aiden lit up. Each thing that brought him joy, I filed away for later. Everything he looked at with longing in the window became a potential Christmas present.

"So, how are your parents, and Alyssa?" Our hands swung between us, partially just out of joy and partially for momentum to keep our hands warm since neither of us had thought to grab gloves. I kept my eyes open for a drug store or something that we could pop into and grab a couple pairs.

That had definitely been a miscalculation on my part. Bad Daddy.

Aiden rolled his eyes. "They're fine. And they love you, which is annoying."

"Sorry," I said with a smirk. I'd never met a significant other's parents before, mainly because I'd never had one, so I'd been nervous about them liking me, but I was happy that things seemed to be going well on that front.

Up ahead, there was a small shop where I knew we could get some hats and gloves, so I tugged him behind me and we made our way inside. They were right by the door, so we quickly rooted through the options. Aiden was always cold, so I should have anticipated that he would have needed to bundle up and I felt terrible for suggesting the walk when he didn't have proper outer wear.

"I'm sorry I didn't think of these earlier, little bird." Guild ate away at me when I saw his trembling, red fingers struggling to grab the set he wanted.

"Here, let me."

I had just worked the second glove onto his hand when a man came barreling up to me, red-faced.

Shit.

My arm went around Aiden to turn him away and guide him toward the register so I could pay and hopefully get out of the store before he would notice the man, or before he would get to us.

But I wasn't so lucky. I'd only gotten us a few steps when I heard my name.

"Nathan Turner."

I froze, caught between the past and my future. Twisting to look behind me, I gave the man behind me a cold stare. But Aiden gave him a curious look.

"Hmm. Still dating pretty boys, I see."

Aiden bristled.

My hand on his shoulder tightened just the slightest bit. A warning to let me handle this. I could see him fighting between wanting to step in and intercede and also letting me handle my own shit.

As he should. Especially considering I was the Daddy here. It was my job to protect him. Not the other way around.

"What do you want?" My voice was cold and flat, not something I had hoped for Aiden to ever have to hear. But especially not this early in our relationship. Not when there was still so much he still had to learn about me.

And so much he never would.

"Oh, me? Nothing. Just doing a bit of shopping. And when I saw you, I thought I must absolutely say hello and introduce myself to your new *friend*."

My eyes narrowed. There was no way he just happened to be in the same store as me, when I was with Aiden. Was there?

Aiden shifted uncomfortably from the tension. This was not how our date was supposed to go.

"Detective Colby Chase, Metro PD." He extended his hand to Aiden, but I moved between them.

Snarling, I hissed, "Do not touch him."

"Detective Aiden Cooper, Sheriff's Department." He reached around me and shook the asshole's hand while shooting me a questioning look.

I wanted to rage at the way he disobeyed me and it forced me to swallow the lump in my throat.

Detective Chase looked surprised, glancing back and forth between Aiden and myself before he shook my little bird's hand. Then the asshole had the gall to *smirk*.

"Keeping your *friends* close and all that, huh, Detective?" he said with a wink. "I'll be seeing you around, Turner."

With that, he walked out of the store.

Fucking asshole.

Aiden turned to me, a wary look on his face. "Nate, what the fuck was that?"

"Nothing to worry about." I gritted my teeth and grabbed our stuff and walked to the register, ignoring his questions.

Fuck. Why the hell had Chase shown up when he did? What did he want?

Nothing good.

Aiden remained quiet, too quiet, all the way back to the car. Which, I shouldn't have been surprised that when we left the store that was where he started walking. But a guy could hope.

My heart sank when we got there and he buckled himself, refusing to allow me to do anything for him.

Once I had the car started, he turned toward me again.

"Nate, why the fuck is a cop from the Metro PD threatening you." His arms were crossed over his chest and he was in full detective mode, waiting to catch me in a lie. I was so fucked.

I shook my head. "That was barely a threat, little bird."

"Don't give me your bullshit, Nate. I asked a question and I want an answer."

Glancing over at him, I shook my head. "It's nothing like what you're thinking. I promise."

My head fell back against the headrest and I wondered how this was my life. The one cop in the city who wasn't looking for me because of me being a serial killer had to be the one we ran into.

"Then tell me what it's like."

"I fucked his son, okay? We met at a bar last year and hooked up. Apparently, he didn't know his kid was gay, or bi, or whatever. Somehow, it was my fault that he ended up at a gay bar before he even met me and that I went home with him."

My hand came up and tugged at my hair as I looked over at Aiden, praying he believed me, considering it was the truth. But there were so many lies between us, I wouldn't blame him if he didn't.

"How did he find out?" His face had softened a little, but he was still reserving judgment against me.

I shrugged and gave a bitter laugh. "Fucking walked in while we were in the middle of having sex. Apparently, his dad had been trying to get ahold of him because of some family emergency, so he came over and let himself in. Neither of us heard him."

Aiden's shoulders relaxed. "I still don't get how it's your fault?"

"Join the club." I rolled my eyes. "He said because I was older and bigger, not to mention the top, that I pressured his son into it."

"That's fucking bullshit." Anger flashed in Aiden's eyes, and it was nice to see him get mad in my defense. Even if I didn't want him to have to defend me. But to know he believed me meant a lot.

I shrugged. "Yeah. He's tried to make my life hell since."

Honestly, I was surprised he hadn't uncovered the fact I was a serial killer, with how much he seemed to be digging into my life.

"I'm sorry, Daddy." He looked so sad as I pulled him into my arms.

Fuck. If he was this emotional over some asshole going at me over sleeping with his son, I didn't want to think about how much it would break him to find out that his Daddy was a serial killer.

24

AIDEN

Life was going well. Almost too well. The last month had been a whirlwind with Nate since we had started dating. I still got embarrassed over how quickly I introduced him to my family, especially when I considered the first time we went to my parents' house.

The second time hadn't been much better. While Thanksgiving had started out normal enough, the snow had proven to be more than what the meteorologists had expected and we'd gotten stuck there overnight.

In my old bedroom. On a full-size bed. Where my Daddy decided he was going to have his wicked way with me, repeatedly. While I'd been a willing participant, what I had failed to factor in was that my sister, who had also gotten stuck there overnight, was in the bedroom next to mine.

Breakfast had been a mortifying affair, to say the least. Thankfully, she kept the teasing to a minimum in front of our parents.

But they loved Nate anyway, so it didn't seem to matter, since he could do no wrong.

We'd already gotten over some big milestones, like meeting the parents and dating for a month.

Despite the fact we didn't get to see each other as often as I would have liked, that was as much my fault as his. When we did get together, we tried to make an effort to actually leave my house. Sometimes, we were successful, but more often than not, we barely left the bedroom and had food delivered.

Not that I was going to complain.

Well, I had some complaints about not getting to see my boyfriend as much as I would like, but we talked every day—*a lot*. Sometimes, I wondered how he got any work done. Then again, I also wondered how *I* got any work done.

I definitely had Victoria to thank for a lot of that.

She was also who I had to thank for helping me plan our anniversary dinner.

"What are you so worried about?" Victoria's voice asked from the phone speaker on the other side of my bedroom.

As I perused the dress shirts in my closet, I thought about how to answer her question. She was one of my best friends and if there was anyone I could talk to about Nate, it was Victoria. Yet I hesitated. Because there were things I couldn't tell her, things that would have her seriously reconsidering my sanity.

"Well, first of all, there's our date tonight. I keep second-guessing how I sprang it on him at the last minute. Because he doesn't seem to like being spontaneous. He's so… I don't know. Neat and organized. The opposite of my chaotic mess."

One of her patented bitch sighs was the response I got. "You are not a chaotic mess. It's just you've just been through more than most people. And he should respect that because you have different boundaries."

I sucked in a gasp between my teeth. Of course she was able to hit the nail on the head without even knowing all the details.

"He does respect me." Boundaries, on the other hand, I

wasn't so sure he understood what those were. But that wasn't something I was ready to discuss with Vic.

"Then what's the issue?"

Honestly, I wasn't sure. And I didn't know how to put the feeling in the pit of my stomach into words. But I knew I had to try.

"Sometimes, I wonder if he's too perfect," I admitted. "I wait for the other shoe to drop and the universe to laugh and tell me that, of course, I can't be that happy."

"Too perfect?" she scoffed. "Do you think you might be looking for problems so that you can push him away before he can do it?"

The barb stung, but it wasn't unwarranted. I'd done that to plenty of guys in the past. But they'd all given me a reason to think they weren't invested or were about to bail.

"I'm sorry, Aiden. I love you. You know I do. But we both know sometimes you expect things to go wrong and it becomes a self-fulfilling prophecy where they leave or you leave first before they can leave first."

I knew she was right. I'd done that more than once. It was why I hadn't had any serious relationships to speak of. And I also knew Nate hadn't done anything to give me any reason to think he wanted to leave me. Just the opposite. He wasn't always the most in touch with his emotions, but he didn't hold back on what he was thinking—and he thought about me a lot.

"Sometimes it doesn't seem real. And I don't mean in the sense that it's really happening to me." I paused, trying to figure out how to say what I was feeling, to figure out if I even wanted to put those thoughts into words. "Nate is, well, he's intense in everything he does. But sometimes, I feel like I'm getting a glimpse behind it all, and it seems...forced. Flat."

If I ever stopped and was honest with myself about Nate, I would have been able to admit the man was throwing out red flags like penalty markers at a football game. Starting with how he'd choked me. It didn't matter that I had ended up finding it hot and came harder than I ever had before.

Then there was the fact that he admitted to stalking me, though only after I had caught him and confronted him about it. Sometimes, I wondered if he ever would have come clean if I didn't ask outright.

I couldn't quite put my finger on it, but something about the whole package seemed off about Nate. There were some suspicions, but I wasn't anywhere near ready to let them become fully formed thoughts, let alone voice them to someone else. If I was wrong, I didn't want it to bite me in the ass and have those ideas in her head.

"You're right," I said with a sigh, wanting to wrap up the call so I could finish getting ready. "I'm probably just looking for problems when there aren't any." I blew out a breath and turned back to my clothes dilemma. I had ten minutes to pick out my clothes, get dressed, and get my ass out the door.

No pressure.

"Wow, are you actually admitting I'm right? Hold on, let me note the date and time." She cackled on the other end of the phone, and with my clothes in hand, I strode across the room and hung up on her.

Served her right.

But I didn't have time to revel in my victory. I needed to get my ass in gear and get to the other side of town at the speed of light. Somehow, I got ready and was out the door in record time, but just as I went to step outside, I quickly made my way to the kitchen and grabbed the small box out of the utility drawer and slid it into my coat pocket.

I still felt like I didn't know much about Nate, so I hoped he liked his present. With it finally tucked away, I was able to get on the road. Thankfully, traffic was light, so I didn't have to break too many laws to get to the restaurant on time. That wasn't something I'd want to explain to anyone I worked with.

Talk about embarrassing.

Twenty minutes later, I was sitting across the table from Nate with a smile on my face as he thanked me for being so thoughtful and planning an evening out with him. Though, I wasn't sure if he thought I was stepping on his toes as *Daddy* or not. But fuck it, I wanted to do something nice for him and I would, dammit.

"It's not a problem. I wanted to do something for you. We're always holed up in my house, and I know it's only been a month, but it felt special. So I wanted to do something… nice for you."

Nate looked at me for a moment before his expression turned soft and bashful. "I should have thought more about it, realized how much it meant to you, and done something for you."

I reached across the table and took Nate's hand. "No, I wanted to do this. For you. For us. Besides, only one of us could have made surprise plans for tonight," I said with a wink, eliciting a soft chuckle from him.

"I suppose you're right about that. Or else, where would we be?"

My hand slipped into my pocket, and I played with the box inside. I still wasn't sure I had made the right decision, but I'd never know until I gave it to him.

"I got you something. It's nothing big," I rushed out. "I saw it and thought of you." I took a deep breath and slid the box across the table until it bumped into his slightly trembling hands.

"Little bird… you shouldn't have." The way he eyed it warily said maybe he meant that literally and it hadn't been such a great idea after all.

I laughed at his absurdity and tried to play it off. Tried to act like I didn't start dying inside at the thought that he didn't like it.

"You don't even know what it is yet." My eyes rolled, but it was a fond gesture. Sort of. At least, it usually was. At that moment, it was more about hiding my anxiety.

Nate shook his head. "But I didn't get you anything. Fuck," he muttered. "I'm sorry. I'm bad at this whole"—he waved his hands around—"peopling thing. Especially when it's a boyfriend thing." He shifted in his chair, and I felt bad for making him uncomfortable. I wanted to snatch the box back and pretend the last couple minutes never happened.

He sat there, staring at the box as he played with it between his fingers. But he looked at it as though it was going to bite him.

It's just a stupid little gift.

"Would you open it? Please? It's nothing fancy. Just something that made me think of you, that I thought you'd like."

He let out a sigh, but I saw the way his lips twitched as he seemed to fight off a smile.

"Of course. Thank you."

He tugged on the bow on the box and opened it. At first, he didn't say anything, then the way his eyes lit up when he saw the antique cufflinks made my heart melt.

"These are beautiful. Thank you, little bird. Truly." His voice had gone soft with wonder and amazement, and it did things to my insides—things that made me squirm and wish we were back at my house rather than at a restaurant.

"You're amazing, you know that?" My voice was full of wonder as he stared at me like I'd gone crazy.

Maybe I had. I was, after all, sitting in a restaurant with a man I barely knew after a month of dating, who was a self-professed stalker. A shiver ran through me as I wondered what else he could be capable of.

Nate shook his head. "If either one of us is amazing, you're the one. You are a rare gift that I treasure." He put the box back down and grimaced. "Me..." His voice trailed off, and he looked away, as though he wasn't going to finish the sentence. "I'm just a pathetic schmuck who imprinted on you like a baby duck, and now I can never let you go."

"Hmm. Well, if you're a schmuck, then you're *my* schmuck." I offered him a grin to let him know I was serious.

"No one should be stuck putting up with me." He let out a huff and quieted as our waiter came back with our food. But I found I was no longer hungry after whatever this was with Nate.

Every instinct in me told me to ask what he meant. To push and prod and ask. But in the end, I didn't want to make him uncomfortable, and I knew he'd tell me if he wanted me to know.

Turned out, I didn't need to wait long at all.

"I don't get people, or relationships. Not because I don't want to, although most of the time, I couldn't give a fuck. But I just don't understand them or the power people give to them."

I sat back in my chair, a slight frown on my face as I contemplated his words.

"I don't know how to give you what you want or need. Not because I don't want to but because I don't have any references to look at. Things..." He hesitated and looked down at his plate with a frown. "Things that seem to come easy or naturally with other people, some things, I can't even begin to comprehend. Facts, rationality, routine, those are things I can understand. But people and emotions... Those things are difficult for me, even when I try."

Nate resembled a puppet whose strings were cut as he finished his little speech. In fact, I'd never seen him look more like a dejected puppy than in that moment. Not even when I'd asked him to leave after he dropped me off at home when we were supposed to have breakfast at my parents'.

His words replayed in my mind, along with some of the things he'd done and said since we met. The thoughts I tried to keep from forming, not wanting to admit the truth to myself. Things fell into place, pieces slotted together, and the picture started to look a bit clearer. Part of me winced at the epiphany I'd had, but I could never let him see that, especially since he was already feeling uncharacteristically vulnerable.

"How old were you when you were diagnosed with antisocial personality disorder?" I was proud of how steady my voice was as I scrambled to remember the more polite term than *sociopath.*

Nate's eyes snapped up to mine, and I let out an involuntary whimper as I got what I assumed to be my first look at the *real* Nathan Turner.

25

NATHAN

Aiden's words made my blood go cold as I snapped my attention to him. I wasn't sure what the look I had on my face had been, too stunned to school my expression. But I assumed it wasn't good based on the noise Aiden let out.

Fuck.

I knew he would probably figure it out one day. He was smart and a homicide detective. I was sure I wasn't the first psychopath he'd encountered. I'd been playing a dangerous game, and it looked like the time came when I would have to finally raise the stakes or fold.

Then my heart did a weird little flutter inside my chest. He hadn't called me a psychopath. The realization turned my gaze to wonder and, perhaps stupidly, to hope. Because while the terms *psychopath* and *sociopath* weren't really used anymore, it was the more well-known term.

"Ten," I answered honestly. "Though, not for lack of my parents trying to find out what was wrong with me before that. It's not really common for children to be diagnosed as a psychopath, but money really can buy anything."

The urge to be honest and purge my sins to him was too great. I had to be careful, or I'd be admitting to a lot more than just my mental health diagnosis to him.

Aiden frowned, the crease between his eyes deepening.

"There's nothing *wrong* with you, Nate."

My eyes widened at not just his words but the scowl that marred his beautiful face.

"Little bird," I said with a sigh as I signaled to the waiter for our check. "I'll take you home now."

There was no way to explain things to him without explaining *everything* to him. While I'd never regret our time together, I knew I should have let him go after I left his hotel room the morning after the wedding. It had been stupid to continue to follow him and then insert myself into his life.

"What the fuck, Nate?" He seethed.

I'd made him angry again, which was to be expected. He'd just found out he'd been wasting his time with someone who couldn't feel the same about him as he did about me. That thought stung because I did have feelings for Nate. And I was sure, in my own way, that it was love.

Just not in the same way he loved me.

And I knew what the sting of rejection felt like as it burned in my chest.

"I'm sorry," I said as I kept my head down and slid my card to the waiter without even looking at the total. "You have every right to be mad at me for wasting your time."

There was no way I could tell him how I felt, even if I wanted to. Not only did I not know how to put it into words, but it would also be incredibly unfair to him when he was already upset.

Aiden sputtered. His cheeks grew even redder as his eyes narrowed at me.

A sense of unease filled me, as I got the feeling I had missed something important along the way.

"So, what? Now you're going to sit there and try to explain my own feelings to me? You couldn't possibly understand what I'm thinking or feeling right now, Nate!"

His eyes went wide, and he slapped a hand over his mouth at his words.

"Shit. I'm so sorry. That wasn't... I didn't... That came out wrong."

I couldn't help but let out a chuckle. Everything about Aiden was a breath of fresh air—from his anger, his honesty, and even his embarrassment.

"You're right," I conceded as I cocked my head and studied him. "I shouldn't have assumed anything. Just, I know from past experiences what comes next when people realize I'm... different."

I shrugged, trying to feign indifference, but the buzz of vulnerability made my skin feel itchy. I wasn't used to feeling so exposed. To make matters worse, I was sure I wasn't fooling him. "It's a lot and not something most people want to stick around and deal with."

"That sounds... lonely," he said. His expression was soft and sorrowful enough that I couldn't help but nod in agreement with his words. "I'm sorry."

"It's not your fault, little bird. It is what it is." I let out a sigh and stood. "Come on, let's get you home."

He frowned but said nothing else as we walked out of the restaurant. When we got to the parking lot, I remembered we had driven separately. The pang of sorrow was like a punch to the gut as I realized I didn't even get to take him home one last time.

My eyes tracked him as he walked through the lot, before he stopped between our cars. I wasn't sure what I expected him to do, but I hadn't expected him to roll his eyes and tease me.

"Are you going to wait until next month's anniversary to unlock the door so I can get in?"

My legs carried me over to where he stood before I even made the decision to go to him. His words bounced around my head as I tried to wrap my mind around it.

Next month's anniversary.

But there wouldn't be a next anniversary, would there?

"I thought you would take your car." It was the stupidest thing I could have said, and from the soft look on his face, he knew it too. But he didn't call me out on it.

"Unlock the damn door, Daddy."

My head swam at his words, and for a moment, I considered asking him to drive.

But just call me a genie in a bottle, because his wish was my command.

I wasn't sure what he expected when we got to his house, and the drive was filled mostly with tense silence as I contemplated all the things that had been shared during dinner.

The most logical thing for me to do would be to kill him, and soon. A small part of me craved to feel his blood on my hands for the way he made me feel. But I knew it couldn't be that night because his partner knew we'd gone to dinner, and that would have made me the prime suspect.

And it wouldn't take a genius to be able to put the pieces together when he was hunting a serial killer and his boyfriend was a psychopath.

Then again, there were plenty of psychopaths—many more than most people realized—who were able to live full and productive lives and never hurt anyone. When I looked at Aiden, I wished I could be one of those people. He deserved better than me and my defective brain.

"Aiden—" I tried to leave him at the door, nice and safe, but he cut me off by pulling me against him and slamming the door closed as our lips connected.

"Shut up," he mumbled as he let out a sigh when my tongue snaked out of my mouth to seek entrance to his.

I officially shut up. If this beautiful and intelligent man wanted me despite my flaws, I didn't think I was strong enough to walk away on my own.

My hands cupped his face as I slowed the kiss and walked him backward toward the stairs so we could get to his bedroom. I might not have had words for him, but I could show him how I felt by making my little bird fly.

When we made it to the bedroom, I picked him up, and he immediately wrapped his legs around my waist, rotating his hips and igniting sparks as our cocks glided together through the fabric.

"Fuck, Daddy," he whimpered in my arms as he let his head fall back and began to rut against me in earnest. "You always make me feel so good." His voice was full of awe, and his eyes were already blown and glazed over.

I leaned forward and nipped his lip as I walked us to his bed and gently laid him down, as though he were something precious. Because he was. Somehow, Aiden had become the one thing I couldn't live without.

He was more than just an obsession. He was *everything*, and it scared the shit out of me.

"Little bird," I choked out as I settled between his legs, my voice thick with unnamed emotion. Reaching up, I unbuttoned his shirt without breaking eye contact. He leaned up and let it fall off his shoulders and down his arms. A sound I couldn't identify broke free from my throat at the sight of all of his skin on display.

It wasn't the first time I'd seen him naked—and he wasn't even naked yet—but knowing he still wanted me, even with what I'd revealed about myself, was more than I could have ever hoped for. It was a gift I truly treasured more than he would ever know, more than he *could* ever know.

"You're amazing," I said as I lightly teased my fingertips over his exposed flesh, making him gasp. "I promise to work to be worthy of you every day."

Aiden looked up and stopped my hand's exploration by placing his own on top.

"Daddy, you don't need to work on anything. I love *you*. There's no reason for you to do anything different. And you're already worthy. I don't know who told you that you weren't, but you deserve everything. Don't let anyone tell you anything different. Ever." I heard his words and they warmed my chest. But I couldn't help the doubt that crept in. No one wanted me for me.

And he wouldn't either, not if he knew my darkest secrets.

Rather than potentially spoil the evening, I didn't say anything and instead captured his lips in a searing kiss that shook me to my core. As I leaned back, something caught my eye, and I hesitated.

"Do you trust me?" It was a big leap. He could like me, love me, or have whatever feelings he felt. But trusting me, that was a whole other ballgame. Especially given what he now knew about me.

"Always," he said without missing a beat, and it snatched my breath away. His confidence in me was unfounded, given how we had originally met. But I couldn't tell him that. He could never know, because I could never let him go.

I needed to get out of my head, though, and regain some control. So I pushed the thoughts aside and reached down and grabbed the tie he'd discarded when we got into the room. Gently, I wrapped it around one wrist before I wove it between the bars of his headboard and then secured his other wrist.

"Move your wrists for me and make sure it's not too tight." He did as I asked without saying a word, but from the way his eyes were closing as he rotated his wrists, I didn't think he had any complaints about being tied up.

Good to know.

Using my tongue, teeth, and lips, I made a wet trail as I explored his body. When I reached his pants, I quickly worked them down his hips. I needed him naked and writhing beneath me. His cries as I impaled him with my cock instead of my knife would be the balm I needed to soothe my corrupt soul.

I bit his exposed hip and smiled at the way his body jerked. My palms ran up his sides until I reached his hips, and then I held them down so he couldn't squirm or move as I made my way down first one leg and then the other, ignoring his leaking cock that begged for attention.

"Such a good little bird," I praised as I licked a stripe up his twitching cock that was weeping almost as much as he was.

"Fuuuck, Daddy, please. I need you." My heart soared as I made soothing noises, and my hands caressed his heated skin. It was a novel idea, wanting someone to feel pleasure—to be the one to bring someone pleasure—rather than pain. Truth be told, I was usually rather indifferent to their pain as well.

Killing was just an itch that needed to be scratched.

But bringing Aiden pleasure was a mission I wanted to pursue for the rest of my life.

My lips wrapped around him as I took him into my mouth, and if my hands hadn't been on his hips, he surely would have thrust himself right into the back of my throat. I let out a chuckle at his eagerness that made him whimper and shiver. While working his cock, I grabbed the lube and rubbed some on my fingers before I reached down and teased his entrance.

"Shit! Fuck!" Aiden shouted, his eyes glassy and wide as he stared at me. His wrists tugged on their bindings as he struggled. He wasn't one to force my movements when I was giving him a blowjob, but from the way he liked to fist my hair or clasp his hands around my neck, I thought it was grounding for him. But now, with his hands bound, he was being denied that.

It made me smile. It was a reminder to both of us as to who was in control, even though we both knew it was always me.

This was the closest I'd ever been to having him trussed up like prey since that night. My eyes shut at the memory, but I tried to shove it away. I didn't want to think about how I'd wanted to kill my little bird. Instead, I wanted to concentrate on making him fly higher than ever before.

Without much finesse, I worked two fingers into his tight hole, and he let out a shout. It wasn't that I'd never been rough with him, even with prep. I knew he could take it. And I was too worked up and scattered to spend the time I usually did to make sure he was ready, so I needed to speed things along.

My fingers scissored inside him, only briefly brushing against his prostate. After a minute, I pulled my hand back and added another finger, and let him work his hips so he was fucking himself on my hand. It was a marvelous sight to see, not to mention the sounds he made as he worked himself open for me.

"You're so beautiful." I leaned up and captured his lips, licking at his lips as he panted and groaned.

"Please, Nate. Now, I need you to fuck me now."

Who was I to deny my little bird anything, especially when he begged so beautifully? The way he tripped my wires with his pleasure, usually only satisfied with death, left me feeling breathless and in awe. For a brief moment, as I stroked lube on my shaft, I wondered if I could be the type of man he deserved. I could try for him.

I'd do anything for him.

My hands splayed across the globes of his ass as I lifted his legs to thrust into his tight hole in one smooth, deep stroke. I didn't have the patience to fuck him gently as I felt my control slip.

He cried out, his head thrown back as he chanted my name over and over as I rotated my hips and found the small bundle of nerves I had been looking for. His screams were music to my ears as I pounded his prostate with each snap of my hips. I was relentless and wild.

I was staking my claim.

My little bird was *mine.*

Forever.

He'd only leave me in death, and I prayed it wouldn't be by my hand. Though I would if I had to. If it was the only way to keep him.

I'd been obsessed with him for too long. There was no escaping me this time.

"You are mine, little bird. You'll never get away from me." I watched in awe as his back bowed at my words, and hot, thick ropes of cum erupted from him as he came untouched. His reaction set off my own, and I emptied my load inside him.

I thrust my cock deep inside him, working us both through our orgasms until I was soft. As I slipped out, I leaned back and watched where we were connected, my cum dripping from his gaping hole.

Couldn't have that. I dropped to the bed and thrust two fingers back inside, fucking my cum back into him. I'd marked him, in every way possible, as mine. While still finger fucking him, I leaned over and took Aiden's soft cock in my mouth to clean him.

He was mine. That meant everything he was, belonged to me—including his cum, and I didn't intend to waste a drop. As I worked my way up, lapping at the mess on his abs and chest, I reached into his drawer with my free hand and felt around until I found what I was looking for.

With a smirk, I went back between his legs and slipped the plug into his hole, sealing my cum inside.

Aiden let out a groan. "Fuck, that's hot."

"I aim to please," I quipped as I leaned up and tugged on his tie to release his hands. I rubbed his wrists and placed a soft kiss on each of his palms.

"Was... was that okay?" I asked, hating how he made me feel vulnerable and unsure but wanting it all the same. He was the only one who could make me feel that way.

He reached out and cupped my face in one of his smaller, calloused hands. His smile reassured me more than any words could.

"I know you'd never hurt me, Nate."

And just like that, I felt like I'd been doused with a bucket of cold water.

26

AIDEN

This case was going to be the death of me. It was beyond frustrating.

And on top of it, I couldn't even concentrate if my life depended on it over the bombshell Nate had dropped on me during our dinner two nights ago. Then again, it wasn't like we had much evidence in our case, so maybe it didn't matter. At least at work, I could pretend my frustration was over the case and not my boyfriend.

I leaned back in my chair, tapping my pen against the metal of my desk, and stared into space. There had been a lot on my mind since Nate and I had our unusual anniversary celebration. He had shared a lot, and I was thankful he felt he could open up and trust me. I also felt I got some glimpses he hadn't meant for me to see.

He didn't want me to pity him, and I didn't. But I did feel for him, because growing up is never easy. I couldn't imagine being the way he was as a child and having an easy time in school. Kids were assholes, especially to other kids who were different. But I had a feeling he wasn't the type to get bullied, that they might have given him a wide berth because they didn't understand him and were afraid of him.

That must have made things lonely. No wonder he said he didn't understand people and relationships. People probably didn't give him a chance. The thought made me sad, knowing how wonderful he actually was.

I marveled at the fact I wasn't afraid of him. And I wondered if that was wise. The night of the wedding, he had choked me during sex, even if I'd ended up liking it. The anger he'd had at the club with the guy I'd been dancing with. At times, I'd felt someone watching me, and then him leaving the present. Him admitting he'd stalked me

There had still been those moments, flashes, when I felt uneasy around him, even if it never turned into fear.

Then again, it could just be because he was... a psychopath.

I hated that word, but it was the word he used to describe himself. While I didn't know much about people with that condition, I knew they were good at mimicking people and it could leave people feeling uneasy around them. Some defense mechanism perhaps warning that it's not real.

Not real.

The thought made me bolt upright. There was no way what Nate and I had wasn't real. He was so intense I swore it bordered on obsessive. He couldn't have faked all that, right? Especially once I knew the truth, there would be no reason to.

Right?

Fuck.

I was in too deep, and I was drowning.

The smack on my shoulder pulled me from my thoughts and startled me to the point where I almost jumped out of my chair. Victoria laughed and plopped in her chair as I scowled.

"God, you're such a pain in the ass." I turned away from her. I wasn't sure if I was ready to talk to her about any of this. I knew she was the best one to ask for advice, but she would also be the most judgmental.

But did I really have any other options?

"Part of my charm," she assured me, and I rolled my eyes. "All right. Spill. How did the anniversary date with Nate go? Considering I didn't hear from you all weekend, I assume it was good."

Victoria leaned back in her chair. The smile on her face dropped and her eyes narrowed as she took in what I figured was my haggard appearance. "What went wrong?"

I let out a sigh and tried to think about what I could, or should, tell her. Logically, I knew there was no reason I couldn't tell her the truth. There was nothing to be ashamed of. Plus, she had a background that could help me.

But still, I hesitated.

"Dinner went well. He loved the cufflinks but felt bad because he didn't get me anything." I chuckled, thinking about that night. "But he made it up to me," I assured her with a wink.

Victoria made a fake gagging sound, but her smile at my words told the real story.

"All right. All right. Enough." I waved her away. "We still have a psycho to catch." I winced at my words.

Shit. Being with Nate and knowing he was a psychopath really opened my eyes to how people with personality disorders are unjustly vilified. I had to do better, not just for him but for the others out there like him.

"Hmm. Yeah. What have we got?" She turned to her computer and pulled up the file.

"Do you think this guy is an actual true psychopath? You went to school for this shit, right?" I schooled my face the best I could so she wouldn't read anything in my expression.

"It's hard to tell if he's someone who has been, or would be, diagnosed with Antisocial Personality Disorder." She cast a glance at me with narrowed eyes. "You know the terms *psychopath* and *sociopath* aren't really used anymore, so watch it."

With a sigh, she shrugged. "But it's possible. He's methodical. There's no hesitation in the cuts. These cuts—there's skill there. But it doesn't feel like he's experimenting, so I think this is just who he is. He's probably considered a loner and shy, though brilliant and perhaps has a successful career."

"What do you think he does for a living?" Why did my breath sound so hollow and tight? Just because I was asking about ASPD and the killer in the same sentence didn't mean anything.

Nate wasn't violent.

Was he?

"You do know this isn't the FBI, and I'm not a behaviorist, right?" She chuckled.

I shifted, uncomfortable, in my seat. "Yeah, I know. I'm just curious."

Her eyes narrowed again and I knew I was tripping some of her alarms, but she didn't say anything for a few minutes.

"It's not like you see on TV and in the movies. They're not soulless, mindless killing machines. At least, not most of the time. Some learn to channel impulses in creative or practical ways that make them useful members of society and never cause a problem."

I let out a huff. "Yeah, I know," I said with a scowl. "I know they can feel and have emotions. It's just different."

"Mmmhm. It still can be a concerning diagnosis."

Her eyes stared at me like she was looking into my soul and I needed to turn away.

"Yes, Mother," I teased, but it sounded wrong. Tight and forced.

With my back to her, I worked on the case to see if there

were any leads we could hit up or follow up with. But I could feel her eyes on me the entire time.

"Aiden." Victoria's voice was equally annoying and supportive. It was the one she used when she was done dealing with my bullshit. "What's this really about?"

I let out a sigh, let my head fall back, and stared at the ceiling. But I didn't say anything. I didn't know how.

"You know you can talk to me, right? About anything."

All I could do was nod. I didn't know how to tell her I wasn't asking because of the case but because of my boyfriend. So we sat in an uncomfortable silence for several minutes before she cut to the heart of the matter.

"You told me Nate seemed too perfect. That you weren't sure if it was real or not. Is this… is this really about him? Did he do or say anything that upset you or made you question things even more?"

My best friend asked me to trust her, to unburden myself, and to let her in. She had already figured it out, even without meeting him. So what was I scared of?

"Do you think he's manipulating you? Using you?" she asked cautiously.

"No," I said, shaking my head as I bolted upright. My body turned to face her, so she would know I was serious and not hiding or trying to defend him when I wasn't sure of the answer.

She put her hands up in surrender, but quirked an eyebrow at me. Leaning back in her chair, she folded her arms and gave the space I needed to find my words and continue.

"I think he's been refreshingly honest, actually." And he had been from the start. Nate always said it like he saw it, though maybe he didn't always see it right or have the best perspective. "I don't think he's using me, but I do feel like he's hiding something."

"Like being a psychopath?" she joked.

I snorted. "No, like I said, he's refreshingly honest, including about that. So I'm not sure what this feeling is."

Victoria's mouth dropped open, and she tried to speak several times before she found her words. "Wait, wait, he actually *told* you that he was a psychopath? And you're still dating him?" she hissed.

I stared at her, my eyes narrowing in confusion. My heart tried to beat out of my chest at the venom in her words. This was why I hadn't wanted to tell her. She was judging him without knowing him.

"Look, I love you. You're like family to me. And I don't want to shit on your parade, especially since you've been so much happier lately—"

"Then don't," I ground out, cutting her off. But the scowl on my face didn't dissuade her from continuing to speak her mind.

"Aiden." Her stern mommy voice came out—and not the sexy kind like Nate got when he went all Daddy—and I hated it. I wasn't a child, and I could make my own decisions.

"You need to listen to me. I know what I just said, but people with ASPD are highly manipulative to where you might not even realize it's happening. They can be violent and dangerous, just like this guy we're looking for."

I held up my hand. "Stop. Please. I have things under control. I shouldn't have said anything."

"Like hell, you shouldn't have!" She practically growled, but kept her voice low so no one around us would hear. "What do you really know about this guy, Aiden? I mean, *really* know? That you've been able to verify independently?"

I opened my mouth but then closed it. The truth was I hadn't looked into Nate at all, but I wasn't about to admit that. Not when she had been on my case already to look into him from the start.

Her eyes narrowed as she leaned across her desk and grabbed my arm, pulling me toward her.

"You did look into him, right?" Her eyes blazed as she stared at me. I couldn't look at her. Even though I was an adult and had no reason to feel guilt or shame over not investigating my boyfriend, I couldn't help but feel a tendril of dread at the way her eyes bore into my soul.

"Jesus Christ, Aiden. You swore to me that you were looking into this guy and had gotten information on him."

I wasn't sure what was worse, Victoria's hurt or anger. But then again, I was hurt and angry too. Because there was no reason for anyone to be treating me like a fucking child. Just because something terrible had happened to me when I was a child didn't mean everyone had to treat me with kid gloves.

Everyone was driving me insane with their shit.

Instead of answering her questions, I turned the topic back to work. My non-answer would be enough for her to know the truth. And I knew it wouldn't be long before she cornered me again.

"I want to go talk to that witness again, the one who found the last body. So, I'm going to head out." I stood and grabbed my coat, hoping to put some distance between Vic and me.

As I tugged my coat on, I ignored the concerned looks she sent my way. But I couldn't talk to her about what I was thinking or feeling, and I shouldn't have opened that can of worms.

Because the truth was so much worse than she thought. The answer was simple—it didn't matter. I didn't care who he really was or what he was capable of. I had fallen in love with Nathan Turner and he was mine. Not to mention, when he told me I was his and that he's never let me go, I believed him.

I couldn't walk away from him even if I wanted to. And God help me, I didn't want to.

"What are you doing?" I spat out as she got up and put her coat back on.

She looked at me in confusion, as though I was the crazy one.

Maybe I was.

"You said we were going to talk to the witness." The way she said it, slow, like she had to draw it out for me to understand, made me want to scream.

I took a deep breath and tried to calm the raging storm that swirled in my chest. "No, Vic. I said *I* was going to go talk to the witness."

With a huff, she grabbed my arm and dragged me out of the precinct and onto the street, away from the prying eyes and ears of our colleagues. When we got into the blistering cold December air, she pushed me against the side of the building, with a finger against my chest.

"You listen to me, Aiden Cooper, and you listen good. I don't care what the fuck you think or say right now. I am worried about you. And I have every fucking right to be worried about you. I think you're making a huge fucking mistake with this guy."

My face slid into an impassive mask. She was my best friend and I never thought I could be so angry with her, could hate her.

"Back up, Victoria. Now." My voice was low and dangerous. I'd never spoken to anyone like that before in my life, and certainly not to her. The way she backed up, eyes wide and darting around the street said that maybe I'd gone too far.

Then again, so had she.

I needed to get myself back under control. She was just trying to look out for me, and I knew that. So, I didn't know why I was reacting like a crazy person.

Like... like someone who was *obsessed*. Fuck. Maybe I was. Maybe I was just as obsessed with him as he was with me.

My head fell back and scraped against the gritty stone of the building at my back, but I didn't wince at the pain. I deserved it for being such a shitty friend. But my head was such a mess, I didn't know what was up or down anymore.

But I did know she had one point, though I'd never admit it. I did need to find out more about Nate. Because I realized in all the time I'd known him, I'd never even been to his house. Hell, I didn't even know his goddamn address.

Closing my eyes, I dug my nails into the wall, letting the sting ground myself. "Let's just get to this guy. He should be at work. We can ambush him there, where he can't ditch us."

Victoria eyed me like a specimen under a microscope but didn't make any further comments as we made our way to the car. Smart woman. Of course, that made the drive to Star Bird Realty and Development all the more uncomfortable, but I knew I had no one to blame but myself. Okay, maybe she was to blame a little. But it was mostly on me.

When we walked in, I whistled at the opulence that greeted us.

"Holy shit," Vic whispered and I couldn't have agreed more.

There was a long, white marble desk with several receptionists, or secretaries, I wasn't sure, who glanced up and smiled at us as we walked in. The floor was black be-speckled black granite and the walls were a soft baby blue. There were a few white plush couches and chairs strategically placed for visitors who had to wait, along with a gray stone and glass coffee table and some plants to make it look welcoming.

My eyes were drawn to the paintings on the wall, even though I wasn't sure who the artist was or what they even were. It was abstract art, but they provided vivid splashes of color: reds, purples, and blues.

Victoria had left me to gawk and had gone to the table as I tried to get my bearings. Something about the place threw me off, but I couldn't quite put my finger on it. But I did my best to shake off my unease and joined her at the desk.

"I told you, Mr. Carter isn't available at the moment. He's in a meeting and I don't know when he'll be able to speak to you. But you're more than welcome to leave your card or make an appointment, though as I stated, he's booked until next month." The woman looked frustrated and two seconds away from calling security. It made me wonder what Victoria had said before I had approached. Usually, she was the calmer one of us.

"Ma'am, I understand you're just doing your job. But so are we. And we are investigating a murder. And we need to speak to him. Now." I hated to barge into people's lives and throw my weight around, but someone was dead and Christian Carter was going out of his way to evade us and it was going to end now.

Behind the desk, a door opened and our witness stepped out, looking just as frustrated as I felt. I went to take a step around the desk, ignoring the woman who tried to stop me. Until my eyes locked onto the man who followed behind him.

What. The. Fuck?

Our eyes locked and all the breath left my lungs as my mind swirled with a hundred thoughts. But none of them made any sense.

"Mr. Carter!" Victoria stormed off toward our witness, unaware of my inner turmoil.

Nate's eyes snapped to her and he whispered something to Mr. Carter and with one more glance my way, slipped back behind the door before closing it behind him.

My feet carried me over to where Victoria had stopped and I looked at the witness in a whole new way as I tried to figure out how he was connected to Nate, and how Nate was connected to this place.

Fuck. I really did need to find out more about him.

"Detectives." Mr. Carter sounded weary as he greeted us, arms crossed over his chest. "I already told you all that I know. I don't appreciate being harassed in my place of employment."

I raised an eyebrow. "I hardly call one visit, where we haven't even said anything yet, harassment, Mr. Carter."

"As I've said, I already told you everything I know. If you have anything else you'd like to discuss, you can do so through my lawyer." He reached into his pocket and took out a business card and handed it to Victoria, who stared at it, lips pursed, without saying anything.

"Good day, Detectives. I'm sure you can see yourselves out. Unless you need security to do it for you."

27

NATHAN

I shouldn't have stormed out of that meeting. But the last thing I had expected was to be confronted with Aiden and his partner.

Fucking hell.

Then again, maybe I should have. Christian had said they had left him a couple of messages and they knew where he worked.

While the investigation was ongoing, I should have distanced myself from Star Bird, with Christian being the one who *discovered* my latest victim. But I had been so sure that things had been going my way.

Hubris. That was how most serial killers were caught.

It was how I found myself sneaking out the side door of my office while my project manager was being confronted by my boyfriend, by my little bird, about the murder I'd committed. Despite wanting to know what Christian had told them, I couldn't stick around and find out, so I got out of there.

Even if it was a dick move to leave him alone with the wolves.

And now, my wolf would be hounding me about my connection to Christian. To the victim.

It was all closing in. Crumbling.

I let out a bitter laugh as I marched toward my car, not caring who might be around in the underground garage to witness me spiral. While I knew I was being childish and reckless, I couldn't seem to stop myself from wanting to lash out. I needed to channel everything that threatened to consume me. Even if it exposed me.

Ask me if I cared.

With a swift motion, I yanked my tie from around my neck and undid my cufflinks, stuffing them in my coat pocket so I could roll up my sleeves. I felt itchy, constricted, out of control.

I knew what I needed, but I had promised myself I would be better for Aiden. That I would be the man he needed me to be. Apparently, I couldn't even go a week being that man.

"Nathan!" Christian called to me from across the garage, but I ignored him as I unlocked my car. There was nothing he could do or say that could help or soothe me. The monster that lived under my skin was too close to the surface. It needed to be unleashed.

Bad things happened when I ignored the monster and I couldn't let that happen, not now that I had found my little bird.

The urge to kill was like a living thing crawling under my skin. If I didn't give in, then things would be bad. That was the last thing I needed. I didn't need Aiden becoming collateral damage to my urges. And I knew what would happen if I kept ignoring what was inside of me.

I'd only done it once, shortly after my parents died. I tried to contain it, to hold it at bay. Then I blacked out and woke up fourteen hours later with a body count of over a dozen. I'd been drenched in blood from head to toe as if I'd bathed in it, at some cabin in the middle of nowhere.

Every day I still wondered if someone would knock on my door looking to lock me up for what I did that night. But no one ever did.

The alternative would be forcing Aiden's hand to put me down. And I didn't want to do that to him either.

Christian came up from behind me, a dangerous move, and slammed his hand against the door of my car, just as I started to open it.

"Jesus fuck, Nathan. What are you doing?" He sounded out of breath and I wondered just how fast he'd had to run to catch up to me. Or how out of shape he was. It would make him easy prey.

No. He is my friend, not prey.

Unless he got in my way.

"Let me go, Christian," I growled as I turned to face him, ready to push him away so I could get in the car and disappear.

Was that what I was going to do? Disappear?

"You're not thinking clearly." I let out a huff and turned away, not willing to let him see any vulnerability. "I didn't say anything. Just gave them O'Keefe's card and told them anything further would have to go through him."

That was smart. And probably what we should have done from the start. But I hadn't expected a witness, let alone one I planned on leaving alive.

"Doesn't matter. He's connected us now. It's over." It almost felt like a weight being lifted off my shoulder. Every day it had gotten harder to lie to him. I hadn't anticipated that.

"Don't do anything stupid, man." Christian gave me a look, knowing full well I must have already planned on doing something stupid.

I threw him a grin. "Does that sound like me?"

He huffed out a laugh. "Normally? No. Lately? Yes."

Unfortunately, he wasn't far from the truth. "I just have

some loose ends to tie up. And then I'll let you know what's up."

That was probably a lie. If I disappeared, we both knew it would be best if he had no idea where I was going, or that I'd even left. But I knew the lie would make him feel better, at least for a moment.

After an awkward moment of silence passed between us, he gave me a fist bump and I slid into the driver's seat of my car and peeled out of the garage. I needed to get to Clint and take care of him. He needed to go. Once I purged the desire for his blood, then I'd be okay for a little while.

Maybe I could come up with some believable lie to keep Aiden off my tail for a while. Then when I could work on trying to go longer between kills.

But I knew it was a lie. I'd never be able to, never be able to do it except how I'd always done it. Especially if I didn't want to risk my little bird.

I'd kill Clint, then go back to Aiden, and everything would be fine.

For the moment.

As I drove to Clint's house, I went back and forth on whether I should go back to Aiden or run. But I knew if I immediately ran, he would know I was guilty. There would be no coming back from that, no making him listen.

I let out a growl as I sped through the streets and stopped a little ways from Clint's house. There was a light on, so I knew he was home. Not that I didn't already know he'd be there. That was the point of stalking and finding out everything I could about my victims.

My thoughts raced, and I knew I was spiraling. I needed to calm myself. But the only way I could do that was by having someone at the end of my blade. As much as I hated it, having Aiden at the end of my cock only did so much. He could only sate my hunger for so long before the need to kill became overwhelming.

I sat and watched, waiting for the moment my prey left his house so I could grab him.

An hour had passed when my phone rang. I glanced down, my heart squeezing as I knew there would only be one person it could be. Unable to deal with him at the moment, I let his call go to voicemail.

And the next.

And the next.

The slew of text messages with previews asking where I was and what I was doing, or saying that we needed to talk, all went unread and unanswered.

My mind was a mess and I couldn't untangle the web of emotions I had become since I had met Aiden. In so many ways, my life had become so enriched with meaning. But in others, he was my downfall.

I shook my head, needing to clear my head. Murder required concentration and focus, otherwise mistakes were made.

With a glance at the time, I was surprised to realize several hours had passed since Aiden's first call.

It was almost time for Clint to be getting ready to leave any minute. Not wanting to miss my opportunity, I got out of the car, hands in my pockets, and made my way down the broken sidewalk and past the vacant houses and those I knew had residents who wouldn't want to notice what was going on around them.

That was one of the good things about the neighborhood Clint lived in. No one saw anything. Ever. Even if they did, they didn't.

Just as I got to the front of the house, there was movement in the front window. I slowed my pace to give Clint time to get out so I could grab him. Thankfully, I didn't have long to wait as he scrambled out a minute later.

I pulled out my phone and pretended to be preoccupied, so we bumped into each other when he got to the sidewalk.

"Sorry, dude," I offered, giving him a crooked smile. He looked taken aback and tried to take a step away, but I clutched the needle in my fingers, brought my arm around his neck in a friendly gesture, and let the needle slide into his skin, easy like butter.

Clint's eyes went wide, and he pushed me away right before he started to lose his balance. I grabbed him to keep him upright and laughed like we were old friends. Acting like I was his buddy and I was there to help him made things less suspicious. Made me less memorable. He clutched at me and tried to swat me away, but I paid no mind.

We walked to the car, and I got him seated and buckled in with no problem. He leaned to the side, up against the door, but to anyone passing us, he would just look like he was drunk or passed out.

While I had a house conveniently across the street, it was too close for comfort. After I took care of Clint, I'd come back and clean the place out of my equipment so it would look like no one had been there except maybe for surveys and inspections. No need to lead the police right to my door.

It was obvious Aiden was already suspicious enough. I was just thankful the house was in the name of one of my other businesses.

It only took ten minutes to get to my kill house on the other side of town, and by the time we arrived, my passenger was slumped against the door, passed out but still breathing. While it would be easy to do a quick, no-fuss kill with something like a drug that couldn't be detected, I needed the blood. I needed to feel their lives slipping away from them.

That passive shit didn't do it for me.

I parked the car in the garage, and when I got out, I grabbed Clint and carried him down to the basement that had already been set up for the evening's activities. Tying him down to the table took no time at all, especially since he couldn't struggle.

A smile crossed my face a few minutes later as he woke up, trying to scream behind the gag I'd shoved in his mouth, to the feel of my blade slicing from his armpit down to his hip. It was a deep cut, but that alone wouldn't kill him.

Probably.

I ripped off the tape and gag with a smile as he let out a blood-curdling scream.

"Fuck you, you fucking psycho! Let me go!" He spat at me, though he missed by a mile.

It only made me smile more.

"You can scream all you want. We're in a secluded place with no one around for miles. So go ahead. In fact," I said, looking around, thoughtful, "if you scream real good for me, then maybe you'll make it go faster. I do actually need to consider the time since I want to be able to call my boyfriend and talk to him before he goes to bed."

My words made me giddy like a schoolgirl. I had a boyfriend. Someone I'd do anything for and who would do anything for me in return. It was a heady feeling. A novel feeling of knowing there was someone for whom I'd burn the world down if I needed to, or if he asked. It was something I thought I'd never get to experience.

But the thought made me sober as I remembered him showing up at my office earlier in the day. Everything was being ruined before it even really started.

Son of a fucking bitch.

I needed to figure out a way to get him off my trail. My desperation was going to make me sloppy, which would get me caught. I couldn't have that.

The last thing I wanted to deal with was being faced with the choice of it coming down to me or Aiden. Because I didn't know which one of us I'd choose, no matter how much I wanted to be able to say I'd pick him.

"Please, whatever you want, you can have it. I don't have much, but I'll get you whatever you need." Tears streaked down Clint's face as I swiped my blade across his chest, creating long, shallow cuts. "Please, please."

His begging lit me up from the inside. Not in a sexual way, the way Aiden could light me up. Killing was more like the satisfaction of a job well done.

"That's it. Just like that," I encouraged. But my words only seemed to turn the other man into a blubbering mess, unable to form coherent words.

I continued to slide my knife through his flesh and swiped a finger through his blood as though it were finger paint. I wore gloves, but I hated them. There was nothing like feeling the blood on my skin. But I had to be careful. I couldn't get caught.

Clint's breaths got shallow in what felt like no time at all. Pity. I wanted to play longer, but I also knew that since I had Aiden, I couldn't spend as much time with my victims.

Another pity.

But he was worth it. I'd rather be with him anyway.

"Goodbye, Clint." I moved behind his head, flicked my knife across his throat, and reveled in the blood spray that covered him and the plastic sheeting that surrounded us.

My phone went off again while I watched the life drain from his body, along with his blood. I glanced over at where it sat on the other table and saw it was Aiden. Thinking about him texting me while we were both working made me smile.

I stared down at the body before me and frowned. There was no satisfaction over Clint's death. No elation or release of endorphins or whatever the fuck it was that made me feel good after a kill.

Instead, I just felt as cold and empty as the body in front of me.

Fuck.

28

AIDEN

It had been two days since I last saw him, and I could say without a shadow of a doubt, Nate was officially avoiding me. And that was *not* a good sign.

I sighed as I threw the phone onto the counter and braced my hands against it, with my head hanging between them. I had no idea what the fuck I was doing.

He had me lying to everyone. Victoria could tell something was wrong after we had left Star Bird, but I couldn't tell her that the man who left the office with our witness was my boyfriend, my *Daddy*.

A choked sob escaped from my chest as I collapsed on the floor and curled into a ball.

What the fuck was he doing there? Did he know the witness?

I wanted to go back and ask the receptionist about him, but we had already been iced out. Not to mention, if I mentioned Nathan's name, it would have set off all of Victoria's alarms. Hell, it had set off all of my alarms.

No, there had to be a perfectly good explanation.

He was in real estate development. It was a real estate office.

He was probably just there for a meeting about a property he was interested in purchasing and developing.

As I rocked back and forth on my kitchen floor, one thing became clear. I needed to pull myself together. The behavior I was exhibiting was not befitting a homicide detective. I knew how to uncover people's secrets.

I just never thought I'd have to dig into Nate like that.

But I knew I had to do it. Because if I kept avoiding the truth, if I kept my head in the sand because I didn't want to know what was really going on with him, then I would always wonder.

But fuck, I wanted to trust him.

With a shake of my head, I pulled myself up onto my unsteady legs and grabbed my phone and stormed into the small bedroom I'd converted into a home office. Firing up the computer, I sat down and instantly lost my nerve.

Shit.

No. I had to do this. I deserved to know the truth. And I knew, deep down, I should have done all this into Nate's background when he admitted to stalking me. The fact that I hadn't, had been stupid and reckless and was what had gotten me into the mess I found myself in. I knew better and I had to do better.

Every time I tried to look him up, I'd always find an excuse to turn away, to turn back. But I couldn't anymore. There were too many inconsistencies and variables that weren't adding up, too many things that didn't make sense.

They say the truth would set you free. Now, it was time to hope it would set me free, rather than bury me.

I tried not to take it personally, that he was ghosting me. But all evidence pointed to *something* shady. And I needed to know. If I had to take another day of Victoria and her looks while we were at work, I was going to lose my fucking mind.

The last thing I needed was to blow a gasket in a fucking police precinct with a bunch of other armed police officers. I'd be fired on the spot. Charges pressed. And I'd be lucky if I didn't end up in the psych ward.

Because I felt like I was going goddamn insane.

My heart raced as I pulled up a private, untraceable browser. I could do this. Even if my hands shook as I typed his name and hit enter.

While I scrolled through the results, weeding through what I already knew and what was irrelevant, I tried to tell myself that we hadn't been together that long. That I could handle whatever I found.

If there was anything bad, if he had any skeletons he was hiding, then I would deal with them the right way. Or, if it turned out he was just an asshole, then I would break up with him.

But deep down, I knew that wasn't true. He was *mine*. There was some deep, dark, possessive part of me that had latched onto him and didn't want to let go. I didn't know where it had come from, and it scared the hell out of me. But it knew what it wanted, and that was *Daddy*.

I came across an article about his parents' deaths and looking at a picture of young Nate shook me to my core. My eyes closed, breathing ragged as I tried to reconcile the boy in the picture with the man I knew.

He looked so young, so lost. And so *cold*. There was nothing there. Looking in his eyes, it was like no one was home. I'd gotten a glimpse or two ever since he told me the truth about his diagnosis and he felt comfortable enough not to put his walls up so high with me. But that little boy hadn't learned to put up any yet and it was chilling to look at.

The most shocking thing to discover was his family history. Apparently, they came from money. It was obvious he was wealthy from the cars he drove and the clothes he wore, but I hadn't realized it was something he had inherited, not that it made a difference to me.

I loved him either way.

The thought rocked me and I fell back in my chair.

Despite everything, I still loved him. Part of me had known that. But to think it as though I didn't have a care in the world, it pulled me up short and made me think.

It brought up another question. With all that wealth, what were they able to hide?

But I knew the only way I'd get real answers was to confront him. I had to ask him directly and not let him evade.

As I trudged to my bedroom and finished grabbing what I needed to head to work, I wondered if I was really ready to face whatever answers he gave me. I had no idea what sort of Pandora's box I would open.

But I was more determined than ever as I pulled out of my drive and headed to the precinct. I was going to get my answers, whether Nate wanted to give them to me or not.

I pulled up to the precinct, only to have Victoria waiting for me in the lot.

She slid into the passenger seat and gave me an address. "Drive. Our guy dropped another body."

"Shit." That wasn't how I wanted to start my day. Especially considering I had hoped to clock out at a decent time and confront Nate. I really didn't want to have to put it off until the next day. But I knew the job came first. It had to.

The whole way there, she didn't say a word, letting me know she was still pissed off at me.

Well, then, fine. She wasn't the only one who could give the silent treatment.

I pulled up to a house in a run-down neighborhood and shot her a questioning look. "You sure this is the place?"

All of the victims had been found in remote locations up to this point. So, finding someone in a neighborhood, even one as derelict as this one, seemed out of character for our killer.

She shrugged. "That's what they said. And from all the

crime scene tape around that residence, I'd say we're at the right place."

I rolled my eyes at her and got out of the car, slamming the door. Pulling my badge out, I flashed it to the officer on the perimeter and walked into the house, wrinkling my nose.

The house was disgusting and it was obvious that it was from the way the victim lived and not anything the killer had done. Although, it could make finding anything the killer left behind all the more difficult.

"Well, this looks lovely."

Victoria shot me a look as she shoulder checked her way past me.

"Tough crowd," Ramirez joked as he came around the corner.

"You have no idea." I sighed.

For the first time in a very long time, I felt restless. Maybe it was all the bullshit going on with Nate or maybe one person could only deal with so much death and murder before it really started to get to them.

Either way, I was starting to think I needed a vacation.

A *really* long one.

"Just as well," he said with a shake of his head. "This one is baaad. The vic is actually up in his bed. But he wasn't killed there. It's definitely been staged."

Fuck. I hated when we had to find a secondary location. Usually, it was like trying to find a needle in a haystack.

"Not only that," he continued, "the body is in really bad shape. Guy's been brutalized. Half of his face is gone. Preliminary ID will be based on the homeowner, but we'll need DNA and dental records to confirm."

I blinked at him in confusion.

"Sick fucker. Our guy is definitely devolving and spinning out of control," Victoria muttered, popping up from out of nowhere. "He'd been going months between kills, and now it's barely been a couple of weeks before another body dropped in our laps."

I nodded as we walked from the foyer into the living room, my thoughts a million miles away. Things weren't sitting right with me over this one. And it wasn't just from the additional carnage done to the victim. Something about the guy sent off warning bells as soon as I'd walked onto the scene and heard about his body.

"You check out down here and I'm going to go up and check out the body and see what forensics have to say." I turned and walked away from her without giving her the opportunity to answer. While it might have been a dick move, I didn't particularly care. I was feeling dickish.

"Casey," I greeted the one tech who was leaning against the wall in the upstairs hall. "That bad?"

She nodded, her eyes looking haunted. "Yeah, Aiden. It's that bad. I'm going to have nightmares about his face for a long fucking time."

I grimaced. She was a tough cookie who didn't toss her cookies easily. If she was spooked and feeling squeamish over the state of the body, it was definitely not pretty.

"Why don't you go get some air?"

She nodded, though I didn't think she really heard me. I pulled on a fresh pair of gloves and entered the bedroom where the victim was, but stayed back, since forensics was doing their thing and one of the guys was getting pictures.

I fist-bumped Oliver, their lead tech, who was standing back as a guy I didn't know worked on getting the pictures they needed.

"What are we working with?"

"Hard to tell." He shrugged and had the same look in his eyes as Casey. "I'd say they're mid-thirties, maybe a little younger. Good shape. From what we could see, there were at least a dozen stab wounds, not counting the mess that was made of the guy's face—or hands and...dick."

A shudder wracked Oliver's body and my curiosity had me trying to catch a peek, but there were still too many people in the room for me to get much of a glimpse of anything.

"I'm sorry, what the fuck, what?" I stared at Oliver, mouth wide open. "What the hell did he do to the guy's dick?"

Oliver glanced away and grimaced. I could practically see him brace himself before he answered. "He cut it off."

"Fuuuck. Is it possible this isn't our guy?" I asked, then grimaced. "Never mind. I don't think I want to know if we are looking at more than one person who is capable of *that*." A full-body shudder went through me. "But I think you're right. Either that or this was personal."

The thought stopped me dead in my tracks.

Personal.

I stared at the body on the bed, my thoughts taking a dark turn.

"Thanks, man." I left the room, not paying attention to where I was going. But I needed to get out of there.

Downstairs, I did a cursory walkthrough to see if anything caught my eye.

"Aiden?" Victoria called my name, but I couldn't find it in myself to answer until she was right in front of me, snapping her fingers.

"What?" I snapped.

Her eyes narrowed as she gave me a once-over. I wasn't sure what she'd find when she studied my face, but I didn't think I'd like it.

I shook my head. "Sorry? What did you say?" I tried to act nonchalant, but I knew I wasn't fooling the partner I'd known for almost a decade.

"What the hell, Aiden?" she hissed, keeping her voice low

so she wouldn't attract the attention of any of the other dozen cops or crime scene technicians who were milling around.

She grabbed my arm and tried to pull me away, but I was able to easily get out of her grasp.

"Are you okay? You are white as a sheet. You look like you've seen a ghost." She grimaced. "Was it that bad upstairs?"

I looked away, unable to make eye contact.

"It wasn't great. But we have a job to do, so let's do it." My voice was firm and held a tone that was non-negotiable. At least, I hoped it did. But she let out a sigh and followed me through the house.

There was nothing unusual in the house, unless you counted all the garbage and the piles of dirty dishes. I was pretty sure there was something alive scurrying around—and I didn't mean a cat.

"This is gross," Victoria muttered as she dug through the guy's belongings, trying her best not to touch anything more than she had to.

Even with the gloves on, it still made me squeamish.

"You're telling me." I made a face as I stared at a pile of gay porn DVDs. "Didn't anyone ever tell this dude he could watch this stuff for free on the internet?" I joked.

She rolled her eyes and ignored me. Which was good. Because I felt like *I* was devolving.

I moved away from the living room and wandered around, but there was nothing that told me anything about the guy or who would want him killed.

Except that he was gay.

Then I came across his office and on his desk were photographs.

Photos of a man I recognized.

My stomach churned. Thoughts racing, I fled the room. Except, I couldn't run because that would look suspicious.

It would also look suspicious if anyone found out that I met the victim at a gay club and had danced with him.

And that I had a stalker who chased him away.

A stalker, who I then started dating.

That boyfriend also knew the witness who discovered the last victim of the killer.

Fuck. Fuck, fuck, fuck.

I was so fucking screwed for not saying anything sooner.

There had to be a reasonable explanation. I didn't accept any other possibility.

Needing air, I went out to see if any of the other techs found anything, but they had just started to get to work, so there was nothing yet. I wandered around and let my thoughts drift, which was not a good idea. They kept going back to Nate. But he couldn't be involved.

Could he?

Had Victoria been right all along and he'd been manipulating me? Using me?

Just as I tried to rein in my thoughts and go back inside, something caught my eye a little farther down the street, nestled perfectly in the crack on the sidewalk.

I glanced around, but no one was paying attention to me, so I made my way down the street and bent down to see if it was anything I should grab a tech about or just more broken concrete. When I got close, I felt like someone had punched me in the gut. My heart raced so fast I was sure it would leap right out of my chest.

No. No, no, no. That's impossible.

With trembling fingers, I reached down and picked up the antique cufflink that had been left behind at the house of the latest victim of the serial killer I'd been hunting for almost a year. My vision swam, and I thought I'd pass out or throw up. Perhaps both.

But I pulled myself together and stared at the tangible proof

I couldn't deny any longer. I'd known something was different from the start about this victim.

Personal.

"Hey, Cooper, you find anything?" one of the techs asked.

I slid the cufflink into my pocket, spun around, and shrugged. "Nah. Nothing but broken concrete here. Thought maybe there'd be some scuff marks or something, but nada." I looked around. "I'm going to canvas the neighborhood. Let Coleman know, would you, if she starts looking for me?"

He nodded. "Of course, Detective."

I gave him a nod and was glad I had an excuse to walk around and dispel some of the anxiety and tension that had gripped me after I found the cufflink. There had to be a reasonable explanation.

We need to talk when I get off work. No more ghosting me.

The words made me grimace. I wasn't sure I even wanted to confront him about it. Maybe I'd be better off being an ostrich with my head stuck in the sand.

Except, that wasn't a viable option. I was a homicide detective. I was hunting a serial killer. And my boyfriend's cufflink was at the victim's house.

Or near, rather.

No! I had to stop rationalizing what I'd found.

But I also had to get back to work, so I slipped my phone back into my pocket and started knocking on doors. Even though I knew no one would answer for the police.

29

NATHAN

I might have had very little experience in dealing with people, and even less when it came to relationships, but even I knew it was never a good thing when your boyfriend said you needed to talk and then brushed you off.

Okay. I knew he didn't brush me off. He was at work.

Hunting a serial killer.

No, he was hunting *me*.

We'd been avoiding each other the last few days. It didn't bode well for our relationship, or for my anxiety over whether or not he suspected me of being the killer after our run-in at the office earlier in the week.

Fuck. I hated lying to him. But there was no way I could tell my homicide detective boyfriend the truth. I didn't even want to imagine how that conversation would go.

But I did know how it would end. With me in prison for life.

He had to know.

So, that begged the question, what was I still doing in town? Why hadn't I fled? There were safe houses I had prepped all over the country. I could easily flee.

It all came down to Aiden.

I couldn't leave him. Just the thought made my chest feel tight, like I couldn't breathe.

There had to be a way to get him to accept me. But I knew it would be impossible. The ethics violation of his job alone would keep him bound to the law and turning me in. No matter how much I wished to the contrary, his whole life didn't revolve around me and he wouldn't choose me.

Even if I would choose him.

Though, maybe I could figure out a way to get him to quit. I had enough money that he didn't need to work. Hell, I didn't need to work. It wasn't like I did much of the work; it was more like overseeing—making sure the things I wanted to get done actually got done. And that they were done correctly.

Of course, that didn't solve the problem with his *morals*, but it would solve the problem with the ethics of his job.

Who was I kidding? He'd never go for it. As soon as he had confirmation, he'd think I was a monster.

He'd *know* I was a monster.

Despite the fact it had only been a couple of days since I'd killed, my skin felt tight and itchy. The kill hadn't been satisfying at all, even though I'd killed someone who had dared to touch my little bird and made him uncomfortable. I had thought he would have been the most satisfying.

Instead, I felt empty.

I'd killed for Aiden, but I could never tell him about it. He could never know what I did for him. But I wasn't stupid enough to believe he'd never find out, even if he wasn't the one working the guy's case. He was smart. Finding killers was his job, so did I really think the two of us could have a forever, especially one where he never knew the truth?

The thought was nothing but a fantasy.

But I couldn't kill him. I should. But I couldn't. I'd already proven that time and time again. I set my little bird free every time I'd set my sights on him.

Frustrated from the lack of thrill from the kill, my thoughts drifted back to Aiden, and the knowledge that one day I might have to kill him, even if it killed me.

No. I knew I couldn't do it. I'd already proven that fact. For whatever reason, I couldn't touch him.

The war raged within me. This kaleidoscope of fear, doubt, and even what I dared to hope was love. But it was all crashing down on me. And I was powerless to stop it because even though I had the means to escape, I no longer had the will. Not when it meant leaving my little bird behind.

I grabbed my phone and tried to doom-scroll my worries away. But nothing could distract me. The longer it took to hear back from Aiden, the more my agitation and fear grew.

After a half-hour of cat videos that did nothing to soothe my nerves, I finally decided I needed a way to expel some of the excess energy. The last thing I needed was to unleash some of that onto Aiden when we talked.

Because that was all we could do. I'd have to be strong and find a way to deny him when he undoubtedly asked me to come over. There was no way I could have this conversation face-to-face. I didn't need to see the heartbreak and betrayal on his face.

Or be an easy target for him to arrest.

Not that I would resist if, or when, he found me. I'd never risk hurting him.

Growling in frustration, I made my way to my home gym and taped up my wrists and unleashed on my punching bag. I worked up a sweat for over an hour, throwing punch after punch. But while I was physically drained, my mind still raced.

Thoughts of Aiden were still there, at the forefront of my mind. All the lies I'd told him. The half-truths. The scars.

And there'd be so many more I caused him. Because not all scars were visible on the skin.

I flinched at the thought of inflicting any more damage to him.

Leaning against the wall, I ripped the tape off my hands and wrists and slid down until I was sitting. I'd never felt so alone, so unsure. My whole body felt like it was being torn apart. But I had no one to blame but myself.

Didn't I?

I knew that I really couldn't blame myself. That I'd been born the way I was and no medications I'd been prescribed were able to curb my impulses, no matter how much my parents, or I, tried.

A sob escaped my lips and I reached up a shaky hand to my face, surprised to find tears wetting my cheeks. I'd never cried before. Not even when my parents had died, and that had been the first time I had felt true emotion, a sadness that had dug its claws into me and didn't want to let go.

I wiped the tears away and refused to dwell on what they meant. There wouldn't be another incident like that time. I couldn't go into another meltdown, not with Aiden so close.

My stomach growled and it gave me something to focus on. I stood and went over to the bench, where I'd tossed my phone, and scrolled through a food delivery app for something appealing. Finally, I settled on Chinese, still ordering enough for two, even though I had no intention of seeing Aiden.

But I couldn't stop myself from getting his favorites. Maybe I could sneak it over there and have it waiting on his porch, or even his counter, for when he got home.

With plenty of time until the food arrived, I eyed the rest of the equipment but shook my head, deciding against working out any more. My shoulders had started to feel the burn and I didn't want to overdo it, especially since I didn't know what *the talk* with Aiden would entail. Instead, I wandered back to the living room and fell onto the couch, letting my head fall back.

As I sat there, worry churned in my gut. I couldn't believe that I was at the point where I was considering myself *lucky* if it was only a breakup talk. Though, before our run-in at the office, I thought things had been going great. Not that I was a good judge of any of that.

I let out a sigh and scrubbed my hands over my face.

Maybe it would be for the best if he did break up with me. I was dangerous to be around, especially with the way I'd been feeling the last couple weeks. My control had been slipping and I didn't know how to get it back. The only difference in my life and routine had been Aiden. Having him near messed with me, but not having him near messed with me even more.

A few minutes later, the doorbell interrupted my spiral. I walked to the door and opened it to see a man who looked to be in his early twenties, probably in college, if I had to make a guess.

"Hey," I greeted the man at the door, who held the bag with my food as I put my hand in my pocket to grab my wallet, but it wasn't there. "Sorry, I think I left my wallet in the kitchen. Would you mind following me?"

He looked around and shrugged. "Sure."

I walked back the way I'd come, past the living room and dining room, toward the kitchen. It didn't escape my notice that the man gawked at the place as he trailed after me. I smirked, knowing I had a great house where the interior had been fully customized with exposed beams, hardwood, and polished concrete flooring, with large throw rugs around. My furniture was plush and extravagant, as I was a creature built for comfort.

The perks of being rich. Not to mention, a developer and having the best contacts for contractors, designers, and architects.

Sometimes, it was great to be me.

"This is a really nice house," he gushed as we made our way into the industrial kitchen with the double stoves, large farm sink, and an island that went on for days.

If I had a kitchen like this, I wouldn't be ordering takeout," he joked as he put the bag on the island and turned to get a view of the rest of the house while I grabbed my wallet.

"Thanks. And yeah, I know what you mean. The kitchen is fabulous. And I do love using it, but some days, you just prefer to have someone else do the cooking." I chuckled as I reached for my wallet. But then, at the last moment, I changed course and grabbed a short, thin, and very sharp knife from the block and quietly made my way to where he had moved to the doorway to continue admiring the house.

I snuck up behind him and had one arm wrapped around his neck, tilting his head back just as I brought the knife up, before he even knew what was happening.

"What?" I could feel him struggle and my monster roared to life. Anticipation bloomed under my skin, eager for the kill.

"I'm sorry. It's nothing personal." My blade had just started to slide across his delicate throat when his hands grabbed at me in a vain attempt to pull me off.

At that moment, I also heard the front door slam and the sound of a single set of footsteps pounding on the floor, getting closer.

But I couldn't stop. The knife was already across his throat, his blood spurting from the open wound and coating my hands. There would be such a mess to clean up. Not to mention, there would be a trail from me ordering the food and the driver coming to my house.

Shit. I hadn't thought this through. I hadn't thought any of this through.

"Jesus! What the fuck, Nate?" Aiden's panicked voice cut through my thoughts, and my eyes darted up at him as he pulled his gun and aimed it at me.

For a moment, I wondered if he would shoot me on sight. But not my little bird. He was a good cop. A fair cop. Even though I was clearly armed and in the middle of a murder, he still would give me a chance.

"Drop the fucking knife, Nate. Now." His voice wavered almost as badly as his hands as he stared at me like he had no idea who I was.

Fuck.

30

AIDEN

"Jesus! What the fuck, Nate?"

There was no way what I had just seen was real. I didn't just watch my boyfriend slit some random guy's throat in his kitchen. I didn't.

Fuck. This can't be happening. Please let this be a nightmare I'm going to wake from any second.

Nate's eyes were cold and flat when he looked up at me. I didn't recognize the person who looked back at me, and it had me drawing my gun and pointing it at him. Even with shaky hands, it was better than nothing. Especially since he still had the knife, and the dead body, in his hands.

"Drop the fucking knife, Nate. Now." My voice shook, and my mind rebelled. I had no idea what he would do, but I still didn't want to believe he would hurt me. He had to still be the guy I knew, the man I'd fallen in love with.

Fuck. I love him. How can I still be thinking that I love him?

The realization hit me like a ton of bricks and I almost went to my knees from the weight of the knowledge.

I loved him, but he was a serial killer. A serial killer *I* was trying to catch. Fuck, Victoria had tried to warn me, but I didn't want to listen. All the signs had been there, red flags waving in my face, and I had actively ignored them and all their potential meanings.

Glancing back, I tried to judge if I could get out of the house before he could get to me.

Probably not. Plus, he knew where I lived. He knew where my *parents* lived.

Shit. I'd put everyone I loved in danger.

Tears slid down my face at the realization that I'd fucked up my life and the lives of everyone around me.

Worst cop ever award to this guy right here.

A thud jerked my attention back to Nate. And I realized I'd taken my eyes off him for too long, distracted by my own internal struggle. I needed to be careful or I would end up like the guy Nate had just tossed to the ground like a sack of potatoes.

"It's okay. Put the gun down, little bird. I don't want to hurt you." Nate still had the knife, but his hands were out at his sides, as though he were trying to appear unthreatening.

"Fuck you," I sputtered. "God, I am such a fucking idiot. You were using me this whole time, weren't you?" I ignored the shake of his head and let it all out. "Did you know I was on the case? On *your* case? Is that why you came up to me and pretended to be interested in me?"

Nate didn't move or even try to defend himself. I snuck a glance around his house, taking it in for the first time. When I first arrived, I thought for sure I had the wrong address. Sure, Nate said he was wealthy, and from what I'd found online showed he'd inherited wealth from his parents, but this was some Bruce Wayne shit.

Except, instead of being the hero, Nate was the villain. He was a monster, a murderer.

"What are you doing here? How did you even find me?" His voice was low and level, as though he asked about the weather rather than the fact I'd just walked in on him committing murder.

"Are you fucking serious? You stalked me and found out where I lived." I let out a bitter laugh at the memory. That had been one of the first red flags I'd ignored.

"I'm a fucking cop. You think I can't easily find people's addresses?" I scoffed. "Nice place, by the way. You pay for it with blood money?" The pitch in my voice told me I was close to losing it and I was sure Nate heard it too. I needed to take a deep breath and get myself back under control.

"And I'm here," I said, pausing as I fished around in my pocket, never taking my eyes off him, "because you left this at the house of the guy you threatened at the club." My hand shook as I thrust it out and opened up to reveal one of the cufflinks I'd gotten him for our one-month anniversary.

"You know, when you killed him," I finished, gritting my teeth.

He didn't reply, but then again, he didn't need to. He knew I had him dead to rights. The evidence was literally in the palm of my hand. Nothing he said or did could make it any better.

A cold shiver ran through my body as I realized I was never making it out of the house alive. This time, the monster was going to kill me.

It made something in me snap. Made me braver as I unleashed everything that raged inside of me.

"You fucking asshole. You couldn't have just tried to befriend me?" I yelled, as if that would have been any better. "No, you had to go and make me feel like I mattered? What even was the point of our talk over our anniversary dinner? Why did you even bother to admit to being a psychopath?" I was so stupid.

There was a scream bubbling up inside my chest. Nate told me he'd never hurt me, but this hurt worse than any physical pain he could have inflicted on me.

"None of it was real." My voice was so low even I could barely hear it. My body trembled, but not just from fear.

And that was what I hated the most. The emotional pain he'd dealt me, the betrayal. I shook my head, trying to clear the thoughts away that tore at my heart. "You told me you couldn't feel the same way, but you still were able to make me believe like you cared, like I mattered. As if I were someone important. But it was all lies!"

Nate flinched. It was barely there, but I caught it.

"It wasn't. I know this all seems... impossible. But I never lied to you. And you are important, so don't you dare start that bullshit."

I nodded, taking his words in but not believing them. "Answer me one question honestly. Just one."

"Anything." Nate's shoulders sagged as though he thought we were finally getting somewhere. But I knew better.

"Did you know who I was when you sat next to me and started talking to me at the wedding?"

I watched as Nate's mask slipped into place. He said he never lied to me, and maybe that had been the truth. But I'd never asked such a blatant and direct question before. Maybe it was his way to keep from lying. It was unnerving to see and I shuddered at the sight.

"Put. The. Knife. Down." I said each word on an exhale as I steadied my gun at him. "Don't make me shoot you, Nate. Be smart about this." Despite my bravado, I wasn't sure if I could actually shoot him if it came down to it. But I hoped he didn't know that.

"Let's talk about this," Nate said, as though I were being unreasonable.

"Sure." I shrugged. "We can talk about this down at the station once you're processed."

Nate threw me a wry smile. "Now, now, little bird. We both know that isn't going to happen."

My heart pounded in my chest. He was going to make me shoot him. Or he was going to attack me and kill me.

Fuck.

The next thing I knew, Nate was taking a step toward me, and I pulled the trigger. But he was too fast, anticipating my move and the shot went wide as he spun out of the way.

I blinked as my brain tried to process the movement, and that gave Nate the opportunity to turn things around on me. He came up behind me and wrapped one strong arm around my throat while the other grabbed my hand and pried the gun from my grip, causing it to drop to the floor with a clatter.

As his body molded to mine, my stupid brain's first instinct was to lean into him and tilt my head to the side to give him access. But it only took a second for reality to sink in, for me to remember that it wasn't a lover's caress but the threat of a murderer.

I threw my head back and caught his nose. He grunted but didn't let go, his grip on my throat tightening.

Unfortunately, I had forgotten about the knife in his hand until he moved the position of his arm so the blade was pressed against my jugular. I swallowed past the lump in my throat and immediately stilled.

"Good, little bird." Nate chuckled, his breath tickling my ear. Despite our situation, my traitorous body lit up at his praise. "We can either fight or fuck, whichever you'd prefer, though I think you know which I'd rather."

Bile rose, and I gagged as I swallowed it back down.

"Actually, I'm not sure I do," I threw back at him.

His nose nudged at the soft skin behind my ear, and he licked a stripe up my neck. A playful bite to the hinge of my jaw made my cock twitch.

No. No, this is not *sexy*, I reprimanded my traitorous dick. The last thing I needed was to get hard as a serial killer was trying to kill me, though I guess I couldn't be faulted for the crossed signals when it was my boyfriend.

"There's a hint," he whispered as sparks lit up my body, betraying the fact that I, too, would rather fuck than fight. But I wasn't naïve enough to believe he wouldn't kill me as soon as he was done.

With Nate's mind on sex, I took the opportunity to throw myself to the side. It was a risky move, and I still got nicked by the blade, but it was better than getting my throat slashed. I scrambled toward the kitchen that was in front of me, figuring there had to be more knives I could use to defend myself.

But I didn't get very far before I felt a burning in my side. I ignored it and kept going but quickly felt something damp against my shirt. When I looked down, I noticed my side was covered in blood and there was a large slit through my shirt.

No, not just my shirt. My fingers probed, and I let out a hiss as I realized the asshole had sliced my side open. The blade had been so sharp I hadn't even noticed.

I looked up at him, shocked. Though, I wasn't sure why. Maybe I had still hoped he'd been telling the truth when he said he'd never hurt me. Maybe I'd been lying to myself and trying to make myself believe he loved me, too, and that meant he couldn't hurt me.

Either way, I'd been wrong. He didn't care about me and he was going to kill me.

I backed up and leaned against the island, never taking my eyes off him as he made his way toward me. But I was getting weaker the longer I stood there. I knew it would only take him a few seconds before his long strides brought him into the kitchen with me.

Then he'd kill me.

"You don't have to do this, Daddy," I whispered as I started to sag, my elbows braced on the counter behind me.

There was a flicker of sadness in his eyes before he shook

his head. It should have given me some sort of comfort to know there was a part of him that didn't revel in killing me. But it was a poor consolation prize.

"I'm sorry, little bird," were the last words I heard before pain and blood loss pulled me under into the cold, unfeeling darkness.

31
NATHAN

I watched in a daze as Aiden slumped in my arms. The blood oozed out of him and mixed with the blood on my hands from the nameless man I'd killed earlier. I grimaced at the realization.

Aiden deserved better than the desecration of having his blood mixed with that of someone who didn't matter. The other man had been a nobody, while my little bird was my everything.

But he was slipping away, dying in my arms. And I felt myself slipping away with him.

As gently as I could, I laid him on the ground and went to the sink to scrub the blood from my skin. There wasn't much I could do about my clothes, but they weren't a priority at the moment. When my hands were as clean as I could get them, I made my way back to where I had left Aiden.

My heart raged at the sight of him hurt and bleeding out on my floor. Well, that wasn't a fair statement. The likelihood of him bleeding out from that wound alone was pretty small. Didn't change the fact I didn't like to see him hurt—even if I was the one who had done it to him.

I needed to get him up and moved somewhere else. Then again, the high polish and sealant that was put over the industrial concrete flooring in the kitchen was probably the best place for him to be while he was still bleeding. Not that it was comfortable, but it provided easy clean-up.

"What am I going to do with you, little bird?" I asked his prone body as I leaned down to check his pulse. Still steady. That was good. Logically, I knew I should kill him. It would be easy, with him unconscious. But the thought made me want to throw up.

Just like every time before when I thought about killing him. I didn't know what it was, but I'd already proven I couldn't do it.

Which was utterly ridiculous!

I'd killed dozens of people without remorse. Yet Aiden had proved difficult from day one. I pushed myself up from the floor and paced as I contemplated my options, of which there really weren't many.

Either I killed him and I fled or I didn't kill him and when he regained consciousness, I'd go to prison. Unless I ran.

Looking down at his prone body, I didn't know if I could find it in me to run. Even faced with the knowledge that he knew everything.

Fuck. I was so screwed.

Why did he have to show up at the moment he did? Even if he'd had the cufflink, if he hadn't watched as I slit a man's throat, then maybe I could have come up with some sort of excuse. Though I wasn't stupid enough to believe *he'd* be stupid enough to believe in any coincidences in the matter. Especially given that he already had Christian as the person who discovered one of the bodies.

He'd never believe it was *all* a coincidence.

But I could have stalled, bought some time to come up with something.

Except I'd promised to never lie to him again. Something I never should have done because it had painted me into a corner.

With a heavy sigh, I went to the small supply cupboard in the hallway and pulled down my heavy-duty makeshift first aid kit. I'd had to improvise, seeing as how, on occasion, I needed more than what a standard first aid kit could provide. I took it back over to Aiden's prone body and laid out the supplies I needed.

After I settled on the floor next to him, I took the scissors and cut off his shirt so I'd have easy access to his wound. Once that was out of the way, I got the gauze and disinfectant and was thankful he was already passed out as I wiped the wound.

The tricky part was going to be the stitches.

Subconsciously, my hand went to Aiden's other side, and my fingers traced the faint lines of the scar that was sure to match the one he'd get once tonight's wound healed. I shuddered at the thought.

With the needle and thread in hand, I set out to stitch the wound. It was harder than one would think, since I didn't have anyone to help. It made the work difficult and uneven. Though it was much easier than stitching my own wounds.

Another person to hold the skin together would have been ideal while I worked on him. But there was no one else. There never was. That was the way I liked my life. It was what I'd strived for.

Though, I supposed I could have called Christian, but there wasn't time for him to get to the house. The stitches needed to be done as soon as possible. Aiden couldn't wait.

Shit. Christian.

By the time I sewed him back up, he had thirty-seven stitches in total. It wasn't a record by any means, but there were more pressing matters calling my name.

Once I had the wound taped and covered, I gave Aiden a

shot of painkiller. There was no doubt he'd be in agonizing pain, and I wanted to do whatever I could to help ease his suffering when he woke up. Even if I couldn't do that for him in the long term.

I got up and cleaned myself off and reached for the phone. The thought struck me that maybe Aiden had changed me, because a part of me felt guilty for upending and potentially ruining the other man's life. Especially since he had become a friend, and more. Though, not in the sense of a lover like Aiden, even though we had that history.

Waiting for the call to connect, I wondered what I was going to tell him. But I didn't have to wait long.

"Nathan?" Christian sounded like he had been asleep and I snuck a glance at the clock and winced when I realized it was the middle of the night.

"Hey. Sorry for calling so late." I rubbed the back of my neck as I tried to find the words that I still struggled with.

"Fuck. What happened?" He sounded more alert, near panicked, and I could hear rustling on the end of the phone. A door slammed and I wondered if he hadn't been alone.

My gaze wandered to where Aiden's prone body lay on the floor and I shuddered as the thoughts of what could have been flooded my mind. "He knows, Christian. Everything. Aiden knows it's me."

There was a long pause on the other end and I wondered if we got disconnected before I heard Christian swear.

"Fucking hell, Nathan. How did that happen? What did he say?" Then another pause. "How are you calling me now?"

I let out a chuckle that I didn't feel. "Well, he sort of caught me in the middle of a kill."

"What?" Christian practically shouted. "Jesus Christ."

The panic in his voice was evident. And I wasn't sure anything I could say would ease it. Because we were totally fucked.

"Yeah, it definitely wasn't ideal." There was a throbbing that had started in my temples and I rubbed it, trying to ease the pain, despite the fact I knew it wouldn't do any good.

Christian's voice was a low hush when he spoke next, as though he were afraid of the answer. I couldn't blame him. I would have been too, if I were in his shoes. "What did you do to him?"

Guilt struck me as I glanced back over at him again and I sighed. "I stabbed him."

Once again, silence stretched out over the line. "Fuck, Nathan. Tell me you didn't kill a police officer."

"I didn't kill a police officer."

He made a sound like he didn't believe me. Again, not that I could blame him.

"Aiden will live. He'll be fine. I patched him up. He's out cold at the moment. And he'll be out of commission for a little while, but he'll be fine." It was the question of what came after he woke up, for me, that I didn't know the answer to.

There was a noise of frustration from Christian, and I agreed. It was less than ideal and very frustrating.

"What do you need from me?" he asked with a resigned sigh as I took a seat at the kitchen island, turning the chair so I could watch the rise and fall of Aiden's chest.

This was the hard part. "To disappear."

Christian choked out an, "Excuse me?"

"It's less than ideal. I—"

"Less than ideal? You think me packing up my life in the middle of the night—no, in the middle of a *murder investigation*, is less than ideal?" His frustration quickly morphed into anger, but I needed him to trust me, and to listen to what I needed him to do. I didn't want to add him to my body count.

"Christian. I need you to stop and listen." My voice was calm and controlled, despite the fact I felt neither of those things. "My boyfriend, a cop whom I just stabbed, knows we are connected. We, who includes you, a man who found a man I murdered."

I stopped and let that sink in for a minute. "Fucking hell, Nathan."

"There are businesses and safe houses set up all over the country. Pack up and get on the road. Text me in three hours and let me know where you are and I'll give you the location of one in the direction you're headed. You can lie low there, or start over there, until I figure out what is going on here."

"Until you... Nathan. Are you seriously going to stick around and see what he does with the information he has?" When I didn't say anything, he started cursing again. "You fucking *stabbed* him. What do you think he's going to do? Be fucking smart about this."

"I am," I snapped, banging my fist on the counter. "I am," I repeated, calmer.

"You don't understand, and that's fine. I don't expect you to. But this is what I have to do. You don't need to ruin your life over what I did, though. So, let me protect you."

Christian sighed and I knew he wanted to argue more, but there was nothing to argue against. It was my mess and I needed to clean it up.

"Good luck, Nathan." The line disconnected and I stared at the phone as I lost the only person I'd ever truly considered a friend.

"Goodbye, Christian, and good luck," I whispered to no one as I stood and went back to my little bird.

I checked his pulse again and was happy it was still strong. But I needed to get a move on because I couldn't leave him on my floor indefinitely. Plus, I had a hell of a mess to clean up.

After I put the first aid kit away, I moved him away from the pool of blood he'd been lying in, and got the body wipes and cleaned all the blood off Aiden's body before gently putting him in one of my oversized jackets. It was still on his pants and shoes, but I'd have to take care of that later. His pants were dark enough that it wasn't noticeable unless you knew to look for it, at least.

So, for the moment, I just worried about what I could see.

He looked so young and fragile. I bit my lip, hating that I had done that to him. He shouldn't have been in that position. I was his Daddy. I was supposed to take care of him, protect him.

And I'd failed miserably.

Heaving a sigh I felt down into my weary soul, if I even had one, which I seriously doubted anymore, considering what I had done to my sweet little bird, I gathered his prone form in my arms and made my way to the garage. When I got to the car, I gently placed him in the passenger seat and made my way back to his house.

The whole drive, I half expected to be swarmed with police cars stopping me. But there was hardly any traffic and I pulled up to his house without incident. When I got there, I let myself in and did my best to drag him in without looking suspicious. Not that he had many neighbors around.

Mindful of his injuries, I carried him to his bedroom and got him changed into his favorite pair of pajama pants and a loose tank top that wouldn't cling to his body and press against the stitches.

He grumbled and pushed me away as he slipped in and out of consciousness, but he was weak enough he didn't get very far. Given everything he'd been through, I didn't think he would be so eager to get a start on his day as he passed back out.

Not wanting to leave him, I tucked him in before I settled on the bed next to him, but I remained careful not to touch him. Pain laced my heart as I leaned over and placed a gentle kiss on his forehead, knowing I'd never be that close to him again. He'd seen the monster and he rejected me.

And I couldn't blame him. I'd reject me too, if I had the option.

I let out a sigh and wondered if it was going to be the last time I'd see him at all. Or, if I'd let him catch me. At least then, I could see him when he interrogated me and at the trial.

But then I thought about how the embarrassment and the pain of seeing me, the reminder, would continue to hurt him. It would be a festering wound. *If* he caught me, maybe I'd just plead guilty so he wouldn't have to deal with any of that.

Wouldn't have to deal with me.

There was still the option of fleeing, but every moment I spent with him, that seemed less and less likely. No matter how much he didn't want me, I still couldn't find it in me to desert him.

With that thought, I couldn't fall asleep. Instead, I lay there, watching his fitful sleep, and wished he looked peaceful.

More than that, I wished I could undo everything I had done to hurt him. But that was beyond my capabilities.

Just as dawn broke, I gave him another shot of the painkiller and gathered everything I'd ever left behind, removing any trace that I'd been there. Before I left, I took one final look at him and smoothed his hair out of his face.

"Be well, my little bird. I love you," I said as I leaned down and placed a gentle kiss on his lips.

32

AIDEN

Fire. I felt like I was being consumed by fire.

Every time I moved, the pain in my side felt like it was going to engulf me, consume me, destroy me. Or, maybe that was just my wishful thinking.

Since I woke, I'd felt like I had been living a nightmare I couldn't escape no matter how much I tried.

When I first woke up in my bed, I'd been terrified and confused, wondering where Nate was. I had remembered being with him, that something had happened, something bad. But the details were foggy and I couldn't remember what had me so scared.

I didn't know where my Daddy was. It wasn't like him not to still be in bed with me when I woke.

Then, I moved to get up, and the searing pain cleared the fog away. With a gasp, I sat there, partially hyperventilating and partially dry-heaving as the memories assaulted me. Instead of clarifying the situation, I'd only been left more confused.

I didn't understand why I was alive, or in my own bedroom, for that matter. As I'd passed out, I had been so sure Nate would kill me—that he'd technically already had, and my body just had to catch up.

Now, I just wished I were dead. I felt like I was. My body was a living ghost walking in the shadows of my life, not really living my life, or registering anything that was going on around me. It wasn't as though any of it mattered anymore anyway.

I gingerly made my way through the house, needing to stop every few steps to take a break due to feeling winded and waiting for the pain to subside. Not that it ever went away. He must have given me something strong, though, because it got worse as time went on. But as I went through the house, there was no sign Nate was still there, waiting for me.

And I wasn't sure how to feel about that, which was all sorts of fucked up. But there was a part of me that was pissed off that he had done this to me and then just left me alive and alone to deal with it by myself.

He had to have been the one to leave me in bed because nothing looked out of place. Even my car was in the driveway.

And there was no way I had driven myself home.

What the hell happened?

I didn't know what sort of twisted and fucked-up mind game Nate thought he was playing, but I didn't appreciate it. Did he expect me to thank him for not killing me? That I wouldn't turn him in just because he had spared my life?

Well, he could go to hell.

I paced around my living room the best I could, grabbing onto furniture and anything sturdy enough that would help keep me on my feet, until I was too tired to keep standing—which, in my condition, didn't take long at all. But the movement, the pattern of my steps, helped me to think.

At least, until my thoughts consumed me and were too much. They took me in a dark direction I didn't want to think about and I shut down. Nothing mattered anymore. I was fucked.

The first thing I should have done when I woke up was call it into the station. To report I knew who the killer was and I was injured, needing medical assistance. Instead, I did nothing except ignore Victoria's calls. Though, I did call my captain and took a couple sick days so I could heal a little bit before heading back into work.

Thankfully, I had a three-day rotation off, so I'd only missed one day so far.

But I knew eventually, Victoria would get tired of me ignoring her and show up before I even had to report back to work. But until then, I needed to figure out what I was going to do. I needed a plan, because there was no way Nate was going to let me go. I knew too much.

Which begged the question why he even went through this charade to begin with. We didn't have any evidence he toyed with his victims like this before he killed them. So, it didn't make any sense. Leaving me alive, alone, with access to resources, it almost seemed like a test in trust.

But that couldn't be right. Because he had to have been long gone by now. And I still had no idea what the fuck I was doing.

It had been four days since I'd discovered Nate's secret, and I was no closer to deciding anything. I was also uneasy, because it had been four days and he still hadn't made a move against me. And I still didn't know why he had brought me home and then disappeared.

Logically, at this point, I knew I *couldn't* report anything. Not without some suspicion being cast on me. If I said anything, it would look like I'd been protecting him to give him time to get away. Especially since I'd called in with the flu, not because I was reporting that I had a serial killer boyfriend.

Ironically, it wasn't a complete lie. I'd barely been able to function since I'd woken the morning after finding Nate with a body and getting stabbed. Things like washing up, changing my clothes, or even changing my bandages seemed too big and incomprehensible. So I ignored them. Hell, I barely ate or drank anything in the days that followed.

Functioning seemed too much to ask for. The world outside the walls of my house could stop existing for all I cared, because it had for me. Everything seemed like it was upside down. I didn't know what to believe anymore, what to believe *in*.

Because of my inability to take my head out of the sand and confront what had happened, it meant that I hadn't even *looked* at what Nate had done to me. Which also meant I hadn't cleaned the wound, either. And I was pretty sure it was infected, if the fever and chills were any indication.

I was so screwed.

The flu excuse, as predicted, only got me so far with Victoria. But at least the infection made me look and sound like I was telling the truth.

Could I count that as a win?

Probably not.

On the sixth day, my phone rang for what felt like the hundredth time and I didn't have the strength to ignore her anymore. Every ignored call and text pushed my luck that she would show up at my door, asking uncomfortable questions that I didn't know how to answer. Not to mention, one look at me, and I was sure she would know the truth.

Or some version of it. While I was sure I looked sick, it was also obvious I was hurt. And that Nate was nowhere to be found, doting on me as a loving boyfriend should.

So, I finally broke down and answered.

"Hey, Vic." I sat on the couch and winced, hoping she didn't hear the gasp I tried to bite back. Moving still hurt like a motherfucker, no matter how gently and slowly I did it.

"Where the hell have you been? And don't you dare say you've been sick with the flu. I know better than that. You still came to work with a fucking ruptured appendix."

I swallowed thickly after having been caught so easily over my lie. Except, it wasn't a lie. I *was* sick, but I just wasn't honest about what led to getting sick.

"That was just a pain in one spot. This is a fever and my entire body feels like it's on fire and going to fall apart."

Her sympathetic noise made me realize maybe I'd laid it on a little too thick. The last thing I needed was her trying to come over and play nurse to make me feel better.

"I swear, V, I'll be fine," I muttered as I pulled another blanket over me on the couch.

My refusal to go back to bed had nothing to do with Nate or the memories there. It was just easier with the wound on my side to sit on the couch rather than lie in bed, or at least that was what I told myself.

"Maybe I should come over and take you to the doctor or at least one of the urgent care clinics." Her worry was appreciated, but I couldn't let her bully me into that. I couldn't explain to a doctor what had happened to me.

Or to Victoria.

"I already told you, it's the flu. There's nothing they can do. I have some cold and flu medicine I've been taking, and it's helping a bit." That wasn't a complete lie. I did have the medicine, not that I had actually taken any of it.

The lies were getting to me. I wanted to tell her so badly, so why didn't I? Why was I still protecting him?

I also still didn't understand why he didn't kill me. I was a loose end, a witness to his crimes. Instead, he stitched me up and put me in my bed, making sure I had a bottle of ibuprofen and a bottle of unopened water on my nightstand for when I woke. He could have come back at any time to finish the job, but he didn't.

Would he answer if I texted? I had so many questions that I needed the answers to. Would he finally be honest with me if I asked?

What if he ran and he's gone?

The thought made my blood run cold. Did he leave?

Of course, he did. He would have to be stupid not to have fled, as he would have had no reason to believe I didn't report him the moment I woke up.

Because it was what I should have done.

"Aiden? Are you listening to me?" Victoria's impatient voice cut through my thoughts, making me wince.

Shit, I'd spaced out and forgot I'd been on the phone.

"Sorry, Vic. What did you say?" I grimaced at how much of a bad friend and partner I had been recently. But I couldn't worry about that when I had more pressing matters to attend to.

Like healing from a knife wound. That had been inflicted by my boyfriend. Who was a serial killer.

Just as she started to repeat herself, there was a knock on the front door.

Jesus Christ. Would no one leave me alone today?

"Sorry, V, someone's here. I'll have to call you back." I hung up and winced as I pulled myself off the couch. I had to take a moment to catch my breath before I stumbled through the house to get to the door.

Whoever was at the door banged a few more times. Each time, my heart raced faster and faster.

I couldn't help but fear that it was the police. That they had found out about Nate and what he had done. Maybe someone had seen him bring me into the house, but then never saw me leave, and reported a welfare check.

Fuck.

Or, whoever he had killed at his house had left a trail. We had said the killer was devolving, spiraling. And killing in his own home would have been the epitome of desperation. I thought I remembered seeing a food bag on his counter.

Oh, Nate, what did you do?

The timing of Victoria's call and the knocking made me suspicious. Had she been checking to see where I was? To see if Nate was with me?

When I got to the door, the large blanket trailing behind me, wrapped around my shoulders. I pulled it tighter around me, like a shield as I yanked the door open without even bothering to look to see who it was.

When I saw him standing there, my vision swam, and I had to grab a hold of the doorframe to keep upright.

"What the fuck are you doing here?"

33

NATHAN

I agonized over what to do, even going as far as changing my mind at least a half-dozen times. It was so unlike me. Normally, I didn't care about such things—about people. When I made my mind up about something, that was it. I didn't care enough to change my mind.

But when it came to Aiden, he mattered.

I waffled between the urge to run and find somewhere new to settle so that I could maintain my freedom and the desire to make sure he was all right. Of course, I didn't think it would be four days later, and I still wouldn't have heard from him—or, more likely, the police.

To be honest, I'd been pretty certain that within twenty-four hours, the SWAT team would have been breaking down my door, and a big man with a gun in my face would have been begging me to give him a reason to shoot. But none of that happened.

In fact, it was as though none of it happened. The radio silence from Aiden was the only clue to the reality of the events from that night.

Unable to take the silence, the unknowing, any longer, I did the only thing I could.

I decided to head to his place. I wasn't going to knock or let him know I was there, but I needed to make sure he was okay. That resolve lasted until I actually got to his house and parked my car.

The next thing I knew, I was knocking on his door like the idiot I was. But there was no answer. His car was in the driveway, so I knew he was home. So, I knocked again, louder. And again, even louder.

My heart raced in my chest as a thousand scenarios bombarded me of what could have happened. Of everything that could have gone wrong. Maybe the wound had reopened and he bled out without anyone knowing. What if he had fallen and got injured and no one was there to help him?

Fuck. I never should have left him alone. Especially for so long, without checking on him. If anything happened to my little bird, I'd never forgive myself.

I went to knock again, praying he was just asleep or in the bathroom and would open the door any minute.

But as I raised my hand, the door swung open, and my heart sank.

"What the fuck are you doing here?" Aiden spat out.

His body immediately recoiled when he saw me, grabbing onto the doorway to keep his balance. Though, from the looks of him, I wasn't sure it was due to the surprise of seeing me. He looked like shit, all pale and sweaty, with a blanket pulled tight around him.

I let out a sigh and grabbed his elbow to usher him back into the house. He tried to push me off, but he was barely able to keep himself standing, let alone fight me off.

"You're sick." My words were obvious, but he tried to argue anyway.

"I'm fine. You need to leave." Aiden batted away my hand that was trying to feel his clammy forehead.

I stopped and stared at him, frowning. Something wasn't right. Okay, a lot of things weren't right.

"You're still wearing the same clothes." My head tilted to the side as I assessed him, trying to piece together what happened in the last four days. "Shit, you haven't done anything to take care of yourself, or the wound, have you?"

Aiden flinched, and I wasn't sure if it was because of the reminder of what I'd done to him or because I called him out about his lack of self-care. Either way, it didn't matter. If he wouldn't take care of himself, then I'd do it for him.

"Go sit on the couch. I'll get what I need to clean the wound. Then, after I wrap it up, you're taking a shower and putting on some clean clothes." My nose wrinkled at the smell wafting off him.

There was another jiggle of guilt at my conscience, at the knowledge I had done this to him and then just *left him*.

"I'm fine, Nate. Go away." The way he tried to assert himself was cute. Or, it might have been if his body hadn't been wracked with chills so hard his teeth practically gnashed together as he tried to talk.

I let out a sigh and led him to the couch. Despite his attempts at protesting, he moved with me and obediently sat. Ignoring the glare he shot me from under the blanket, I set out to get what I needed.

On the way over, I wrestled with what I should do or tell him. I wanted to be honest. More so than ever, after seeing what my lies had done to him—even though I knew if I had been honest at any point, we would not have gotten to where we were. And I couldn't find it in me to believe that was a bad thing.

It was selfish, but I liked that he had wanted me and loved

me. And I had to believe a part of him still felt that way. How could I not when he hadn't turned me in?

When I got back to him, I sat on the floor at his feet and spread the stuff out next to me.

"I know you're cold, but we have to remove the blankets and your shirt so I can get you cleaned up."

Aiden jerked away, as though I'd slapped him. "F-f-fuck y-you," he bit out.

I let out another sigh and sat back on my heels. "We can do this the easy way or the hard way, little bird," I told him sternly as I caught his gaze. "As it is, you're going to be lucky if you don't need an antibiotic in order to get rid of the infection."

He winced at my words, but I didn't have time to wonder what he'd been thinking about when I said that. The only thing that mattered was getting him better. He could hate me all he wanted when I was done and he was still alive. Because a wound like that being infected had the possibility of being life threatening.

"I'm not leaving until I know you're going to be okay. So you might as well just let me do it, if you want me to go." I changed tactics. Not that I wanted him to kick me out. But I'd do or say anything to get him to listen to me.

Not giving him any other options, I reached up, ignored how he cowered from me, and moved the blankets to the side of the couch and then eased his tank top off. He was so weak, he had no choice but to be compliant in the way I moved him around.

I took a deep breath, steeling myself for whatever I was going to see, and quickly peeled off the tape that held the bandage I'd put on his side before I'd brought him home. When I saw the red puckered skin, I let out a sigh of relief. After I poked around a few times, and there was no sign of any discharge, I looked up at Aiden and offered him a smile.

"You're lucky. I don't think the infection is that bad.

Cleaning it regularly, keeping it dry, and changing the bandages for the next couple of days should do the trick."

Aiden didn't say anything and barely flinched as I applied the disinfectant all around the area. It wasn't until I had the tape in my hand to secure the bandage that he spoke up.

"Why are you doing this?" His voice sounded small and defeated. "Why didn't you just kill me?"

I looked up, but he was looking away from me. I wasn't sure if it was because he didn't want to see my expression or because he didn't want me to see his.

At first, I didn't say anything as I secured a waterproof bandage and tried to think of how to answer him. But it wasn't an easy question, and it didn't have a simple answer.

"How about you get that shower and get dressed? Then, when you're done, I'll tell you everything." I couldn't keep lying to him. More so, I didn't *want* to keep lying to him. When he didn't say anything, I took it as an agreement.

"Can you manage to shower yourself, or do you need help?"

"Yes," he spat out, but then he slumped back against the couch.

"I don't know," he admitted with a sigh. "Maybe."

It sounded like it pained him to admit he needed help, but I was pretty sure it was just *my* help he didn't want. But I didn't want to make him uncomfortable, especially since we had a difficult talk ahead of us. So, I stood up, hooked an arm behind him, helped him off the couch, and walked him to the bathroom.

When we got there, I leaned him against the sink and went to get the shower ready. Then, I herded him over to stand next to it. I kept my eyes on him in case he started to lose his balance, as I quickly shed my clothes and pulled his pants down in as clinical a manner as I could manage.

"Time to get in," I told him softly. "I've got a hold of you, so go as slow as you need to." As promised, I kept my hand on his upper arm as he got under the warm spray. Once he settled in, I quickly followed behind him.

"Keep your hands on the wall while I wash you and get you cleaned up, little bird."

He did as I said, but I could see his shoulders and arms shaking slightly as I squirted his shampoo into my hand.

"Don't call me that." His voice sounded wet and raspy, and I realized his shaking was from silent sobs wracking his body.

I didn't know what to do as I watched him, my hands going to his head and massaging his hair clean. His head fell back, but I tried not to take the reaction personally, given how else he'd been reacting to me since I showed up unannounced.

Not wanting to make him suffer more than I already had, I quickly lathered up his soap and washed him, being mindful of the tender flesh on his side. Once I was done, I grabbed the shower head and rinsed him off. Getting him dry and dressed was a little harder as he started to sway more, having been on his feet for too long.

Instead of taking him back out to the couch, I tucked him into bed.

"You said you were going to tell me everything." His words were an accusation, thinking I was trying to get out of my promise.

I had no intention of doing so, but I needed to collect myself. So I walked out of his room without a word and went to grab us each a bottle of water. When I came back, I let out a sigh when I saw he'd moved and sat up. No doubt ready to get out of bed and hunt me down to make me talk.

"Settle down and stay put." I handed him the water, and my eyes traveled over his naked chest and torso. If he'd been anyone else, I would have admired my handiwork.

Without thinking, I reached out and traced the scars on the opposite side of his fresh wound. "You're the only one I've ever let go."

Aiden's brows furrowed, his lips downturned into a tight frown as he put my actions and words together.

"It was you." It wasn't an accusation or a question, just an acceptance of fact. He sounded resigned. "You're the one who took me when I was seventeen."

"Yes," I admitted as I sank down to my knees in front of him.

His eyes filled with tears, but he turned his head, refusing to let me see them fall. "Why?"

That was a much more difficult question to answer. Then again, maybe it wasn't, given our recent history.

"I was drawn to you. It felt different than what it did with my victims, but I didn't know how to differentiate it. I didn't know what it meant, only that when I saw you for the first time, I knew you were supposed to be mine."

I took a breath and tried to rein in my swirling thoughts. "I'd never felt like that before, but I didn't have the words. I didn't know what emotions to associate with the way you made me feel."

He nodded, still turned away from me. I wanted to take it all back. He'd been so understanding and accepting of me when we had that talk about who and what I was. And while I knew he wouldn't have been able to understand and accept it as a child, if I'd never crossed his path back then, then maybe things could have been different for us.

"I couldn't kill you. So I stitched you up and dropped you off at the park, knowing someone would find you and help you."

Dropping my eyes to my lap, I struggled to find the right words. "I set my little bird free."

His shoulders tensed. "That's what you called me, back then. Your little bird. I didn't remember, but there'd been something about when you said it, that night in the hotel. I still didn't remember, but it triggered, I don't know, something."

My hand itched to touch him, to comfort him. But I knew it would be unwanted, and that knowledge broke my heart.

"Where—Did you stalk me this whole time? Ever since you let me go?" Aiden turned to look at me. His eyes were still wet and shiny, but he hadn't let a single tear spill.

He was so brave, so good. I wished I could have protected him from all this—from *me*.

"No. You moved away, and I thought I'd never see you again." My voice cracked as I was overcome with emotion, remembering how I'd felt all those years ago, thinking I'd lost my little bird forever.

"What now?" Aiden asked.

He finally looked up and met my eyes. "Are you going to kill me now that I know the truth?"

34

AIDEN

I couldn't believe I had just asked a serial killer if he was going to kill me. Then again, I couldn't believe my boyfriend was not only a serial killer, but the same one who had kidnapped me when I was a teenager and let me go.

He let me go twice already. I couldn't be lucky enough to believe he'd let me go a third time.

Sure, I didn't remember the actual events that happened during the time I'd disappeared when he'd kidnapped me, but I wasn't stupid. There was the scar and the questions from the cops, not to mention the reporters and their news stories. I knew I had somehow escaped death.

My heart raced as I watched him stand and start to pace. There was nothing I could do but sit there and wait for him to seal my fate.

"You still—" he started, but cut himself off. "Fuck."

Nate spun away from me and shoved his hands through his hair, tugging on the strands. When he turned back and looked at me, his eyes were full of sorrow, and my heart sank.

He shook his head as he slowly made his way back over to

the bed, but he didn't kneel or get on it with me. Instead, he looked down at me as though I'd just broken his heart.

"Little bird..." His voice cracked. "I could *never* kill you. Don't you see?"

He let out a resigned sigh. "Because it might have taken me a long time to figure it out, but I was finally able to put words to how you made me feel. And those words were that I love you. Or, at least, in the only way I can this time. Though, I guess I can't blame you if you couldn't believe someone like me."

A shudder ran through my body, but it wasn't one of fear or disgust.

The worst part was I did believe him. But we could never be together. I was a cop, and he was a serial killer. We could never work.

"Right." His mask started to slide back in place, his voice going cold and distant as he took a step away from me.

"Well, I suppose this is the part where you tell me you have no choice but to turn me in and ask me not to do anything stupid."

Confusion clouded my thoughts. He was right. It should be what I did next. He was in my home, admitted to being a serial killer, and kidnapping me as a teenager. So why hadn't I thought about it before he mentioned it?

"No," I said, shaking my head. My heart raced, and there was a lump in my throat that made it damn near impossible to swallow. My limbs felt like rubber as I slid off the bed and my heart gave a triumphant fist pump at Nate's instinctual reaction to make sure I was able to stand without falling over.

"Stop." I had no idea what I was saying, but I didn't want the mask, only the real Nate. "Just stop, Nate."

My hand reached out to the nightstand at my side to steady myself.

Nate's shoulders slumped, defeated. He glanced around, but from his expression, he couldn't find what he was looking for. With a sigh, he reached into his pocket and pulled out his phone.

"Here," he said, holding out the phone to me. "I don't know where yours is, but I guess you can use mine to call whoever you need to. And don't worry, I won't do anything stupid."

Shocked, I stood there, not moving. Even when he took a tentative step toward me and placed his phone in my hand before he turned and walked out of the room.

"What the fuck?" There was no one left in the room to answer me, though. I looked down at the phone in my hand and frowned.

He really thought I was going to turn him in.

Fuck, he was an idiot. Or, maybe I was an idiot.

I threw the phone on my bed and walked as quickly as my throbbing body would let me, which wasn't anywhere as fast as I would have liked. I let out a relieved huff when I found him sitting on the couch, where I had been earlier.

"You're a real stupid son of a bitch, you know that?" I practically yelled the words, making him jump, his eyes wide as he stared up at me.

"Why didn't you kill me? You had my unconscious body bleeding out in your arms. Instead, you took care of me, brought me home, and tucked me into bed. Why?" Tears pricked my eyes and blurred my vision as I stood my ground and waited for him to answer me.

Nate cocked his head, confused. "I told you why. I said I couldn't."

"Exactly!" I threw my hands up, well, as best I could before I winced and wrapped my arms around myself instead.

"You couldn't do it. You couldn't kill me. And you didn't think, that in the four days I sat here, alone and confused, that I didn't come to the same fucking conclusion?" I stared at him as though he were missing a few marbles.

"Dumbass," I muttered.

"Wait. What?" His eyes went wide as he stared at me and tried to make sense of what I said.

I shook my head and let out a brittle chuckle. "I couldn't do it any more than you could."

My eyes closed, and I took a deep breath. "Believe me, I thought about it plenty. Hell, even now, I know it's the right thing to do."

I bit my lip, looked down at him, and shook my head.

Nate slowly reached up and tugged at my hands, which still gripped my upper arms, and pulled me gently, just enough so I took the couple of steps needed to close the distance between us. His hands rubbed up and down my arms, a look of wonder on his face as he stared up at me.

I knew what he was thinking, because I'd been thinking the same thing ever since I woke up alone in my bed after our confrontation.

That we'd never have this again.

Never touch, never kiss, never love.

But there we were, and it was right there for us, if we were brave, or stupid, enough to reach out and take it.

He let go of my hands and went to my hips, gently easing me down so I straddled his thighs, watching me for any sign of pain or hesitance. But there was none. Nothing ever felt more right than being with him, as crazy as it sounded.

"What does this mean, little bird? I need you to be very clear and very plain about what you want." His words were slow and his caress on my hips and lower back was soft and soothing.

"I... I don't know how we can make this work. But I love you, Daddy, and know I can't turn you in." I shook my head. "But I'm a cop, and I don't know how I can go to work every day knowing what I know." My words were soft and anguished.

A thought struck me and I glanced up at him, surprised I hadn't put the pieces together before. "Wait. That cop. When we had our first movie date. That wasn't really about sleeping with his closeted son, was it?"

Nate let out a laugh. "Actually, it was. Trust me. No one is as surprised as me, with how much he hated me and was hell-bent on ruining my life, that he didn't discover my secret."

I hummed in response. "Dumb luck, I guess. Just like it took so long for the cop you were sleeping with to put the pieces together."

He brought my hands up to his lips and kissed the knuckles. "I worried every day that it would be the last time I would see you."

The pained look on his face was too much. "So, what do we do?"

We didn't have many options. But I couldn't let him go to jail. I couldn't lose him.

"We could leave," he suggested, his warm palms blazing a path of heat and love everywhere they touched. "Fly away with me, little bird."

I scoffed at the suggestion, but his eyes told me how serious he was. Swallowing my words, I considered him.

"How? Where would we go?"

I shook my head, reality crashing down on me. "I can't leave my parents. After what they went through before, I couldn't disappear on them. Not again."

A heavy sigh escaped my lips as I leaned forward and put my head on Nate's chest.

"You could just quit your job. We could stay here for a while, and then go."

When I went to interject, he put a hand over my mouth and continued. "I don't mean run away. We can plan a move, maybe in six months or so. But you wouldn't be able to tell anyone but your parents."

He let out a sigh. "Eventually, though, we would have to

move on to somewhere more permanent, but *no one* would be able to know about that."

Was that something I could do? Could I give up my job?

"I can't just quit my job, Daddy. I have a mortgage and bills to pay." While I would have loved to give in to his idea, it wasn't feasible. Though, that didn't mean I couldn't start looking for a new job right away.

"Sure you can. I'll pay off your mortgage and pay your bills. In fact, you could just sell your house if you want and move in with me."

I barked out a laugh so hard I had to clutch at my side as it felt like daggers were stabbing me. "Fuck."

Nate looked at me with concern. "You okay?"

I nodded and felt him relax under me.

"What was so funny anyway?" The perplexed look on his face made me snort.

"Well, everything we just went through aside, it's kind of soon, isn't it?"

I paused, another question demanding to be asked. "Okay, I need to know. What the fuck is with your house?"

Nate cocked his head to the side. "What do you mean?"

"I mean," I said, drawing out the word, "it's like a fucking mansion. Is that really your house? Why? How?"

Embarrassed, I glanced away. "I mean. I did look you up a little, after I saw you with our witness. Sorry," I mumbled. "And I saw some of the things about your parents and how you inherited some money from them. But like, that seems like *a lot*."

He let out a chuckle, and his cheeks actually turned pink with embarrassment. "Yeah, that's my house," he said with a shrug. "I mean, I don't know why I didn't say anything. I guess I don't really think about it."

"I guess I didn't realize you were secretly rich, even with the clothes and the car." I let out a chuckle as my arms encircled his neck.

"Aiden... I... I didn't think it *was* a secret."

My jaw practically dropped to the floor. "Wait. What?"

"I told you, I own properties, rehab them, repurpose them, and sell them."

"Riiiight. Like a flipper." I was so confused. I'd watched house flipping shows, so I knew there was money to be made, but it wasn't *mansion* kind of money.

Nate shook his head. "Shit. Yes, but no. I guess we never really got into it and talked about it. At the time, it was easier the less you really knew about me. Though, people do know my name in the business world, and know what my name means."

He shot me an apologetic smile.

"So I do residential and commercial properties. There are a multitude of corporations that I operate under—we won't get to that," he said with a *look* that had me biting my tongue. "But I inherited my parents' development company when they died."

"Right. Yeah, like I said. I saw that you inherited that and some money from them. But I didn't see anything that talked about actual figures." I let out a sigh. "I guess, once I started looking, I realized I didn't really want to know too much. It wasn't giving me information that I thought I was looking for, more like stuff I'd rather know by getting to know you."

Nate's face went blank and his eyes glazed over in a way that made me want to throw up. He was shutting down, letting the mask slip back into place.

I reached out and cupped his face in my hands, but I didn't say anything. He just needed to know I was there with him, to ground him, the way his hands rubbing small circles on my back grounded me.

He blew out a breath and then took a deep one. "When they

died, the company was worth just under a billion dollars, and now, just that company is worth double."

My body went still, eyes wide, lungs frozen, and I stared at him.

To be honest, what he said broke my brain. It was incomprehensible to me and I realized then that was a sort of wealth he'd always known. In fact, it was probably what had kept him out of prison.

"Holy shit," I muttered.

I let out a hysterical laugh that had him side-eyeing me. "I guess I know how you stayed off the cops' radar for so long."

He gave me a rueful smile but didn't say anything.

"And you have *other* companies, too."

He started to say something, and I moved my hands from his cheeks to his mouth, shaking my head. "I don't want to know."

My eyes closed, and I tried to relearn how to breathe properly. His hands kneading into my skin helped ground me. When I opened my eyes and stared into his, all I saw was his love for me.

It might not look the same as it would on anyone else, but that didn't make me doubt it. In fact, it made me love him even more. There was nothing he wouldn't do for me, and he proved that by killing for me—even if it had been completely unnecessary.

Because once all the pieces had slid into place, I had realized that was what he had done with Clint. He had touched me. Made me uncomfortable. And Nate had killed him. *For me.*

I wasn't sure how I felt about that. But I did know one thing for sure. And that was how I felt about Nate.

About my Daddy.

Fuck, I was in love with a serial killer.

But as I leaned in and brushed our lips together, I knew no one would ever love me as completely or as fiercely as Nate.

"I love you, Daddy," I whispered against his lips and sealed my fate.

35

AIDEN

The last thing I expected when I joined the force was that I'd one day be handing in my resignation. Especially under these circumstances. That I'd be leaving because of the person I had fallen in love with.

Not that I would want to change anything about it.

In the last week and a half since I had discovered my boyfriend was a serial killer, I'd had a lot to think about. There had been so much he'd finally shared with me and options I'd been left with. I'd been surprised when he had been adamant I had the freedom that if at any point I had second thoughts, I was allowed to walk away, even if it meant turning him in and having him arrested.

The feeling of knowing he thought I was worth that risk, the risk to his freedom, it was a heady feeling. But I knew in my heart that even if he hurt me again, I could never turn him in.

Because for me, my Daddy was worth the risk too. He was it for me, just like I was it for him.

For what I knew would be the last time, I walked into the precinct and gave Enid a sheepish smile as she went to hug me. I shook my head and she stepped back, eyeing me warily.

"Aiden Cooper, where the devil have you been? And what do you mean *no* to my hugs?" Her hands were on her hips as she stared at me over her glasses, which had me glancing back toward the door, wishing I could sprint back out and go back home to my Daddy. But I straightened my spine, determined to get this done.

Today.

"Sorry, Enid. You know you're my girl." I gave her a sheepish smile. "But with all the throwing up and everything, you know how it is. Every muscle in my chest and back feels like I twisted and rearranged it."

She gave me a sympathetic look and squeezed my shoulders. "Aw, honey. I hope you at least let Victoria come and take care of you while you were getting better."

I bit my lip and winced at my best friend's name. "No, but my boyfriend was over and he took good care of me, Enid."

Her eyes lit up like I'd given her the best present. "A boyfriend? You scoundrel! Why am I always the last to hear the good gossip?"

With a laugh, I shrugged and gave her a sheepish smile. "Sorry?"

Looking over toward my desk, where Victoria was eyeing me, I felt my resolve slipping, but I knew I couldn't count on Enid to protect me from Vic's clutches forever. "Well, I better get to it, I guess."

She glanced over and gave a chuckle. "Good luck with that one, honey."

I snorted in agreement. It was time to face the one-man firing squad.

But first, I needed to get past her and the rest of the cops in the precinct, get to the chief, and do what I had come to do.

Easier said than done. Especially when facing Victoria. But I ignored her attempts to corner me and answer her questions.

This wasn't about her. As much as I loved her and would miss her when this was over, I needed to let her go.

Turning my back to her, I greeted my other friends and colleagues. They were all happy to see me up and about, all razzing me about being down with the *man flu* when nothing else would get me. But I accepted their good-natured teasing, knowing it would be the last time. Even if they didn't.

It felt strange knowing that I was never going to be working with them again. There was a pang of longing, as I'd miss the camaraderie that came from our time together, but I knew I was ready for the next chapter of my life to begin.

Slowly, I made my way past them, keeping my eyes forward so I didn't give Vic any ammunition to butt in before I could talk to Chief Vasquez.

With a fortifying breath, I walked past Victoria's and my desks, ignoring her hissed questions she threw my way under her breath. My shoulders were held back, head held high, as I strolled to the chief's office and knocked on the door.

"Come in!" he barked and for a moment, I hesitated.

Not because I questioned whether or not what I was doing was the right thing, but Chief Vasquez was an intimidating man and if anyone would be astute enough to see past my bullshit and call me out on my lies, besides Vic, it would be him.

But I knew what I had to do. It was time for me to quit my job, even if we weren't going to be moving on quite yet.

I opened the door and peeked my head through the opening. "Good morning, Chief Vasquez. Do you have a moment?" Nerves clutched at my throat and stomach, and my hands shook as I opened the door further at his nod.

"Detective Cooper, good to see you're all rested up and recovering well."

My cheeks pinked as I thought of everyone at the station welcoming me back from my bout of the *flu*.

"You could have just faxed your paperwork over to HR." He frowned at the paper in my hand.

It had been a little over two weeks that I'd been out of work while I recovered from the nasty gash Nate had sliced into my side after I'd walked in on him killing a delivery driver. But thankfully, with the way my schedule rotated, I'd only missed five work days. The last couple of those, I'd spent being taken care of by none other than Nate.

Unfortunately, that was enough that they expected some sort of work release from a doctor, which I couldn't provide.

We hadn't been left with a lot of options on how to handle the situation.

The fact still shocked me that he hadn't run and had come to make sure I was all right and took it upon himself to take care of me when he noticed I hadn't been in a state to do it myself. It was things like that that made me love him, despite the fact that he was a serial killer and a psychopath.

"Thank you, sir," I offered with a tentative smile as my fingers played with the edge of the paper in my hand. The fact I was dressed down, even for a plain clothed detective, wouldn't have escaped his notice. Nor did it escape my partner's keen eye, given her incessant questioning once I'd arrived.

"I don't want to take up much of your time, and I only have a moment, but I wanted to give you this." I took a deep breath as I handed the letter over, with minimal shaking to my hands, thank you very much.

"First of all, I want to thank you for all the opportunities you've given me, sir. I've learned a lot from you and the department. But my life is taking a different direction and working here just doesn't fit into my new plans."

"New plans?" Chief Vasquez asked, one eyebrow raised as he frowned at the letter of resignation in his hands, stating that it would be in effect immediately. While it might not have been exactly professional to leave without notice, I couldn't stay on the case that was trying to put my Daddy in jail.

"Yes, sir. My partner is a land developer and an opportunity arose on the other side of the country that the company is looking to acquire and the project is expected to last at least a year. Starting shortly after the new year. And I'm not interested in a long-distance relationship, so I decided to go with him."

"Partner?" The shock on Vasquez's face was obvious. I'd spent a lot of time at my desk bemoaning my single life and lack of dating prospects. "I hadn't realized you were dating anyone."

The frown returned and it left me slightly squeamish, though I couldn't figure out why.

I nodded, trying to keep my nervous fidgeting to a minimum while maintaining eye contact. The chief was a shark, and if he smelled blood in the water, he'd latch on and never let go until I spilled all of my secrets.

"Yeah, it's only recently become serious. But he's not someone I'm willing to let go of." Thinking about Nate made me smile and I couldn't wait to get back home to him and get started on the adventure that our lives would be.

While it wasn't going to be anywhere near what I thought my life would be like, it was the one I wanted. Anything with him was what I wanted. Even if it meant that I had to start helping him. While I didn't revel in using my detective skills for such purposes, I had to make sure Nate minimized his risk of getting caught because I couldn't live without him.

I *refused* to live without him.

Vasquez nodded and gave a heavy sigh. "If this is what you really want, Cooper, then I wish you the best of luck in your future endeavors. Don't hesitate to reach out if you need a reference or letter of recommendation.

"Thank you, Chief," I replied with a smile, even though I knew it wouldn't be necessary. The last thing I wanted to do was join a different police force and still end up hunting Nate. Plus, I couldn't leave a trail as to where I was going once we left town.

Not to mention, Nate was *super rich* and wanted nothing more than to keep me naked and pampered at home. If he could have me naked, barefoot, and *pregnant* in the kitchen at all times, I was sure he would. Especially given once I'd put the idea in his head, he'd gently scooped me up into his arms, mindful of my still-healing stitches, and laid me out on the bed and ravaged me all night, filling me with his cum, not wanting even a drop to spill.

The memory made me shiver and I knew I needed to get out of there fast before I embarrassed myself by having to walk through the station with an obvious boner.

Not that I would see any of them ever again once I crossed the threshold out into the world. The only one I'd miss was Vic and I knew I'd have to be careful about how I extricated myself from her life.

I quickly shook the Chief's hand, then relinquished my badge and gun.

"Goodbye, sir," I said as I opened the door.

I should have expected to find my partner, *former partner*, standing on the other side of the door, arms crossed, with a scowl on her face and toes tapping.

"Well?" she demanded as I walked past her. "Spill it, Aiden. What the hell is going on with you?"

Out of the corner of my eye, I saw her reach for me so I quickly stopped and spun to face her. The last thing I needed was for her to grab hold of me and pull or yank me. There'd be no hiding the sharp sting of skin pulling against the stitches if she got her hands on me.

"Vict—" I started, but she cut me off before I could even finish her name.

"Don't you dare *Victoria* me, Aiden Cooper! What the hell is going on?" She poked a finger at my chest with each word, and while it wasn't ideal, it was definitely better than her trying to manhandle me and pulling on my stitches.

I held up my hands in surrender and sighed. There had been a calculated risk in talking to Victoria first versus after it was already done, and I couldn't help but think maybe I had bet on the wrong horse in this scenario.

"I just gave Chief Vasquez my letter of resignation."

She pulled back, her mouth slack as she tried to process my words. The hurt was clear on her face and my heart plummeted. The last thing I wanted to do was hurt her.

"Resignation? What? Why?" With a frown, she glared up at me and I would have taken a step back if the action hadn't been like waving a red flag in front of a bull.

"This is about *him*, isn't it? Is he making you quit? Trying to control you? I told you—"

"Stop." My tone held no room for argument. I knew Vic was worried about me with Nate and I regretted ever telling her about his diagnosis. Especially in light of the new development of finding out that he was a serial killer.

Her eyes hardened as she stared at me. "So, it's true. You're leaving. Moving away?"

Shocked, I took a step back. "How? Alyssa, did she tell you that? Why the hell are you suddenly all buddy-buddy with my sister?"

It didn't make sense. We had been friends for a long time, but she had never shown an interest in being friends with my sister before. Not until Nate came into my life.

"He's manipulating you, Aiden, and you can't even see it. Isolating you from your family by convincing you to quit your job, move away from your family and friends. This isn't you."

I shook my head. "I had decided to quit on my own. That wasn't his decision to make, Vic. You need to leave me, my family, and my boyfriend alone."

Her eyes blazed as she got in my face, hissing. "He's a fucking psychopath."

"Thought that word wasn't used anymore, Victoria? You're a fucking hypocrite." I tried to push past her, but she blocked my path, drawing the eyes of the other cops around us.

"Get out of my way, Vic." The last thing I wanted was to start something in the middle of the precinct, but I also wasn't going to let her bully me.

"Is there a problem here?" Ramirez asked as he stood from his desk and made his way over.

Victoria glanced back and forth between us for a moment and put her hands up in surrender as she took a step back. "Nope. You know how it is."

"I'm sorry, Vic. You're my friend, my best friend, and I love you. But Nate, he's off-limits to whatever bullshit this is." I waved my hand in her direction.

The fact that she'd never met him and never tried to give him a chance stung.

"I love him and that's all that matters."

I left her sputtering as I walked away. A part of my heart ached for pushing her away, but I knew it was necessary. Not just to protect Nate, but to protect Victoria as well.

36
NATHAN

I paced back and forth as I waited for Aiden to return from the police station. Everything in me told me I could trust him, but that small voice in the back of my head that told me to trust no one, still hadn't learned to shut the fuck up.

When I spotted his car pulling up the driveway, I let out a sigh of relief and went to meet him at the door. I hated any moment I didn't have eyes on him. Anything could happen and I wouldn't be held responsible for my actions if I ever lost him.

I was a possessive, obsessive psychopath, so sue me. He loved it, and me. That was all that mattered.

His smile was dazzling as he jumped out of the car and raced up to wrap his arms around me. I held him tight, while still being mindful of his healing side, my face buried in his neck as I breathed him in.

Fuck, I never wanted to let go of this man. But all too soon, he was pulling back and dragging me into the house.

"How did it go?" I could guess, but I hoped it went well, though from the way his shoulders sagged, I knew it wasn't all smooth sailing.

"It wasn't bad. The police chief accepted my resignation and told me if I needed a letter of recommendation, or even wanted my old job back, all I had to do was ask." He trailed off and had a faraway look in his eyes.

"Vic," he whispered, "on the other hand..." A deep sigh escaped from his lips and he knocked his forehead against mine. "She's not taking it well that I'm leaving."

My little bird pulled away and I felt a chill envelop me as he moved toward the kitchen and grabbed a beer from the fridge. We both knew she had been the wild card and the only one he would actually miss when we left. Not to mention, I knew that she had tried to warn him against me and that there had to be a million alarm bells ringing for her.

For both of them, really.

I sighed as I followed him into the kitchen and watched him grow more agitated as he wandered around. Though I wasn't sure if it was from him worrying about whether she would try to cause trouble for us or from the sorrow he felt about leaving her, and his family, behind. But I had to trust him to take care of his own problems and only offer my support when he asked for it—or, at least that was what he kept trying to tell me.

But honestly?

Fuck that.

He was my man, my heart and my soul, and I'd be damned if I let anyone get in the way of that or let someone hurt him.

"Do you think she'll be a problem?" My voice was soft and I tried to sound unthreatening, but the way his back stiffened as he stared into the fridge told me I hadn't succeeded.

"No," he bit out as he reached in and started to yank things into his arms.

My eyebrow shot up as he kicked the fridge door closed and slammed the pickle jar so hard on the counter, I feared it would shatter. Before he could injure himself, I walked over and wrapped my arms around him and held him against me. The way his body melted against me made my heart soar.

There had been a lot of things in the last couple of weeks that I knew had caused him distress, and I hated to be the cause of it for even a moment.

"Little bird," I whispered as my lips ghosted across his ear. "I know I'm asking a lot of you and I hope you know that every day I thank every deity I have never bothered to believe in, for bringing you into my life."

My lips grazed his jaw, my throat tightening at the twinges of emotion that threatened to shake me to my core. "For letting me love you, and for the miracle of you loving me in return, despite all the sacrifices you have to make for me."

Aiden let out a sigh and his head lolled to the side, exposing his neck to my wandering lips. "Nothing about loving you is a chore or a sacrifice, Daddy. I love you and I'm here because this is where I want to be."

He turned in my arms and wrapped his own around my neck and pulled me into a searing kiss. The type of kiss that is a brand, a claim. I was as much his as he was mine.

I couldn't believe how selfless my little bird was. He was a miracle I'd never deserve but would always cherish. "I love you so fucking much."

He smiled up at me and cupped my cheeks before stealing another kiss. "I love you, too."

My gut clenched with guilt. "I wish I could stop, for you. You deserve that. To be with someone who is normal, who doesn't have these urges that drives him. But I—"

"Hey, hey." He cut me off, squeezing my cheeks together tight as his smile turned to a frown.

Fuck.

"Look at me. And listen to me. Very carefully. I know you would change for me if you could. I know that. I do. You've already explained that you can't, and why, and the consequences if you did try."

He let out a frustrated sigh that left me even more confused. "And it's not up to you to say what I deserve or don't deserve."

"I didn't mean—"

"Yeah, you did."

My mouth snapped shut and I stared at him for a moment. Things had gone off the rails somehow and I wasn't sure how or why. And I didn't know how to get things back on track. I still had so much I wanted to say, but I didn't know how. Not when he was starting to get angry.

I let out a frustrated grunt. "I was just trying to say that while I can't change what I do, I can change how I go about it."

Aiden froze and I pulled away, giving him the space he needed to sit up. He stared at me, blinking like he couldn't comprehend the meaning of my words.

I shoved my hand through my hair and tried not to get agitated with him and take out my feelings on him. None of this was his fault. He had no experience in dealing with any of this. It was up to me to make him understand.

"You're giving up so much. Sacrificing so much. But I feel like I'm just taking from you and not giving anything in return."

When he opened his mouth to undoubtedly rebuke my sentiment, I silenced him with a kiss.

"But there is something I can give you. You're a cop. You have amazing instincts, whether you believe it or not, after your experience with me."

When I shot him a grin, he rolled his eyes and shoved me away with a wet laugh.

"No, I'm serious, little bird. You do. And I can give you the gift of using those instincts to find people who have escaped justice. People who have gotten away with the most vile, heinous crimes. And I can punish them."

Aiden's face drained of color as I spoke and I feared I'd

come up with the worst possible solution. I'd thought being a cop, he would want to see criminals who had clearly been guilty but got away with their crimes, be punished. That he would be happy if I turned my focus from random victims to those who deserved to die.

Clearly, I had misstepped somewhere along the lines.

"Aiden?" My voice came out shaky and unsure when he still hadn't said anything after a couple of minutes. In fact, he hadn't even moved or looked at me.

"If I'm out of line, please tell me, little bird. And it was just a suggestion. You don't ever have to do anything you don't want to do."

He looked up at me, a beautiful frown marring his face, his eyes watery and teeth digging into his teeth. Normally, that would be a big no-no, but given the way I'd just sent him into a tailspin, I figured I could let it go that once.

"Yo-you want me t-to find your victims?" His lip trembled and he caught it between his teeth. For once, I didn't pull it back and scold him.

I smoothed his hair away from his face. "Don't think about it like that, little bird. Think of it more like I want to save the rest of the people who are sharing in this miserable existence."

The questions were there, rapid firing in his eyes. Along with horror and just a touch of intrigue. It was obvious a part of him was more comfortable with me only killing people who were truly evil and deserved to die.

Made things palatable. But if it was something he truly didn't want a part in, then I wouldn't force him. I'd never force him. "If you would rather I do it alone, I will. It's something I'm used to doing alone. But I thought maybe you would want to be a part of this and make sure they truly deserved it."

I almost felt guilty for the war that clearly played out across his face.

Almost. But this was a part of me. And if he was going to be with me, then he needed to be comfortable with all parts of me. Not necessarily being an active participant, or even discussing my victimology, but in having the knowledge of who and what I was.

Or we were going to be doomed before we ever really had a chance.

And I wasn't going to let that happen, not if it was up to me.

It was time I showed my little bird just what he meant to me as I scooped him up in my arms, ever mindful of his healing wounds, and took him up to what would still be our bedroom for the next three weeks.

The deadline loomed over us, and it was longer than I was comfortable with, but I needed to give him time to work on his parents to get them used to the idea that he was moving away and they wouldn't see him as often as they were used to.

I'd give him the holidays, Christmas and New Year's. Hell, I'd give him anything.

But I liked his parents and his sister, and I didn't want to hurt them either, with Aiden moving away. So, I was happy to be able to give them all one more holiday season together before we left. After that, their time together would get briefer and briefer.

Sure, there would be a few visits for the first year or two. But slowly, he would be forced to make them fewer and farther apart. I knew it was going to kill him, but knowing his love for me was that strong left the heart I'd thought to be long-dead beat rapidly in my chest.

I gently lowered him onto our bed, nipping along his jaw as I did. The moan he let out went straight to my cock that ached to plunge back into him. But I had to refrain. He was still healing and the last thing I'd do was hurt him even more than I already had.

After making sure he was comfortable, I helped him get out of his heavy sweatshirt. When he grimaced as I tugged it over his head, I pulled up his undershirt, silencing his protests with a single raised eyebrow.

He let out a huff, but leaned back on the bed, letting me inspect the wound. The stitches had started to dissolve and there was no redness or sign of infection, which was good. All the swelling had gone down as of a few days ago, which I had been relieved to see.

"Do you need any painkillers, little bird?"

He shook his head. There was a mischievous look on his face that had me tilting my head, trying to figure out what he was thinking.

"I just need you, Daddy," he whispered as he sat up and wrapped his arms around my neck. His lips found mine and I was never to deny him anything he wanted and I hummed in satisfaction as his tongue sought entrance.

Mindful of his side and the strain he was undoubtedly putting on it, I shifted our positions as gently as I could, lying down with him on my side.

"You always have me, little bird." I nipped at his bottom lip, tugging it into my mouth and sucking on it. His hips rocked back and forth, rutting against my thigh. He'd been a needy little bird since I'd come back, but I had to be a good Daddy and put my foot down, despite hating to deny him.

He was healing and I couldn't risk hurting him. It would kill me.

"Daddy," he whined as he rocked faster against me, clearly ready to burst. I put my hand on his hip to steady him and he growled in frustration when he was unable to rock against me anymore.

I chuckled at his antics, but he scowled at me, clearly not amused. "Patience, little bird."

"No. I'm done being patient, Daddy. I want you to fuck me."

My heart stuttered. When did my boy become so petulant?

But I couldn't deny I loved him being so bold and demanding of what he wanted.

I reached up and caressed his cheek. His eyes fluttered closed and he nuzzled into my touch. "I don't want to hurt you. You're still healing."

He slumped against me and made a pathetic noise that didn't make me feel any better. I hated to deny him and if he was anywhere near as frustrated as I was, I could understand where he was coming from.

"If it's too much, I'll tell you. I promise. But I feel like I'm going to burst." The look on his face was adorable. I wasn't used to seeing him pout, but it was something I could get used to.

Or not, because I could feel my resolve wavering.

I heaved a sigh and looked at the heavens for the strength to do what was right by him. But he was a grown man, and if he wanted something, I should trust him to know his body and his limits.

My gaze met his and I eyed him warily.

"I need your word that if it's too much, you say something immediately. We can start slow and build up to penetrative sex again. It doesn't have to be that—"

"Yes," he demanded, cutting me off, "it does have to be that. Now."

A laugh tore from my chest at his blatant desire. But I quickly sobered at the way he glared at me. "Sorry, I'm not laughing at you. Not really. You're just too cute."

"I am cute. Which is why you should fuck me, Daddy." He pouted.

Another chuckle escaped unbidden and I leaned up and stole a kiss.

"You want to ride Daddy's cock, little bird?"

His breath caught in his chest as his eyes went wide as saucers. A low whine rumbled from his lips as he nodded enthusiastically.

I smirked as I leaned up and caught him under the arms, gently laying him down. "Stay here, while I get my little bird all prepped and ready for his Daddy."

He threw his head back with a muttered, "Fuck."

Slowly, I pulled his pants down and revealed his leaking cock that bounced back, and I swallowed it down as I reached up and put a hand on his chest to keep him in place so he couldn't jump and hurt himself.

"Fuck! Daddy, yes. Please, fuck." His hands fisted the sheets under him, and I grinned as I bobbed up and down his length, swallowing it whole.

While he was distracted with my mouth, I reached over and grabbed the lube off the nightstand and flipped the cap open and squeezed some onto my fingers. I rubbed them together, allowing the gel to warm a little before I brought them to his entrance.

The first finger found his entrance and he tensed for a moment before he relaxed, letting out a breath to let it in. But I didn't push. Instead, I circled around his hole and teased his rim, driving sounds out of him I'd never heard before. But I wasn't looking to drive him too mad, considering he was hurt.

Having pity on him, I slowly slid the first finger in and he hissed in approval. His head shot up, gaze seeking mine as his teeth bit down hard on his lip to keep from crying out.

I let go of his cock and moved up his body to catch his lips in a bruising kiss. "Don't hold back, little bird. I want all of your sounds. They belong to Daddy, remember."

He nodded and cried out as I crooked my finger, finding that bundle of nerves inside him that lit him up like a firework on the Fourth of July.

My palm had to press down on him to stop him from trying to fuck himself on my finger. "Tsk tsk. Are you in charge, baby?"

With a pout, he shook his head, but it didn't stop him from

trying to swivel his hips to get me to brush over his prostate again.

I gave him a stern look as I slipped a second finger in and began to scissor him open. He threw his head back on the pillow and whimpered.

"Oh, God. Oh, fuck, yes." I hadn't even nudged his prostate again and his cock was pulsing like it was going to erupt.

Not wanting to end things early, I wrapped a fist around his base to keep him from coming and he whined in frustration. I let out a chuckle as I slowly stoked the fist up and down his cock as I continued to work his hole open, adding a third finger.

"I'm ready, Daddy. Please fuck me now." His eyes were wide and pleading, with a tear in the corner that I chased away with my lips.

"So beautiful. And all mine," I whispered as I released his weeping dick and ran my fingers up and down his torso. Tracing his old scars sent a shiver of anticipation through him, but I knew better than to go anywhere near the new wound yet.

"Yours, Daddy. All yours."

I gave him a soft kiss and lay down flat on my back and let him maneuver himself at his own pace to straddle my hips. It took a minute, but I was glad to see him take the time he needed rather than rush and hurt himself.

"That's it, baby. Easy does it." Both of my hands were on his hips to hold him steady and keep him from tumbling as he sat above my waiting cock. "Hold on to my shoulders or the headboard, whichever you need, and I'll hold myself still and you lower yourself down at your pace."

He gave a quick nod, his eyes boring into mine. I wanted to tug his lip from between his teeth again, but I didn't have the working braincells, or limbs, as he started to move down and sheath himself.

"Oh, fuck, little bird. You're so tight."

He keened and whined as he slid down my shaft, his knees

pressing tightly into my hips. When his eyes rolled back in his head, I smirked, knowing he must have found his prostate again. But I had to be careful. We couldn't get too wild or rough and risk him getting hurt.

Once he was sitting flush in my lap, I went back to gripping both of his hips to keep him steady and hold some of his weight as he began to move. I knew it wouldn't take either one of us long to come. It had been too long and we were too worked up. But that didn't matter. Helping him find his pleasure was the only thing I cared about.

"Fuck, Daddy. Breed me," he yelled, his head thrown back as he rocked back and forth in my lap.

I groaned, wishing more than anything that I could. "Yeah, you want to be Daddy's little cum dump? Want to have Daddy's babies?"

"Yes! Yes, Daddy. Fuck, I'm going to come." Streaks of cum spread out up my torso and chest as he came untouched. It was a beautiful sight. And as his ass clenched around my shaft, he drove me over the edge and I unloaded into his tight little hole, leaving my cum deep inside him.

My hips bucked up into him, trying to drive it in deeper, to keep it there. To always have a part of me inside of him.

Aiden went to collapse on my chest, but I caught him before he could. Not only did I not want him to fall into the cum, but I also didn't want him to hurt himself, so I shifted us as gently as I could to the side and laid him on his uninjured side.

He stared up at me with a sleepy smile and I traced my fingers over his face, still unable to believe that he had chosen me.

"You're sure about this?" I asked him again as we lay there, after I'd cleaned us both up and I'd snuggled him against me.

He stared up at me as though I was the greatest prize he could have ever won, and I knew I would always do anything and everything I could for this man.

"For you, Daddy? Anything, always and forever."

I let out a possessive growl and claimed his lips in a kiss, wishing I could claim his ass again so soon, because there was no way I would ever let this man go.

Not even in death.

Ream subscribers get a BONUS EPILOGUE by visiting https://reamstories.com/jo_lovebytes

ABOUT THE AUTHOR

Jennifer O'Malley writes dark m/m romance and prides herself on giving the unlikeliest of relationships the happiness they deserve especially when it's hard won. A voracious reader, lover of the anti-hero winning the heart of his man, and whose ultimate guilty pleasure is fanfiction, she prides herself on creating character-driven books that will make you swoon for the guy all our mamas warned us about.

Jennifer is currently living her own happily ever after with her family which also includes her two fur babies: an Irish Wolfhound Poodle mix named Jack and a mischievous Russian Blue named Freya.

You can sign up for her newsletter and stalk her by visiting https://authorjenniferomalley.myflodesk.com/signup

www.ingramcontent.com/pod-product-compliance
Lightning Source LLC
LaVergne TN
LVHW030909080826
845145LV00010B/2818

* 9 7 8 1 7 3 5 9 7 3 5 2 4 *